White Roses

White Roses

a novel by

Ellen Greenfield

Brooklyn, NY

2017 3Ring Press Trade Paperback Edition

Printed in the United States
First Edition: May 1, 2017
10 9 8 7 6 5 4 3 2 1

Library of Congress Control Number: 2017905684
ISBN: 978-0-9906251-8-6
eBook ISBN: 978-0-9906251-9-3

Book design & cover art: Alex Martin

Antwerp

Berling LT Std

Feijoa Display

Zingha

3Ring Press
191 St. Marks Avenue
Brooklyn, NY 11238

ellengreenfield.com
3RingPress.com

For the ants & the elephants,
& everything in between.
Always, for love.

Maswa, Tanzania

E rica squeezed her eyes shut. *I went on a picnic and here's what I brought: an anthurium. I went on a picnic and here's what I brought: an anthurium and a begonia.* Muscling her fear aside, she willed herself to focus on this variation of the game she had played as a child. *I went on a picnic and here's what I brought: an anthurium, a begonia, and a caladium.* She opened her eyes, but nothing changed. The blackness was total, and terror was a palpable pressure in her chest. The air was viscous with the stench of waste and death. In an effort not to gag, she squeezed her lips tight between her teeth and forced her breath to slow; her diaphragm continued to spasm. The heat in the cramped space was intense. A drop of sweat began its slow, itchy progress down the back of one knee. *I went on a picnic and here's what I brought: an anthurium* (waxy heart-shaped red spathe, larger than her open hand, with its long, pale, suggestively phallic spadex jutting from the center), *a begonia, a caladium and a dendrobium*—each familiar plant a delicate tendril connecting her to rationality.

She fought the urge to reach out and touch the walls, only inches away on all sides. This was Africa. Anything could be crawling there. But a rush of vertigo made her sway dangerously, and the idea of hitting the floor, or the gaping porcelain bowl, was even more appalling. Before she lost her balance completely, Erica braced herself against the walls with her elbows, less intimate than the touch of her palms against the cinder blocks.

How long had she been trapped like this? It might have been

only a few minutes, but Erica's sense of time had lost all forward momentum. She had gone into the small structure, which rose from the grasslands like a hitch-hiker's thumb, to use the toilet. And only out of desperation. For hours they had been bouncing around in the Land Rover along the rutted and rock-strewn roads to the lodge where they dropped poor Bea with her broken ankle. The last animal sighting—a small group of wildebeests and zebras—had been more than an hour before that.

In the stifling cinder block shelter, Erica had squatted gingerly inches above the dirty bowl and comforted herself with the thought that she was leaving something behind, not taking anything with her (putting a welcome lie to the phrase *taking a piss*) and a reminder-to-self that any kind of toilet was an unexpected luxury in this corner of Tanzania. Just as she had finished peeing, though, something covered the screened window from the outside and she was left in total darkness. She yanked up her pants and grazed her knuckles grabbing for the door handle. The knob came off in her hand. And there she was, alone and sweating in the dark. She let out a half-strangled scream—who wouldn't, she assured herself—and anticipated immediate help. Nini was nearby, or at least she had been when Erica entered. She shouted the guide's name, embarrassed, at first, desperate as she continued, in mounting alarm. But there was no response.

I went on a picnic and here's what I brought: an anthurium, a begonia, a caladium, a dendrobium, and an echinacea. An intense sting made her slap at her hip. Tsetse fly. Erica began screaming for real. Her voice ricocheted back at her.

But nobody came. This was no accident. Someone had purposely trapped her in this stinking box. Bile pushed against her throat. Someone was sending her a message that she had no way of translating, as obscure to Erica as if — as if it were in Swahili. She couldn't deny that there had been warnings, although she hadn't any way to decipher them, or to satisfy the demands. Now she would pay the price of her ignorance. Heat and fear threatened to overwhelm her. Of all the ways she had imagined dying, baking in a concrete outhouse at the edge of a desert at the tender age of thirty-nine had never surfaced. Already her head was thick and woozy, and her arms, still braced against the walls, were trembling with the effort of propping her upright. Any minute now she would lose consciousness. Maybe that would be better, actually. Unless she banged her head on the way down. Against everything hygienic that she held dear, Erica allowed herself to perch on the seatless porcelain bowl.

Coming to Africa had been a mistake. She was forced to admit that now, although it was probably too late. So many things had been mistakes. She abandoned all pretense of horticultural distraction—the anthurium, the begonia—and began instead to trace the lineage of her bad choices.

1

First impression: Erica had been beamed onto another planet—one in which the atmosphere was only marginally hospitable to the human life form. Although it was almost completely dark out (as they made their final approach, the pilot told them to set their watches for 9:23 p.m.), the temperature was at least twenty degrees hotter than it had been in the cabin. And as she and the hundred or so other passengers stepped from the aluminum stairs onto the sticky tarmac, her previously orderly fellow travelers devolved into a swarming, jostling mass, bouncing off each other and swerving in every direction like a dropped box of ping pong balls. Just the act of standing still and clutching her bags took all of Erica's strength. Without making any conscious effort, she found herself swept toward a low-slung and dimly lit building: **WELCOME TO KILIMANJARO INTERNATIONAL AIRPORT**, a small sign read.

Erica struggled to catch her breath. The air was not only hot, but smoky, caustic, and for a second she imagined that she had been caught up in the panic of people bolting from a flash fire. To her unwilling mind came the now-infamous photos of dust-covered office workers rushing away from the Twin Towers, and the painfully imagined scenes of those trapped on the upper floors. The pulsing heat, the acrid smoke, the undeniable portent of death.

And of course, Cal. Cal's terrible death, somewhere in that inferno. 9/11. Just over two years ago now, and still the oft-envisioned scene made Erica reel. She shook her head hard to dispel the vision and concentrated on her present situation.

A quick look around made it clear that there was no fire, and in another moment the will of the crowd carried her into the airport's one small building. Here, the smell turned from smoke to sweat. What her childhood friends would have labeled B.O., those letters howled in disgust. It lapped around her like a salt-laced sea; there was no escape, and Erica was acutely embarrassed to find it so distasteful. Not everywhere did people have the option or even the inclination to de-odorize themselves, she told herself firmly, and as she was as slick with sweat as anyone, she was probably a full-fledged contributor to the overall funk. She hoisted her duffel higher on her shoulder, determined to take some control of her situation.

But there was nowhere to go. Every bit of empty space that opened up adjacent to her was quickly filled by another body. Erica pictured the scene from above, like those toys that she had once liked so much: a square frame filled with small flat plastic pieces that could only move if they were next to the one empty space in the frame. Each little square piece was printed with a segment of an overall picture, like a jigsaw puzzle. Hers, she observed, was the white square in the midst of so many shades of brown and black. The object of the game, she recalled, was to slide the individual squares around—upward, downward, side to side—until they formed a recognizable image. She was pretty good at it then, but not now. And although as a New Yorker she felt at home with diversity, this was the first time she'd ever truly been a minority.

Boldly, she stepped into the next bit of space that opened and ran smack into the back of a solid body in a khaki uniform. He spun around and thrust a semi-automatic weapon in her direction. She leaped backward and landed on someone's foot. An elbow jabbed into her ribs and a shout—clear in its meaning though in a foreign tongue—followed quickly.

"Excuse me, excuse me," she blurted, spinning to deliver the words. But their intended recipient had already moved on. Erica was so weary. Her eyes filled with tears. If there had been room to curl up on the linoleum floor, she would have done so, no matter how grimy it was. Her mission here, tracing Cal's path to adulthood—his halcyon Peace Corps years—suddenly seemed like a Herculean effort. But no. That was just the fatigue talking. She had come to Africa to gather the final—and most resounding—accounts of how Cal had grown into the sort of man who would race into an inferno, putting aside fear for his own life to save others. The seventeen hour trip she had just endured was scarcely a minor inconvenience in comparison to what she would acquire on this journey.

Erica arrived at a glassed-in office in the middle of the building. The woman behind the window shoved a printed sheet through the slot under the glass and indicated with a thrust of her chin that Erica should fill it out. A pen dangled from a cord and Erica tried to use it. No ink. The woman stared at her with blank impatience, waiting for the form. Erica quickly rummaged through her backpack and came up with both a working pen and her passport and visa, which she slid under the glass. The form asked how much money she was bringing into the country and whether the purpose of the trip was business or pleasure. This last part stymied her for a moment, until she realized that pleasure would likely meet with fewer questions. And she *was* planning to go on safari for part of the time, which would be a pleasure. *Safari*, she wrote, in block letters, and she passed the form back under the glass.

In another minute she was beyond the checkpoint. She carefully returned her official documents to the zippered compartment in her pack. By now most of the other people had left the building. Erica could see the space around her in its entirety, though there wasn't much to look at: benches tracing the perimeter of a hastily erected prefab building; a scuffed and streaked linoleum floor with an office in the center; a line of windows looking out into the tar-black night. Even the lights of the runway had been switched off. Erica shouldered her duffel once more and headed for the exit.

Outside, one flickering streetlamp lit the small parking lot. A stream of aging cars and minibuses exited slowly, spewing exhaust fumes and lurching across the rutted surface like a line of the afflicted heading to Lourdes. Erica had requested a pick-up from the hotel she'd booked in nearby Moshi, anticipating exactly this sort of situation, but none of the buses sported the name of her hotel. What would she do if no one arrived for her? The idea of standing alone and forgotten in the dark of this place raised goosebumps, even in the heat. A few minutes later, the smell of creosote replaced the last of the exhaust fumes. She was, indeed, by herself. As her eyes accommodated to the dark, she tried to see beyond the parking lot to the vegetation. After so many years of growing tropical plants in containers, Erica was curious to observe the African flora in their natural state, even if all she glimpsed were roadside weeds. But she could make out nothing recognizable. And she dared not walk beyond the paved boundaries.

She was about to return to the airport building when a pair of headlights swung up behind her, illuminating the great expanse of scrub vegetation that surrounded the small paved area. Erica spun around, prepared to leap out of the way, but the lights came to a jerky halt. Beyond the glare, a car door slammed shut, and shoes crunched on gravel.

"Are you waiting for a car to Moshi?" called a musically accented voice. "The Hotel Moshi? You are Miss Erica?"

With great relief, Erica pulled her duffel toward the figure now silhouetted in the brightness. Long, sinewy arms reached out and hoisted her bag into the van. Erica climbed into the back and settled gratefully onto a padded bench seat. Without another word, they took off into the blackness of a world without streetlights. The Dark Continent indeed, she thought. Bleary with jetlag, Erica closed her eyes.

The car she had hired to take her to Cal's memorial service in Brooklyn had been mired in traffic the entire way across town and down the FDR Drive. Erica lay back in the deep leather seat that reeked of cigars and aftershave like an old Mulberry Street don. She was too despondent to urge the driver into a more aggressive approach. She picked at imagined lint at the hem of her skirt and refused to look out the window as they approached the bridge. There was nothing to see. Once, the two thrusting towers had commanded the view, but now there was a gaping hole like the emptiness where pink, raw gums bore witness to the violent removal of teeth.

On the Brooklyn side of the bridge, the driver struggled with a maze of one-way streets until he finally got his bearings. By the time Erica entered the hulking stone church, the sanctuary was packed but the service had not started. A drone of voices met her at the vestibule as she passed through the heavy wooden doors. They waited for me, Erica thought gratefully, and indeed, as she made her way with metered steps down the long aisle toward the altar (like a bride, she thought, with a wince), the loud buzz of conversation hushed. She walked with painstaking awareness, holding herself erect, her shoulders back, head high. Ennobled in her grief. Her usually wild hair was restrained in a tight knot at her neck. The skirt she wore swished against her stockings, like a mother shushing a fussy baby. Breathy whispers floated into the arched eaves from the pews to her right and left. With every step her feet grew heavier; as she approached the first row, she began to feel as if she were slogging through mud.

Erica turned to her left. Cal's mother, his brother and two sisters, surrounded by members of their extended family—a few of whom she recognized from a Fourth of July picnic at his sister Jill's house on Long Island—sat in a tight group. Erica had phoned Cal's parents several times in the weeks that followed the attacks. She wasn't surprised when they didn't pick up. She finally reached Jill and managed a brief conversation before the woman was called away from the phone. She hadn't spoken to any of them since then, but she was certain they expected her at the memorial. Now Erica searched in vain for the space they had surely saved for her. In the front row, Cal's mother stared straight ahead, her head and shoulders trembling slightly. Next to her, his older brother, Ted, who had also been at the picnic that day, studied his hands folded in his lap; wisps of gray hair curled over the collar of his jacket. Erica tried to make eye contact with Cal's sister, Margy—the sister he'd introduced as his Irish twin—who stood and smoothed the lap of her dress with nervous fingers. The woman's searching gaze passed over Erica's head and swept across the crowded nave. Seemingly satisfied by what she saw, Margy began to walk determinedly toward the chancel. In the pew to Erica's right, the many younger cousins clustered, passing tissues down the line. In consternation, Erica scanned the second row. It, too, was completely filled, as was the row behind it and the one behind that. Erica's hands were icy but her cheeks flared. There was no space held for her. They had no idea how important she'd been to Cal. For a moment, she dared not even take a step; her knees felt as watery as her eyes. Finally, she fell back a row or two, as if pushed.

A hand reached out and grabbed hers. Startled, Erica took a moment to recognize Karen, one of her oldest friends. Karen's face, usually chiseled and burnished from her daily run, was puffy and pale, her eyes bare of makeup and rimed in red. Karen wriggled forcefully until the people next to her got the message and pressed together, creating room for one more on the wooden bench. Erica sank into the aisle seat gratefully. The fifth row, she noticed wretchedly. A year ago, they were a couple. A year from now, she was certain they would have been again. But now she was just another mourner, one of many. Maybe Erica shouldn't have been surprised, but she was. Even though they had met only a couple of times, she was sure Cal's family understood the depth of the relationship. Erica wanted nothing more than to allow herself to bawl out loud with frustration and grief. Instead, she sat tall and stared straight ahead. Even without a ring on her finger, Erica was, she had always known, the great love of Cal's life. She was his soulmate, as he was hers. Their recent separation counted for nothing against that irrefutable fact.

A sob struggled up through her chest and Karen's warm arm pulled her close. Despite her need for comfort, Erica shook Karen off. She wanted to be strong. For Cal. For the friends and family who had come to say their last goodbyes. She wanted to model the decorum that he deserved. The dignity that he would have wanted for her, too. And so, she rummaged in her purse for a tissue, dabbed her eyes and prepared to listen to the prayers and memories of others. She hoped that when her turn to speak arrived, her voice would be under control. Shit, she hoped that her legs would carry her up the steps and into the lectern.

Erica had lain awake most of the night before thinking of what she would say: how she could best translate the inchoate into words. Which memories she could bear to share and which would remain hers alone forever. Perhaps the time she arrived home to find that Cal had painted one wall of the bedroom the precise shade of intense lavender nested deep in the throat of the orchid on her windowsill after she'd told him it was the most sensual color she could imagine. Or the time he traded his courtside Knicks seats for tickets to the sold out Rolling Stones *Bridges to Babylon* concert she'd longed to see. Maybe the time they stayed awake all night on the beach at Montauk to watch the sun rise and then fell asleep in each other's arms only moments before it finally did. Erica turned each of these memories around in her mind like an exquisite bloom that obliged viewing from every angle.

Cal's sister Margy ascended to the pulpit and tapped the microphone.

"Let us pray."

In the stillness, the amplified sound ricocheted around the sanctuary like a gunshot. Pray, pray, pray, the stones commanded.

Erica had forgotten that Margy was an ordained Episcopal minister, although she hadn't had a congregation since her third son was born, just before Cal and Erica met. All three boys were sandwiched in the front row between their grandmother and their father.

"The Lord is my shepherd, I shall not want. He maketh me to

lie down in green pastures. He leadeth me beside still waters. He restoreth my soul."

Muffled sobs broke out from random places in the room. Erica groaned quietly. Karen reached around her shoulders and held on.

"We have gathered together today—the family and dearest friends of my beloved brother, Calvin Michael White—to say good-bye, yes, but also to greet one another in loving companionship and to share the spirit of joy and generosity that Cal exemplified as a first responder who lost his life in the effort to save others. Those of us closest to Cal knew that autumn was his favorite season—the colors blazing across the treetops, the clear blue skies, the tang of a wood fire in the air at night—all these gave my brother such happiness. He was taken from us on one such perfect early autumn day."

Erica looked up sharply. Autumn, Cal's favorite season? Cal, who loved nothing more than the lingering light of summer days and the smell of salt water and a baking boardwalk? How little they knew the true Cal.

In the velvet African night, the van lurched to a halt, jolting Erica from sleep. For a moment she struggled to anchor herself in time and space. Everything outside the window was still dark, although somewhere in the middle distance a faint electric bulb was putting up a brave fight.

"We are here at the Hotel Moshi. I hope you had a good sleep," the driver called in a sweet singsong as he opened the rear hatch and took out her bag. "You did not snore."

Erica sat in a daze for another moment. I am in Africa, she reminded herself. I am about to tread the ground on which Cal walked. Her heart beat faster and she held a deep, steadying breath. Erica stepped out of the van and was met by the driver. He was almost a full foot taller than she. High cheekbones. Serious eyes in a broadly smiling face. White teeth against ebony skin. She reached into her pocket and came up with a couple of bills, which she pressed into his hand.

"*Asante sana*, thank you and enjoy my beautiful country," he murmured before turning away, leaving Erica to walk up the short steps to the hotel alone.

There was no one in the hotel lobby. Through the entryway, the room that stretched before Erica was decorated in early Ernest Hemingway: threadbare overstuffed couches and chairs clustered around carved wooden tables, inviting guests to gather for cocktails and conversation, although at this hour there were no takers. A small bar lined the back wall. It, too, was empty. The severed head of a water buffalo glared from the wall. Erica turned away quickly and went to the reception desk and waited. No one appeared. Africa was not exactly welcoming her with open arms. A small glass of pale orange juice and an old-fashioned call bell, the kind a concierge in a B movie might pound with his palm to summon a bellhop, sat on the desk. Was she supposed to ring for assistance? Would that be rude at this hour? As she pondered her options (not many) Erica noticed a small envelope at the end of the desk. *Welcome Erica!* it said on the front, and inside was a key, Room 207 incised on it. Desperate for sleep, she clutched the key, climbed a narrow flight of steps behind the desk and let herself into a small, sparely decorated room where an overhead fan turned lazily. The quilt on a single bed surrounded by mosquito netting was folded back to uncover crisp white sheets. In five minutes, Erica had stripped off her stale clothes and fallen into a deep and dreamless sleep.

2

Summer crept in slowly the year Erica met Cal. She had joined a biking club and was signing up for one trip after another in an effort to combine weight loss with date gain. At thirty-four, it was getting harder to succeed at either one. Just as spring put a promising haze of green on the trees, she had been, there was no other word, dumped by the guy she had been seeing for almost a year. He wanted to end it before they had an anniversary to celebrate, he said. To let her down easy. He called her wonderful and sensitive and a real catch. But the real catch as far as Erica could see, was that he didn't think they had a future.

"Better now than a year from now" was how he put it.

"Screw you" was Erica's terse response. After a month or so of moping around her apartment, fortified by a limitless supply of Cocoa Krispies and premium vanilla ice cream, she went out and bought a bike—a hybrid Specialized with first-rate Shimano components, according to the lean young man in the bike shop—and a pair of spandex shorts with lots of padding where it counted. Erica thanked her lucky genes that her legs were still great, even if her middle had gone a bit pudgy. She splurged on highly-rated biking glasses with three interchangeable lenses—sun, haze, and deep shade, the same guy told her—and a moisture-wicking shirt with a hidden zip pocket across the back for snacks and maps. And she bought the loudest, coolest helmet she could find, the better to be seen in. The salesman threw in the latest issue of *Bicycling* magazine, with a photo of a determined-looking Lance Armstrong and an article on his chances for winning the upcoming Tour de France only a few years after battling cancer. Erica read the issue cover to cover for inspiration.

The club she joined offered early morning and weekend rides in Brooklyn and Long Island, followed by late evening get-togethers in the dive bars of Williamsburg. It was at one of the latter that Cal appeared at her elbow one night, offering to refill her drink. She recognized him from the day's ride across Brooklyn and out to the lighthouse at Long Beach. She hadn't thought much of him before that day. He was loud and competitive, racing past the other riders with his fancy bike shoes locked into the pedals of his sleek racing bike, shouting *Girlie girls!* in a ridiculous faux Teutonic accent. He acted like a frat boy, although he looked at least her age.

It had been a beautiful day for a bike ride. The path ran along the beach on the south shore of Long Island, and an onshore breeze kept the sweat and the bugs to a minimum. Erica was glad she hadn't blown off the ride in favor of an extra hour of sleep. Her body felt fit and electric—a sensation that had been building over the last months since she traded French fries for carrot sticks. Although she started out the morning with a couple of other women she'd met on earlier trips, she had been riding alone for a while, having out-pedaled them but not yet caught up to the lead group. Up ahead, a knot of bikers gathered at the side of the road. As she approached, Erica recognized them as members of her club. Their bikes were circled around what the magazine coverage of the Tour de France called *une chute*, an accident. Erica slowed and joined the group. Here and there, a few bikes lay haphazardly on their sides, wheels spinning slowly in the breeze. Through the tangle of spandex-clad torsos, Erica caught a glimpse of what was going on in the center. On the ground a couple of men hunched over a body. All she could see of the downed biker were his legs, which were twitching spastically. A crying child was trying to push closer. "Dad? Daddy? Dad!" the child called out, the pitch of the cry rising with each repetition. It was hard to tell from the voice whether it was a boy or a girl, but the kid couldn't have been more than nine or ten and was clearly terrified.

"Somebody call 911," a woman yelled. A dozen hands, including Erica's, began rummaging through pockets and zippered seat bags. A woman reached out and wrapped her arms around the child—a boy, Erica could see now—and coaxed him over to one side. His face was blotched with tears and his eyes flew wildly around the crowd like a bird trapped in a greenhouse. Erica pulled her phone from the zippered pocket on the back of her shirt and flipped it open to dial.

"He's having a heart attack," someone shouted. "Get an ambulance." The pair of legs had stopped twitching now, the feet splayed out to the sides. Erica's own heart began to pound.

Suddenly, someone shoved her hard and her phone went flying. She heard the crack of plastic against stone as it hit the ground.

"What the fuck!" she cried out.

She turned and saw that it was the obnoxious Girlie Girls guy. She took a deep breath, preparing to give him hell. But he had already pushed past her—seemingly unaware that he had broken her phone—and was heading for the center of the circle.

"I'm a paramedic, let me through," he barked. Both the men who were with the victim pulled back reflexively. Tossing his helmet to the ground, the guy bent low and tore the shirt away from the victim's chest before he pressed his ear to the man's bare skin. In a few seconds the alleged paramedic lifted his head, the look on his face grim. He knelt astride the unconscious man's hips and placed both hands high on his abdomen. Raising himself slightly, he let his full weight drop into his hands, thrusting upward. There was no response. He tried again. The child broke free and flew at the man, pounding him with tiny fists. Someone from the crowd scooped the boy up and restrained him.

"Somebody, help me lift him up," Girlie Girls demanded, and a dozen hands reached in to assist. Struggling to shift the dead weight, they maneuvered the victim into a sitting position and Girlie Girls positioned himself behind him. He reached around the unconscious man with both arms, grasped his own right wrist with his left hand, and gave a mighty tug. The victim's body bounced several inches off the ground, and his head lurched violently up and then back toward his chest. The child started screaming louder.

"What the fuck are you doing?" a man shouted. In the distance, Erica heard a siren. She hoped it was heading their way.

Girlie Girls gave another wrenching tug, and something flew from the victim's mouth and landed inches from Erica's feet. At the same moment, the man gasped loudly, turned his head and vomited. Everyone around him took an involuntary step back, widening the circle. The cry of the siren grew louder until it was right behind Erica and deafening. A pair of burly, uniformed men rushed past carrying bags and a stretcher. By the time they got to the man, his color had turned from gray to pink and he was breathing, albeit raspily. The child flung his arms around his father's neck.

"Whoa, sonny, don't choke him now," one of the medics said, gently lifting the boy away. The medics and the guy who had administered the Heimlich maneuver slowly led the man and his son to the ambulance and helped them into the back.

Erica, still in the same spot, looked down. At her feet was a giant jawbreaker. She hadn't seen one of those since she was a kid. It was as bright blue as the sky overhead, a deadly jewel, she thought. Not far from it was her busted phone, which she retrieved and stuffed into a jersey pocket.

The ambulance doors opened once more and Girlie Girls, still in his biking gloves, emerged with the little boy. A round of spontaneous applause broke out and he gave a sheepish grin and a little nod. Someone handed him his helmet as he and the child retrieved their bicycles. The boy's was a child-sized trailer attached to the back of his father's touring bike. He struggled to get the linked pair upright and started to cry again as they fell tangled to the ground. Girlie Girls leaned his own bike against a large boulder and helped the child right the tandem.

"Would you like to bike to the hospital with me?" he asked the boy, who shook his head no, solemnly. Without the put-on accent, his voice was surprisingly warm and mellifluous, Erica noticed. The pair loaded the extra bike into the ambulance, and the boy returned to his father's side. Erica could see that the man was sitting up now, smiling weakly and giving a thumbs-up to his son. Then the ambulance doors were closed and the vehicle moved slowly back onto the road. Girlie Girls took off in its wake.

Later that day, as Erica settled in at the bar where the club had gathered, she recognized the first pangs of sunburn on the tops of her knees. The pint of Guinness she'd almost finished had spread its caramel warmth through her muscles like a balm and she closed her eyes briefly to bask in the stillness that always came after a day of hard pedaling. Five more minutes, she told herself, then home for a shower and some aloe vera.

"I'm sorry about your phone today," said a voice inches from her ear. Startled, her eyes fluttered open. Girlie Girls straddled the empty stool beside her. He looked genuinely contrite. So he had noticed after all. Without his helmet and riding kit, he appeared a bit older and less irritatingly brash. His face and hands were tanned and slightly weathered, as if he had spent much of his life on a boat or out in a field. His hair was glossy and dark and flopped over his brow. He periodically reached up in a futile attempt to slick it back. Each time, it promptly returned to his face. It was a battle he seemed comfortable losing.

He bought her a Margarita. She countered by buying him a Heineken. They moved from the bar to a table, from the table to the street, from the street to a quiet bench near the water where the wished-for breeze never quite materialized, but the sky was vivid with sunset.

"You know—one loves the sunset when one is so sad," Cal said. She looked at him in confusion. "Don't tell me you've never read *The Little Prince?* My all-time favorite book. "

She had read it as a high school senior in A.P. French class, but it had seemed a little soppy and maudlin to her. Now, all she could remember was the phrase, *Ce qui embellit le désert, dit le petit prince, c'est qu'il cache un puits quelque part.* What makes the desert beautiful, said the little prince, is that somewhere it hides a well. She and Karen used to race through the phrase like a tongue-twister. It cracked them up.

"Are you?" she asked.

"Am I what?"

"So sad."

He shrugged. "Sometimes. Not right now, though."

Erica and Cal talked until they were too parched to say more.

When dusk fell, he took the subway back to Manhattan with her, although he lived in Brooklyn. As the stations ticked by—Bedford, First Avenue, Third Avenue, Union Square—Erica debated whether to invite him up to her apartment. She could have saved herself the mental gymnastics. Cal told her he had a midnight shift to work—he had to head down to the station. Erica had been surprised to learn that he was a fulltime paramedic with the New York Fire Department—she had pegged him more as an investment banker type with a volunteer side gig. He had a good laugh when she told him that and said that three consecutive days in a suit would probably give him a terminal rash. Cal kissed her goodnight at her building entrance like a chaste throwback to the Fifties and waited for her to push the front door closed before he left. Erica walked up the three flights to her apartment, wondering what it might be like to be resuscitated by this guy.

Two weeks later, she did invite him up. By then, she had been out with him three times, and although she wanted to maintain some distance, she had to admit she was deeply hooked. There was something about Cal that fascinated her. But more than that, there was something about him that made her feel like a seed that had blown halfway around the world but had finally found the climate in which it would thrive.

Now, Erica had flown that distance herself, chasing a ghost, some might say. She preferred to think she was digging down to the roots of what had made Cal the man he was. So many of her conversations with Cal had led back to Tanzania. He said he loved that country more than he could possibly express. The animals of the plains and the mountains, the children he coached in school and the people who taught him so much about love of family, of country, of the natural, wild world.

"Someday, we'll go to Africa together," Cal promised as they lay side by side late into the night. "Maybe Kenya, or Botswana. There's so much I want you to see." He cooked her a spicy stew with chicken and peanuts that he said was practically the Tanzanian national dish, and they scooped bites of it into flatbread with their hands, sitting on the floor. Once, as they were walking along Columbus Avenue, he veered abruptly into the shop of a travel agent after he caught sight of some safari brochures in the window. He stuffed her purse full of them, and as they read them together that night over takeout pizza, he pointed out the wildebeest—an animal made entirely of spare parts, he said—the tiny antelope called a dik-dik, the warthog with its frightening tusks. In an aerial view of the great migration, a phenomenon the brochure called "the eighth natural wonder of the world," animals covered almost every square inch of the photo, trampling the ochre grassland.

As a child, when asked what her favorite color was, Erica invariably said, *green*. Not the green of money, but the green of grass and leaves. A hue with an infinite number of variations. It was no surprise to anyone that she became a horticulturist. Nothing made her happier than a trip up the New York State Thruway in spring, when the hills had broken out in more shades of green than there were stars in the sky. If the Sami people of the North Pole have hundreds of words describing snow, she often thought, then we should have a million names for the color of new blades of grass, bamboo shoots, limes, oak leaves in April and in August, the thousand variations of conifer, and the countless ways in which yellow cozied up to blue on the color wheel.

But Africa had pretty much dispensed with green. On nature's color wheel, it had been shoved aside to make room for myriad permutations of brown, from rust to ochre, from taupe to mud.

On her first full day in Tanzania, Erica realized that Moshi, proud of its designation as "the cleanest town in East Africa" and a self-proclaimed center for Tanzanian higher education, was something of a dud as far as tourism was concerned. Its proximity to Mount Kilimanjaro notwithstanding, the area had little to offer. Aside from a coffee blending plant asserting Moshi the first place to cultivate the Arabica coffee seeds introduced by Catholic missionaries at the end of the nineteenth century, and a rushed tour through a large greenhouse farm for flowers and vegetables (which struck Erica as somewhat inefficient, given the high price of bringing water to such an arid region), there was little to do besides sit around the pool and wait for Cal's old Peace Corps buddies to return her calls.

There were only a few other guests at the hotel, most of them hikers using it as a staging area for their ascent of the great snow-capped mountain, or returning to shower off the sweat and grime of the four-day journey. Most people, she quickly realized, went straight to nearby Arusha before leaving on safari. But she remained at the hotel, eager to receive calls from Cal's friends.

She slathered herself with high-test sunscreen and stretched out by the pool, privy to a view of the magnificent peak during the brief periods when it wasn't shrouded in clouds. She dozed, swam desultory laps, and waited impatiently for word from Drew, Billy, or Anna Marie, the three names that had dropped so fondly from Cal's lips in the many stories he told about his days in this country.

After Erica's first date with Cal, their time together had grown

organically—from Saturday nights to weekends, weekends to mid-
week stay-overs, and, finally, with no more ado than one extra
grain of wheat dropped onto a scale, an arrangement in which they
were basically living at her place, with the occasional separation
for work trips (hers) or outings with biking buddies (his). Erica
was the happiest she had ever been. Cal's jokes made her laugh out
loud, his cooking pleased and sustained her, his lovemaking shook
her to her bones, and his willingness to remember to put down the
toilet seat touched her deeply. If there was a speck of sand in the
ointment, it was only that his work often included overnight shifts.
Sometimes Erica would rouse herself when she heard Cal come in
just ahead of the dawn. Often he was flushed and restless, though
sometimes he was pale and drawn. Asked if he wanted to talk, he
declined. One night, however, he sat on the edge of the bed with
his head in his hands and finally spoke through his palms.

"I brought a man back to life tonight."

"Good for you. Bravo." Erica's heart flushed with pride and
love. She reached out to touch his arm, but he pulled away.

"Maybe good for me, but not for him. He was ninety-four.
Ready to die. Clean, peaceful, serene in his own bed, drifting off
to that endless sleep. Then his daughter peeked in and noticed he
wasn't breathing and called 911. We did what we had to do. And
we broke him into pieces to do it. Now he's trussed up to life support in a sterile hospital room where he'll have to fight tooth and
nail for his own death."

"You became a paramedic to save people, and you do. You
can't also blame yourself for it."

"Maybe I didn't become a medic to save people so much as to
save myself."

Erica knew not to press the matter. When he unfolded himself and came to bed, she curled silently around him until his breaths turned soft and regular. In the morning, he woke hungry, first for her and then for a spinach and feta omelet.

It seemed almost bovine to feel so content, but Erica didn't fight it. Nice not to struggle, not to suffer all the angst and insecurity she'd begun to believe was part and parcel of any relationship. Nice just to relax for once, and be happy, and flick worries about the future away like so many watermelon seeds. At work in the Brooklyn Botanic Gardens, she hummed as she weeded and whistled as she mulched. Her friend Edward, in charge of the local flora garden where she was assigned, had taken to calling her Our Happy Little Moron. "But in a good way."

One evening, Erica arrived home from the Gardens to find Cal standing amid a pile of cardboard boxes. She shot him a questioning look.

"Oh, just a few things I thought I'd bring over," he said, enveloping her in a warm hug. "Just in case anyone ever breaks into my place, or there's a fire or something. You know, things I wouldn't want to lose."

A month later, Cal and Erica agreed he should move in completely. He sublet his apartment to one of his many cousins who had moved to New York for law school and packed most of what was left in the apartment in a trunk that he stowed in one closet there. Erica organized and purged the closets at her place and made space for the things Cal hauled over in a cab. Aside from a few armfuls of clothes, it was mainly books and papers. And one fairly ugly rock that weighed a ton, which he said would be perfect for holding open the off-kilter door to the bathroom. Erica would have preferred an ordinary doorstop, but she kept her own counsel on the subject. Here, she thought, is proof positive that they were embarking on a future. She made way for it all enthusiastically.

"Is there more?" she asked, once the pile was cleared.

"That's pretty much it," he said, and then he swept her out the door for a celebratory curry at their favorite Caribbean place on Ninth Avenue.

For more than two years they shared that apartment, although occasionally Erica lobbed a few hints about looking for someplace a more spacious place. Cal worked a lot of nights and occasional weekends while Erica had more of a nine-to-five schedule, but almost all of their intersecting time was spent together. They biked, took endless walks around the city, taught themselves to cook Thai and Indian food, and they made love until they fell back in exhaustion. They were happy and proclaimed it frequently, which prompted Erica to hint once or twice that they might as well be married. In her eyes, their bikes, suspended side by side on hooks in the small apartment entryway, stood as a metaphor for their parallel paths.

And then, just like that, it was over.

One day in late April Erica came home from work to find Cal once more surrounded by boxes. But this time he was filling them with clothes and books.

"What?" she asked, thinking there must be some explanation other than the obvious, because the obvious was impossible.

"Erica," he turned to face her, his arms loaded with shirts, "I have to leave. I can't give you what you want."

"What is it I want?" she asked, thrusting her chin belligerently.

"You want what we both want—marriage, kids, permanence. Exactly what I can't give you. I have no right to offer that, and no right to deprive you of it."

Erica blinked with disbelief. What could he mean? Her mind raced, grasping at straws.

"Kids? Big deal. We can adopt."

"What?" his brow wrinkled in confusion. "No, no, that's not what I mean!" He laughed abruptly, as if at a private joke more painful than funny. "Just believe me. I'm doing this because I don't want to see you get hurt."

"Then don't do this," she said. "Step away from the boxes, put the shirts down and no one will get hurt."

He didn't laugh.

"Laugh, damn you."

He still didn't laugh. Just layered the shirts into the box and folded the top closed.

He was leaving. Moving out. He couldn't see her any more. It wouldn't be fair, he said. He taped the top of the box with the concentration he might give to bandaging a head wound.

"But why? Can't we talk about it?" she asked him, hearing the tremor in her voice and hating it.

"That's just it. We can't. You're wonderful, Erica, I've been happier here, with you, than I thought I could ever be. But I have to leave. Don't ask me to explain, okay? You deserve someone better." His face flushed and he turned away, his shoulders trembling.

Erica slammed the bag of groceries she was carrying to the floor. The melon exploded with a muted *thunk*.

"*Fuck!* Fuck you, you fucking fuck!"

And with that, she left the apartment and didn't come back until almost midnight. For most of that time she sat in a Starbucks, where she wouldn't otherwise have been caught dead. She had never realized what a sad place it was, with its musty threadbare easy chairs and its tables stained by a million damp paper cups. Rank with the stench of burnt coffee beans and the misery of hundreds of lonely misfits with nowhere else to go. When the barista told her they were about to close, she got up without a word and left. After that, she just walked until a blister on the back of her left foot sent her limping home to an empty apartment. Cal had cleaned up the splattered groceries and thrown out the trash. Erica imagined that he was actually proud of himself for that. The thought only made her angrier.

She gathered the few things he'd left behind and crammed them into a shopping bag, but when she got to the rock in the bathroom, she just stared, her arms limp at her sides. She'd worry about it in the morning. When she woke up she'd remove all traces of him. But the next morning instead she dashed from the apartment, unwilling to be there alone. That night she didn't bother going home after work, but instead headed straight to Karen's apartment, where she broke down and sobbed until her chest convulsed with hiccups. Karen brought them each a cup of tea and folded her tall frame onto the couch beside Erica.

"This is just wrong," Erica finally gasped between shudders. "This is not the way it's meant to be." She picked at her cuticles until they bled. Then she sucked at the wounds.

"Erica," Karen said, rocking her in her arms, "sometimes we just haven't a clue what is going on in someone else's head. Maybe you were so happy you missed the fact that he wasn't."

"No, that's not true," Erica insisted. "No one knows Cal like I do, maybe not even Cal himself. I know I made him happy. It was something else, but he wouldn't tell me what it is."

Karen looked unconvinced.

"Look, he told me, in so many words—I swear—that he loved and adored me. His missing piece, he called me. He said that. Maybe he got scared of how much he was feeling. That can happen to a person. He said I'd be better off without him. That's not possible. Maybe he's running away to protect himself. He's been hurt before. Maybe he was more damaged than I knew. He just needs a little space and he'll be back."

Karen's expression of disbelief mixed with sympathy made Erica furious.

"It's true, goddamn it! You'll see. We were meant to be together and some day we will be. He just needs time, and it's up to me to keep the faith." Erica pulled her shoulder from the strong grip of her friend and struggled up from the deep sofa.

"Even people who seem perfect for each other split up. You'll get over it, I promise."

"I know about people who belong together splitting up. My parents were a prime example." Erica grabbed her jacket from a hook by the door. "And you know what? If my father had been a little more persistent, he might have gotten my mother back and they wouldn't be living their whole bitter lives alone." And with that, she smoothed back her hair, gathered up the rest of her things, and left.

ROSE

*E*ach time I open my eyes, the crack on the ceiling has grown; the picture becomes a bit more distinct. A line becomes a mountain—the mighty Kilimanjaro—another snakes its way into a dry stream bed. A bead of water gathers in one particular crack and I try to stay awake long enough to see it fall to the floor, where it will ping into an empty can that has been placed there to catch it. Around the swelling droplet, a pale brown stain seeps into the plaster that has begun to look like arid earth in the unfolding scene. It is a landscape I know and long for. I have asked for my cot to be placed out in the yard, beneath the fever tree so I can send my last breath through its branches and upward to meet Enkai. But each time I wake, I am still behind these walls.

My children come to me when I close my eyes. They are a pair of lion cubs, my daughter quick, impatient and strong, my son, lean and always hungry. Hunger has driven them from the safety of the den and they've gone out to hunt, although they are too young to be doing so. I call them back to me, but these walls trap my words. I pray that the stories I have fed them on from their birth keep the hunger from maddening them. I told these stories as they nursed, one at each breast. I told them as we walked the cattle to the river for water. I will tell them in the future—shouted across the Great Rift that is death—though I cannot say if they will hear me.

In my village, I was respected for the tales I told. This also served me well as a teacher of young children in these last years. The most challenging part of telling a good tale is the ending, which must be both a surprise and also the only true way the tale could have concluded. So it is with my own story, as well.

This morning, a new spot appeared above my head. A tiny bloom of red, like a solitary flower in the parched savannah. Looking at it was like looking up at myself, Rose, and it reminded me of the stories I used to tell my classes about the strange and surprising world in which we lived.

My young students all walked from sun-up to reach our small school in the grasslands. Two tin buildings, on either side of a neatly swept patch of bare earth on which we played games and formed our *story circles. My classroom was in the larger building. In the smaller one, the older children did their lessons. Through the open window, we could hear them reciting multiplication tables and lessons from history.*

My young ones laughed when the older classes sang songs in English, a language they said sounded like the chattering of weaver birds fighting over a scrap of food. They, too, wanted to sing in this strange tongue, and I taught them the one about Anansi, the eensy weensy spider. Their favorite trick was to sing this in their loudest voices to drown out their older brothers and sisters.

To my little ones, the grassland was the whole world. It contained cows and acacia trees, fierce animals from which to flee, and peaceful giraffes to follow in hopes of dropped tail hairs to wind into bracelets. The blue sky by day and the milky sweep of stars in the nighttime blackness. Inside my classroom I tried to expand that world, with posters of rushing alpine rivers, cool green forests, and cities of towering skyscrapers.

One morning last May, I brought out a globe of the planet Earth, and then a map showing its place in the solar system. Most of the children laughed until they got hiccups while some of them sat silent and disbelieving. The idea that men flew from the Earth and roamed the dark sky to other worlds was almost too much for them to bear. I passed around a copy of Life Magazine *with a picture of Neil Armstrong walking on the moon, and one little girl—Mbizi—began to cry.*

"Why would a man leave his family and his cows to wander in a terrible nightmare land?" she asked. Why, indeed? I had no answer. Instead, I told them this story.

Once, long ago, a seed fell from the beak of a great go-away bird as he flew over the savannah from high edges of the Ngorongoro crater. From the seed, a plant struggled up out of the earth and a rose bloomed, surprised to find herself all alone in an unexpected place. But the sun was there to warm her leaves, the grasses sheltered her from too much sun, and one day a boy came who smelled the rose's sweet perfume and decided to dedicate his life to hers. Every day he left his friends behind in the village to bring her water and cut away the grasses that threatened to smother her. He told her stories of the place he had lived before he came to her country—an island surrounded by water and covered with roads and houses—with many flowers like her (only none, he insisted, nearly as lovely).

One day the boy arrived with a shovel and asked if he could dig up her roots and place them in a large chombo *so that he could take her with him when he went home. The rose trembled at the thought. Petals dropped to the ground and the boy rushed to assure her that he would never force her to go. So every day he continued to visit and she thrived in his care. Until one day he did not arrive. Nor did he come the next or the one after that. At first, the rose shrugged. She did not need any strange boy. Her roots reached deep into the earth and would find their own water. She would not think about the boy or about loneliness.*

In the story as I told it to my class, the boy finally returned to his rose with gifts and tales of the world beyond their land. In his manhood he brought his children to help care for his dearest flower.

But that was not the true ending of the story. Instead, the boy travelled too far ever to return. The rose became angry at the boy and then deeply sad and then angrier still. He had no right to break his promise. To take her trust and leave her behind in the dry ground that was no longer home without him. She questioned her decision not to allow him to gather her up by the roots and keep her beside him. Did that make him stop loving her? Was it something else? Her thorns had pricked him, but he had never complained. She questioned his love: Was it so feeble and inadequate? And, of course, her own: Love that turns so easily to hate must be a weedy thing indeed.

The sun now burned too hot. The grasses crushed her. Her petals became bleached and brittle. Her roots grew feeble and could not reach the water. She shriveled in the heat, and in time, grasses covered all memory of her. Even if he returned, the boy would fail to find her.

Today, the picture overhead is almost complete. There is the mountain that sheltered me, the earth that fed me, the mines that gave me joy and also great sorrow. I can smell the scorched brush, the cattle, the delicious peanut stew my family loved. I feel the damp earth after a storm and see the flicker of the deep blue of the gems that lightning uncovered in the rocks.

I am not in pain nor am I confused, although each breath comes to me only with increasing effort. I know exactly where I am, who I am, the life I have led. From the boma, my people come to visit, though I mostly do not speak to them. Some, like my uncle, bring mangos and apologies. I require neither. Some come only in my mind and they are as silent as I. As one who has been taught by Christians, I see my mother and father in heaven. They appear to be waiting for me, their arms outstretched. As Maasai, however, I foresee no afterlife, but I rest easy, counting on my children's memories to provide my immortality. They are the thread that will bind me to the future. I can hear my laugh as it comes from my daughter's throat and I watch my own careful gestures as my son ministers to a sick calf. I see my girl telling my stories and her own to the children in her future and I feel how my boy has absorbed my respect for all the life around us. I do not question the existence of both these beliefs in one heart. The heart, I have learned, is large enough to hold all.

3

Throughout that spring and summer after Cal left, Erica veered between the belief that time would work its magic and bring them back together and a hard inner voice (that sounded an awful lot like Karen's) telling her to get over it and move on. She went to work, she went on the odd blind date, she went on vacation to Isla Mujeres, where she suffered a painful sunburn. Life goes on, she told herself. Life sucks, she responded, twisting around to apply aloe to her own shoulders.

And then, one morning in early August—4:13, in hard bright digital numbers—Erica's phone rang. She bolted to her feet. Had someone died? Her grandfather? Her mother? Erica had absolutely no firsthand experience of the death of anyone close to her, but she imagined that someday it would come in just this way, the sky an inky starless black, the path to the phone splashed with the dregs of moonlight. A voice apologizing before hammering her with the awful news. When she picked up the phone, however, there was no one on the line. Wrong number, she told herself firmly and got back into bed. But in another minute, the doorbell rang. Now suspicious, she took her time responding, wrapping herself in a robe along the way. She checked to make sure the safety chain was across the door and then quietly tipped open the peephole with its one-way magnifying glass.

Outside the door, Cal was staring down at the hallway floor. His hair was wet—she didn't think it had been raining—and he swayed from foot to foot in a slow, unsteady shuffle. Her first thought was that she was dreaming. Her second was that Cal was so drunk he'd forgotten he no longer lived here. But he never let himself get drunk, or he never had in the time she'd known him. 4 a.m. He must have just gotten off shift. Quickly, she unlocked the door. He looked up but didn't make any move to come in. His cell phone was clutched in his fist.

"I woke you." He continued to shuffle. It frightened her a little. The dislocated, random-ness of the movement.

"No, I was hang gliding." Why would I say something like that, she wondered. She'd imagined this moment—her chance to get in a last word—so many times, but now that it was happening she only felt bewildered. He let out a dry, choked laugh. She opened the door wider and stepped back.

"Come in." Erica turned and walked toward the kitchen to make tea. In a few minutes, she heard Cal come up close behind her accompanied by the smell of smoke and sweat. Once more, she felt a little frightened. She turned around toward him and he turned away, but not before she noticed that his face was dirt-streaked and his eyes as swollen as a pair of over-ripe figs.

"They were only four," he said, although it sounded more like *gey wah olly fo*. With one hand she reached for his arm and steered him to the couch, while the other clutched the handles of two mugs of tea. She sat across from him in a chair, as still as if she were confronting a wild animal she didn't want to spook, and placed both mugs on the floor. Once Cal started talking, he could hardly stop himself.

First he told her about the fire. A women's shelter in lower

Manhattan, probably arson, certainly not up to code. Most of the women and their children got out, but one pair of twins hid and then were lost in the smoke. He found them wedged in a closet on the third floor and carried them together to the street. Their mother was screaming and tearing at him as he bent over the little girl. His partner Frank crouched down and worked on the boy.

"My mouth covered most of her face," he sobbed. 'I got her breathing. Then she stopped. I tried and tried. I couldn't help her. I couldn't help her." After that he was mostly incoherent, although Erica gathered that the mother kept screaming and calling him a murderer. Cal was trembling now and Erica moved to the couch and wrapped him inside her robe with her. She dried his soaked hair. And she kissed him until he stopped crying and started clutching her with more desire than sorrow. The next thing she knew, they were in her bed, their bodies locked in feverish rhythm.

Both of them fell into a sleep of oblivion almost before they had pulled apart.

When she opened her eyes, he was already awake and watching her intently.

"I'm sorry. I should never have done this to you."

What did he mean by that? Arrive here unstrung with grief? Make love to her after walking out on their lives together? She was afraid to ask, and afraid not to. She worked to swallow the knee-jerk "It's okay" that threatened to slip out her tense lips. What, exactly, would she be forgiving him for? She would not offer him instant absolution. But she needn't have worried about a response. He wasn't giving her time to speak.

"I need you, Erica. And I don't know if I can let myself have you. Please don't ask me to explain."

"Cal, this is crazy talk. What do you expect me to say?"

"Before I woke up just now I dreamed of Tanzania," he continued. "Not the country I knew like bones of my hand, but one with rivers sweeping through the grasslands and rain pouring down from brutal gray skies. Still, I knew it was the same place. Two small children rushed by me in the flood, their mother racing on the bank alongside them, her dark cheekbones flashing in each shaft of lightning. I dove in to catch them but they were carried on by the tide. No matter how hard I swam, I couldn't catch up."

Erica cupped his flushed cheeks between her palms. She tried to imagine what it would be like to send her breath into another human being only to have it die beneath her lips. She immediately made the connection between the children lost in last night's fire and those in the dream and was about to voice it when he continued.

"I lost them all. But I don't want to lose you, too." There was a long pause. "I want you to know that I'm working on not letting that happen." He paused. "I'm seeing someone."

Erica startled. Seeing someone? Another woman? Cal must have read her reaction and hastened to add, "A counselor. A therapist. *He* believes I'll be able to tell you everything. Some day."

She took a deep breath and tried to feel brave. "Just tell me one thing now, and swear it will be the truth."

Cal nodded almost imperceptibly.

"Do you love me?"

"Yes."

"I want to believe you. I also don't want to be played for a fool."

"I would never do that to you. I want us to spend the rest of our lives together."

"Then get whatever help you need with this and come home, yeah?"

Cal nodded his agreement. "I don't deserve you."

"And stop saying stupid shit like that."

For the first time since he'd arrived, Cal truly smiled, or at least the muscles in his face relaxed enough to let his lips unfurl. He kissed Erica on the cheek. An innocent peck, like a promise. He nodded again.

"Let's keep this to ourselves until I've got it straightened out, okay?" he said. "I don't know how long it will take. It's complicated."

Erica pulled him closer and felt his body flow toward hers.

"As long as it takes. I'm not going anywhere." She wondered how she would manage to contain this wonderful secret until the time was right.

But then time ran out.

The cab picked Erica up from the Moshi hotel on the dot of 1:00, just as Drew had promised over the phone. It took over half an hour to arrive at the narrow alleyway of tin houses where Drew lived, an area that seemed so disreputable she almost asked the driver to turn around and take her back to the hotel. As she fumbled with the door handle, a short, stocky man with a graying ponytail and a beaten up cowboy hat stepped out from behind the building and strode quickly to the curb, wiping his hands on the front of his trousers. Was this Drew? He looked like some kind of refugee from the Sixties. The man greeted the taxi driver warmly in Swahili and handed him a couple of bills from his pocket while they continued to have a brief conversation. The driver waved away the money Erica tried to give him as she got out of the car.

Following Drew, Erica stepped from the bruising sunlight into the relative darkness of a small tin structure. Inside it was a good ten degrees cooler, but oppressively airless, as though the house had been closed up for a long time. As if reading her mind, Drew reached around her and fastened the mosquito netting into place and braced the wooden door open.

"Thanks, but you didn't have to pay for the cab," she said.

"It was nothing."

Erica held out a small clutch of bills, not certain whether this was more or less than the cost of the ride.

"No, really, *nothing*. Money in Africa goes a long way. I asked him to come back and pick you up in an hour. You'd never get a cab to or from here otherwise. Can I get you a drink? A beer, maybe?" he asked, using his hat to brush a large cat off the one upholstered chair and indicating with a sweep of his arm that she should have a seat.

Erica hesitated for a moment—sit down with cats, get up with fleas, she thought—then lowered herself gingerly onto the chair. She couldn't risk insulting Drew now that she had finally found him. She had called at least four times before he responded. All of them—Drew, Billy, Anna Marie—had been so difficult to contact that she had begun to feel they were ducking her, or never existed at all. Now Drew disappeared into another room and came back holding a couple of bottles of beer with a snow-capped mountain and the words Kilimanjaro Lager on the label.

"I assume you've already been warned off the water. It'll kill you. They drink Kili like it's water here anyway," he said, wiping the open top of one bottle with his shirttails and handing it to her. It was tepid, and the contents smelled strong and yeasty. Erica took a swig and felt the alcohol go straight to her dehydrated muscles. She relaxed a little further into the musty cushions. Drew pulled a wooden chair from the dining table and swung it around, so that he was facing her with his legs straddling the seat back. Exactly the way Cal sat, Erica thought, with a pang of recognition. They drank in silence for a few moments. Finally he growled, "I'm sorry for your loss."

The way he said it made Erica wrinkle her brow. It was almost grudging. An ironic upswing to the final word, a fleeting grimace before he brought the bottle back to his lips. Almost as if what he meant was the exact opposite. This was the friend Cal spoke of most often. The one he said had been like a brother to him during his time here. She was relieved that she hadn't needed to be the one to tell him. When he finally called her back at the hotel, he began the conversation with a reference to "my late friend Cal."

"It was a loss for so many people," Erica said, pausing for another swallow of beer. The brew was reaching deep down her limbs; she could feel its warmth flow from her thighs to her knees to her calves. She wondered what the alcohol content might be.

"Cal spent more than ten years as an EMT, a paramedic, in New York. There's no way to know how many lives he saved in that time. At his memorial service," she winced, thinking of that day, but pushed on. "At his memorial service, a dozen people got up and spoke about how he had given them back their lives or the lives of people they loved. No one doubted for a moment that he ran into that building without a second thought for his own safety. It was the kind of man he was." She stopped and looked at Drew as he sucked down another slug of beer. "But you must have known that. You were here in the Peace Corps with him, after all. I'll bet he was like that even then. That's what I've come to talk about. The story of a hero." She reached down and stuck one hand in her bag for her notebook and pen.

Drew looked startled. Then, deeply pensive. Erica became concerned that he was overwhelmed by the memory of the friend he would never see again. All the potential that would never be fulfilled. The reunion that would never be held. She reached out to place a hand on his arm in solidarity and understanding. But as she did, Drew let out such a wild laugh that both Erica and the cat, which had settled on the floor nearby, jumped and Erica's heart took a little lurch sideways.

"The Peace Corps? Is that what Cal told you he was doing here?" Drew took a big swig of beer and then reached out as if to tap the can in a toast. "Here's to you, Cal, you old bullshitter!" And he let out another howl that sounded less human than baboon.

"I don't understand."

Drew stopped laughing and looked straight at her.

"I don't understand what you don't understand," he said. "Your friend Cal may have died a hero, but he certainly didn't start out as one. Of course, not many people do."

"But the years you knew Cal—the Eighties, right? Just after he graduated from college?"

"Yup, the enigmatic Eighties," Drew said. "You want another beer?" He dismounted from his chair and disappeared once more into the other room, returning with two more bottles, although she hadn't answered or even nodded.

"What, exactly, did Cal tell you about his time here?" Drew asked with apparent amusement as he settled back into the chair.

"He said that you and Billy and Anna Marie were his housemates."

"Well, that much is true. We lived in this very house. Of course, back then it was barely on the edge of town, not deep in its gut, like now. But go on." He tilted his chair back and watched Erica over the lip of his bottle.

"You and he taught English in a school for young Maasai children, while Anna Marie worked on a water treatment project in a building that you all had helped to build. And then he worked there with her for a time. He said he spent two years here—the full Peace Corps stint—and then stayed on another two years before he returned to the States because his father was ill." At this, Drew rocked forward bringing the chair legs into loud contact with the dirty floor. Erica looked up quizzically for a moment and then continued before he could say anything. Drew took a breath, as if he were going to speak, but said nothing, so Erica continued.

"He told me that of the four of you, he was the only one who left. He spoke about you all the time. He wanted to come back some day and see you. I had hoped—" Her voice cracked and she covered with a swig of beer. "I had hoped maybe we'd come back together." What she couldn't bring herself to admit was that she had pictured the trip as their honeymoon. Days with Cal pointing out the places he had worked as a young man, the remarkable flora and fauna. Nights shared under African skies, on a tented safari. She had gone so far as to imagine the photos they would take, pasted into an album and eventually brought out to show their children.

Drew remained silent. He put down the bottle and began rubbing his eyes, then his whole face, making it impossible for Erica to read his expression. She found his demeanor bizarre and incomprehensible and a sudden bolt of anger ran through her.

"So, *what?* You're saying Cal lied?" She closed the notebook and gripped the pen so tightly her fingers ached and grew numb.

"Yeah, I guess it sounds like that," Drew finally said, but not unkindly. "You know, people go through a lot of changes in a lifetime. Cal, he was a wild one back then. A real cowboy. He came here the first time on a college semester abroad. He came back because the first visit whet his appetite for a lot of things. There was money to be made. We all wanted some of it. I started my trade with the Maasai for their beadwork and I've done pretty well." He looked around the shabby room. "This pit notwithstanding, I've got plenty in the bank, and I only have to come here maybe two months out of the year. Rest of the time, I'm in London with my girl."

Indignation made Erica's cheeks flush. She was being mocked. How long had she been here in this sweltering house? The beer had left a sour taste in her mouth and her limbs felt rubbery. She wished the cab would return so she could get away.

"Then what, exactly, was Cal doing here?"

"Oh, this and that." Erica sensed he was skating over something. Or trying to come up with some story.

"We tried to stay out of each other's business as much as possible. There are things you don't necessarily need to know about the people you live with." It was like he was feeling her out before he said more.

"But you're sure that Cal wasn't working with some organization? Maybe he'd used the words "Peace Corps" generically, the way some people said Kleenex or Xerox. But even she could hear the creeping note of desperation in her voice. Drew wore a pitying expression.

"Listen, babe," Drew said, gathering up the empty bottles, "I'd be happy to talk all day about the fun times Cal and I had, but I don't think that's what you came looking for. I can tell you some of his story, but it's not necessarily the part about becoming a hero. You want to hear it anyway?"

Erica remained silent, her anger simmering.

"I didn't think so. Africa is more complicated than most people are prepared to accept. Maybe you should just go on safari and enjoy the wildlife. And remember Cal the way he was when he ran into that burning building."

"Damned right, I will." Erica started to rise, thrusting her half-empty bottle ahead of her. "Remember him, I mean. Cal was an amazing man. We didn't lie to each other, ever. I've heard enough. I'd like to go back to the hotel now."

As if on cue, a car horn honked in the street. Erica struggled up from the chair as if swimming up from the bottom of the ocean. Something inside of her felt brittle, vulnerable. She had to get out of this awful place before it broke. Something malevolent had been set loose in her direction and she needed to escape.

"What about Billy? And Anna Marie? Are they still here?" she asked as she headed for the door.

"I really couldn't say," Drew said coldly, shaking his head. "We don't keep in touch." He opened the screen and called out to the driver, again in Swahili. Then he turned to Erica. "If you see them, tell them Drew says hello. By the way, how did you find *me*?"

"Cal's address book." There was no need to tell him more, or how she came by the book. Drew took the empty beer bottle from her hand as he walked her out.

Erica hit the bright wall of heat that waited right outside the door. She wove slightly as she made her way down the narrow path to the road. The path was lined with spiny Portulacaria plants, which she hadn't noticed before. They were covered in tiny candy-colored blossoms that masked the razor sharp thorns lining the stems. She walked the narrow path with care. One misstep and her bare skin would be pierced. Even the most attractive plants in Africa could draw blood.

Drew had to be mistaken, or outright lying. At Cal's memorial, she could barely take in the many stories of heroism and the outpouring of gratitude from those who bore witness to his life.

Instead, she had smarted from the obvious fact that no one had thought to put her on the program to speak alongside family, co-workers, and childhood friends. Stuck at the back of the line, she never made it to the altar. She stood and wept in silence, as the stranger behind her patted her back dumbly and Karen kept a tight grip on her hand. But all those people who spoke weren't lying. Cal had truly done all those acts of heroism and kindness. So who was this man—living in a tin shack with a flea-bitten cat—to tell her that someone she knew and loved was a cowboy and a liar?

"I spent two years in Tanzania, working for the Peace Corps," Cal told her. Why would he make up a story like that? Someone was lying, but why should she take the word of this stranger over those of a man who would give his life to save others? Still, why would Drew make up such a malicious lie? Did they have a falling out? Was he jealous of Cal? She needed to find Billy and Anna Marie more than ever. For a brief moment she thought of her recent interview with Cal's partner Frank. Frank, too, hinted that there was a side of Cal that Erica was not privy to. But in that case, she chalked it up to the man's own emotional trauma.

"Miss? *Miss?* Is this not your hotel?" the cab driver was asking. She hadn't noticed that the car had stopped before the tall gate that blocked off the large colonial reception hall and the unimposing structure behind it. Once more, Erica rummaged in her purse and shoved some bills toward the driver.

"No, no, miss," he said, ducking his head and raising both hands, palms toward her. "Your way has already been paid."

"The ride back, too?"

"Mr. Drew took care of all that," he said with a happy grin.

"He's a generous man, Mr. Drew." Erica accepted the pronouncement in silence. She had a sudden thought.

"I was wondering," she asked haltingly, "have you known Drew a long time?"

"Oh sure," the driver answered right away. "I've known him since I was a boy. I worked for him when he first arrived in our country. Helped keep his garden and ran errands and taught him to speak Swahili and even a little Maasai. And it's Mr. Drew who made sure I went to school and helped me get my first real job. He's been a good friend, he has certainly." A car pulled up behind them and honked its horn. "Miss? I can't stay here. Will you be needing anything more?"

Yes, Erica thought. There was more she needed and she would either have to ask fast, or lose the opportunity.

"One more thing. Did you happen to know any of his friends? Another man, somebody named Cal?"

The driver nodded vigorously.

"Oh, Mr. Calvin. I do remember him, certainly! Do you know him?"

Earlier in the day, Erica would have answered that question with complete conviction, but now she just slightly was less sure.

"Could you tell me your name?" she asked, in lieu of an answer. Erica's pulse was racing and she was covered in a fine sweat.

"I am Sankei, but my friends call me Sammy."

"Sammy, it's nice to meet you. I'm Erica." She thrust out her hand. He shook it warmly. "I did know Cal," she began. "I loved him very much. We were about as close as two people could be. In America, we call it *soulmates*. I hoped we would share the rest of our lives. Do you think maybe you and I could talk a while? I'd be happy to pay you for your time."

"No miss, I'm sorry, no. I have to get this cab back to the garage quick quick or I will be in big trouble. The next driver is waiting."

Erica felt something akin to the geographic midpoint between disappointment and relief. Here was another person who knew Cal. Who could add to the stories of Cal that she was here to compile. But after meeting Drew, an element of apprehension had crept into her mission. Cal *was* a hero. There were so many lives back home to attest to that. But here, halfway across the world, the facts suddenly seemed less certain. Still, she needed to push on. For the honor of his memory, she told herself.

"I understand," she said now to Sammy. "But how about tomorrow? We could talk while you show me the city. Would that work?" The car behind them honked again, louder and more forcefully. Sammy reached out his window and gestured abruptly.

"Sure thing, Miss. What time would you like me to be here?"

"Nine o'clock?" The driver leaned on his horn and did not let up. Behind them another driver added to the cacophony. Erica opened her door and stepped outside, where the heat added to the oppression of noise.

"I will be here," Sammy promised. He gunned the engine and left her standing in a cloud of fumes.

Erica turned and went into the hotel. For the first time since her arrival, the lobby was full of people, most of them hovering around the age of retirement, virtually all of them clinking glasses in full celebratory mode. A man dressed in well-worn khaki shorts and a loose plaid shirt turned and offered her a drink.

"We made it," he boasted. "To the top of Kili and back to tell the tale. And all of us survivors."

"Survivors?" Erica echoed, quizzically.

The man pressed a cold beer into her hands. "Yes. We're all survivors of one sort of near-death experience or another. Myself, it was a pituitary adenoma. My wife, here," he indicated a petite woman with curly blond hair streaked with gray, "had a pulmonary embolism that would've felled an ox. Brad, over there by the bar, walked down ninety-six floors of the World Trade Center and got out the door moments before the end. And yet, here we are. To us!" The others raised their drinks in his direction.

Erica took a polite sip of her beer. It bubbled up in her throat.

"Congratulations," she murmured, when she stopped coughing. A week ago, a day ago, she might have told them about Cal. Now, she extricated herself from the group as quickly as she could and fled to her room.

4

The tape clicked on:

Inevitably, somewhere between the end of August and the middle of September, summer in New York City turns to fall with something as distinct as the tap of a pebble against glass. You go to sleep one night with the soft mugginess humming outside the screens and you wake to the crystalline tang of autumn tapping at the pane. The smoldering haze of the summer sky is wiped away, and what's left is a blue so sharp you could cut out paper stars with it.

Erica had noticed the change as soon as she opened her eyes. Even though her bedroom window opened only on a wide alleyway with limited access to the sky, the shift in the quality of light and the briskness in the air were immediately apparent. Summer's end. Time to get busy and make something of yourself. Time to strip away the dead foliage and replenish the soil with compost and nutrients in preparation for the next growing season. She wouldn't miss this past summer much, Erica thought, all hung about with frustration and heartache (right up until the last few weeks), but she would miss the lingering evening light and half-day Fridays at work. Today was Tuesday, her day off, and she had plenty to get done. The lights on her clock radio informed her that it was already 9:02. She sighed and got up to shower and dress.

The insistent howl of sirens, close by and continuous, penetrated her windowless bathroom. Dressing quickly, she raised the
blinds over the living room window that offered the apartment's
best view, straight down Ninth Avenue and into the southern sky.
What she saw dwarfed the global shift of the solstices, crushed it
to a fine powder and blew it away.

Erica stared, lightheaded, unwillingly rapt. At the far end of
the island, the silvery skin of one of the elegant towers that punctuated the downtown skyline was ripped in two by a jagged slash
of darkness. Plumes of gray and black billowed from the wound
and merged with more of the same roiling from the top of the
building's twin, before tailing off across the blue sky. Five minutes
went by. Fifteen. This is the most awful thing I will ever see in my
life, she thought. Then slowly, silently, in a herky-jerky motion like
an old magic lantern animation, both buildings began to cave in
on themselves, one and then the other disappearing into a heaving
pillow of black smoke that rolled upward into the soot-mottled sky.

Erica's hands, clutching her robe, trembled.

In the background, the radio kept up commentary on the horror that she was witnessing. Two planes. Not an accident. Witness-
es shouted over each other into the mic. Sirens and cries of anguish
in the background. She hadn't heard a crash. How could she not
have heard it?

She turned on the television. The first image she saw was foot-
age of firemen and paramedics dashing from the street through the
shattered entry to the doomed buildings. In a daze, she walked into
the bedroom, grabbed the phone and dialed Cal's number.

"Hi," she heard, and the relief surged from her body in a groan.
He was home after all. She inhaled. "This is Cal. Leave a message
at the beep and I'll get back to you," his voice continued, and she

dropped the receiver to the floor as the reality closed in. Sure, he could have been in the shower, or the supermarket, or out voting—it was Election Day, after all—but Erica knew with absolute certainty that Cal was at the scene of the devastation. She turned back to the window, staring hard, as if her vision might burn through the steel and glass and smoke to catch a glimpse of him.

On the news, people who had fled at the very first impact were being interviewed, reporting stories of racing down one hundred flights of stairs through smoke and terror, lending an arm to colleagues and strangers; others were haunted by the sight of bodies sailing thousands of feet to certain death rather than allowing themselves to be overtaken by the inferno that was bearing down on them. Erica's knees shook as she finally stepped away from the window.

The drone of the sirens became deafening, unbearable. She clapped her hands over her ears, squeezed her eyes shut and tried to will the sound away. But another sound broke through—her phone ringing. She glared at the empty place on the base where the receiver should be and then remembered she had dropped it. It had lodged half under the couch, and she snatched it up on the fourth or fifth ring.

"Hello," she shouted into the mouthpiece only to hear the click of the call disconnecting. She imagined it was Cal, calling to say he was fine; calling to say he wasn't. Clumsily she punched at the buttons, trying to retrieve the dialer's number. *Private Caller* appeared and she moaned in frustration. He would probably be using his FDNY cell phone, she realized, and she'd have no way to get the number. She pressed *69 to redial the last incoming call. Again and again, a rapid busy signal gave her no satisfaction.

The phone rang again, and this time she snatched it up on the first ring.

"Hello?" she panted.

"Are you watching this? Are you seeing this?" The pitch of Karen's voice veered toward hysteria and Erica had to sit down. Karen was in the library of the law firm where she worked in midtown, gathered with the entire staff around a television. She and Erica didn't speak for the longest time—just listened in tandem as reports continued to emerge on the constant news feed. When they finally hung up, she remained rooted to the chair, breathing into her closed fists and staring unseeing at the room before her.

Everything that happened over the next several days was like a dream—fragmented and shrouded in haze. Erica was out in the street, walking downtown, turned back by the police. Then what? She was at an ATM drawing out money. Why? She woke up on her couch, the television still on, the sky now dark, the sinister smell of smoke and electricity choking the air. Karen came and went from this blur. Also, Edward from work. She was in Brooklyn. She was in a church, lighting candles awkwardly. She stank; she was wearing the same clothes she had put on days earlier. She was at the front door of Cal's apartment building, ringing his bell. She was at St. Vincent's Hospital Emergency Room, spelling his name for a nurse at the front desk. She was at the fire station where his rescue team was based. There were flowers and flags everywhere. No one spoke to her.

At one point, she found herself standing on line for the 8:00 p.m. showing of *Shrek* at a theater on 23rd Street. She made it all the way to the ticket seller's window and then realized she had neither the desire to see this picture nor her purse.

Public radio broadcast stories about people who had been missing and then turned up hours later, stunned and exhausted. Erica found this sufficient reason to walk the streets night and day, looking for Cal. Over and over again she raced up to the back of a stranger only to be disappointed. Eventually, she made her way home and fell into a feverish sleep for a full twenty-four hours.

When she woke, she felt empty and fluttery, as if she were recovering from a bad case of flu. She didn't have the strength to open the bottle of ginger ale someone had left in the refrigerator and instead lay on her back, willing her thirst away until she passed into sleep once again. The next time she woke up it was raining. She got up and walked around the block, wondering if grief, like tar, would stick to her forever.

That's the way it was for months. She walked, she talked, ate, drank, but most of it was un-recallable even hours later. She felt like a shadow, or like she had no shadow—she thought of Peter Pan, tapping at the window of the Darling household trying to recover that shadow part torn from him and locked away. She thought of the little prince, adrift through space with no way to rescue his beloved planet. For the first time in her life, her houseplants withered and died. She left their twisted, blackened bodies in the dry soil of their pots, crusted over with mildew and salts.

At work, things were even worse. Asked to install a bed of tulip bulbs, she mourned for all those who would never see tulips or spring again. She felt too guilty to go to the gym or ride her bike—pleasures denied to Cal and the other victims for eternity. Her skin grew pasty, and climbing a single flight of subway stairs left her breathless.

"Do you know how extreme this is?" Karen asked her over the phone one night the following spring. "Do you realize how badly you need help?"

"Yes," Erica admitted, tearfully. "I'll get help."

But the next day that promise, too, was forgotten.

Shortly after the first anniversary of the attacks, Edward handed her a newspaper article about something called "complicated
grief," a syndrome in which certain people find it impossible to
move beyond the initial stages of loss—denial, anger, depression—
and to progress to some level of reconciliation. This type of grief
lost its redemptive value and became a prison that locked the person away from the rest of humanity. Erica read the article dutifully,
recognized herself even, but then swept the pages into the trash.

Fewer and fewer friends called. Erica realized that people had
passed the point of understanding and had relegated her to that
level of hell reserved for the willfully insane, a circle of suffering
that was both crowded and lonely. Every night, in a ritual bid for
comfort, she touched each of the items that Cal had left behind
when he moved out: the books, the Black Watch plaid flannel shirt,
the pair of quarter socks that had been in the hamper and, finally,
the rough hunk of stone that still propped open the bathroom door.

All that was left from what Erica thought of as *Before* was her
job, and she threw herself into it. The gardens were her haven,
the only place where she might, for a few minutes or even hours,
engage in physical work hard enough to prevent her brain from its
obsessive looping. Each morning she rose at 6:00 a.m. and was on
the subway to Brooklyn by 7:20. The trains were relatively empty
at that time and she almost always had a seat. She plugged herself
into her music, focused on a crossword or book and managed some
forty minutes of blessed non-awareness. The ride home in the evening, crowded with rush hour commuters, was almost as numbing.

And then, one evening, Erica glanced up from her book and
spotted him in the next car. Beat-to-shit black leather jacket, collar
turned up, fringe of dark hair dipping over his brow. He grasped
the pole, then swiveled and moved further down the aisle and out

of sight. A jolt of adrenalin charged through her and left her fingers and cheeks tingling. It was Cal. Alive and on the subway. She stood abruptly, treading on the foot of a woman clutching the bar above her head.

"Excuse me, excuse me." The woman looked at her sourly, then pivoted and took the vacated seat. Erica forced herself through the line of straphangers to the door between the cars. It was locked, and all she could do was stare. In the next car Cal lowered himself into a seat, and the crowds closed around him, cutting him off from her view. In frustration, she ground her teeth—a habit from childhood that she thought she had long ago squelched—and continued to stare through the dirty window, willing the crush of bodies to part. The train picked up speed and rounded the bend before the Chambers Street stop, and Erica readied herself to make a hasty exit.

The doors opened, and slowly—maddeningly slowly—people began wedging their way onto the platform, pushing against the mass of bodies waiting to board. Despite her best efforts with elbows and hips, Erica was the last person off and in desperation she shoved and bumped her way toward the car in which she had spotted Cal.

"Please stand clear of the closing doors," the conductor warned and the doors began to slide shut just as she reached them. Without a second thought, Erica thrust her arm and shoulder into the narrowing gap and found herself snared—one arm inside the car and the rest of her on the platform's edge—as the rubber-edged metal clamped shut. Trapped, she crooked her elbow tight to keep her purse from dropping to the floor. In a panic, she swung her head from side to side, searching out the conductor, trying to catch his eye. He was two cars down and facing the other way.

"Hey!" she called out. "Hey!" but her voice was lost in the din. Desperately she pushed against the doors, which failed to give. She had to get them to open. She had to get to Cal. Alive! He was alive. She saw him—could still see the turned up collar of his jacket. The nightmare was over—if only she could get into the train. The crush of people around her forced her against the dirty skin of the subway car. She twisted her face away from the grimy window.

"This is a Seventh Avenue Number Three Express. Next stop, 14th Street."

Suddenly, Erica realized fully the danger she was in. Her bag was inside the train, making it impossible to extricate her arm if the train began to move. She struggled and called out again. Around her rose a buzz of concern. Wasn't there some kind of alarm that would tell the conductor that a door wasn't completely closed? There was, right? Would it be working? Would he bother to look? The doors remained tight against her arm. Cold sweat broke out on Erica's face and despite her deeply ingrained reluctance to cause a fuss, she was about to scream, when the bells binged and the doors bounced open once more. She yanked her arm back and in a flash, they closed again, leaving her safe, but on the platform. The passengers nearest the door turned to glare at her for causing the delay and for one more moment, her view of Cal opened up. He turned, too, and with a sickening jolt, Erica realized that it wasn't Cal at all. Just some guy with a leather jacket, five o'clock shadow, and dark hair. The train pulled away.

Erica stamped her foot. Tears blurred the sight of the red light as the train receded into the tunnel, stealing hope from her once more.

"What the hell?" a man behind her shouted. "You could have got yourself killed!"

Erica wanted to turn and scream in his face. A wave of grief crashed over her, swollen and furious as a tsunami, only this time her tears weren't just for the loss of Cal but for the loss of the person she had once been. The loss of hope, of a core belief that life was an open road and all she had to do was keep stepping in a forward direction. Ahead of her now was only the drop to the tracks, the filth of the city and the tunnel of darkness. She turned and shoved her way past the man who was still railing at her and the swarm of people who couldn't have cared less.

For almost two years she existed in something close to a fugue state. By the time Erica broke down and made an appointment to see a therapist—a specialist in "prolonged grief disorders"—she had lost twenty pounds and silver had begun to thread through her auburn hair.

The woman's office was on the top floor of an Upper West Side brownstone. To get to it, Erica had to climb four flights of steep stairs, leaving her winded and flushed. She figured it would take up something like thirty dollars'-worth of the woman's fee for the time it took to stop panting and get her breath back if she got there just in time for her session, so she arrived early and composed herself while waiting on the tiny landing outside the door. The problem was that the room was far from soundproof. Standing there, the plight of the patient before her each week became all too clear. His name was Paul, and he had lost his wife in a car crash. He had been the driver. In the years that had passed since the accident, he'd been unable to drive or ride in any motor vehicle. His children, all married, had lost patience with his guilt and suffering—the accident hadn't been his fault—and apparently they came to visit him less and less. On the other side of the closed door, he cried and he raged. Each week, he emerged thinner and grayer.

But when Erica glanced into his eyes as they passed each other on the landing, she saw only pity. She realized that she must look even more pathetic than he did.

The therapist, Elizabeth, employed a technique she said worked for many people in Erica's situation. The problem, from Erica's point of view, was that the treatment required her to revisit the day of Cal's death—recall it down to the minutest detail—and tell the story out loud while a tape recorder captured the entire session. It also required her to play back the tape on her own, several times a day, if possible. In this way, Elizabeth stressed, Erica might finally come to realize that her grief, like the recording, was a tale that could be listened to or could be put aside while she moved on with her life and created new goals. For weeks, Erica danced around the issue, close to quitting, and then one day she began, speaking softly but clearly, facing the microphone on the doctor's desk, her eyes closed:

"Inevitably, somewhere between the end of August and the middle of September, summer in New York City turns to fall with something as distinct as the click of a pebble against glass."

She continued to speak until the tape ran out with a snap.

At first, just the act of slipping the tape into the player and pressing Play brought on a bout of ragged sobbing. She dreaded the appointed hour after dinner when she had committed to listening. Instead, she lingered in the greenhouse or dawdled at the market after work until exhaustion drove her home. Eventually, though, the words on the tape began to lose their power to wound and became more like those horrid German fairy tales in which ghastly things happened to children. Those, too, gave up their power to terrify after constant retelling. Finally, it was the tape itself, or rather the revelation of the power of storytelling, that planted the seed of an idea that gave Erica a beanstalk upon which to climb out of her depression.

Four months later, she quit therapy with a well-worn cassette and a new goal: even in the face of his absence, she would get to know Cal more intimately by tracing the story of how he grew to be the man he was. The idea had come to her one day as she was staking a bed of hollyhocks that had been felled by a storm. Painstakingly, she worked her fingers through the tangle down each toppled stem to its strong base – bent to the ground, but not broken – at which point she was able to lift it back upright and offer it support. It was a large bed and the work took some muscle, but when she was done, she could once again enjoy the bright and formidable blooms and appreciate how her work brought them back to life. She would do the same for Cal's story. She'd follow his path as he grew to manhood, visiting the places and interviewing the people who had been so important in shaping the hero he had become. She'd travel to Africa, as they'd planned, and find his friends there. The finished story would stand, strong and erect, and their words would support and preserve his memory. As she mapped out a plan, her entire body filled with warmth and energy she had almost forgotten was possible.

She went into her next session with Elizabeth and announced she was ready to move on. The woman looked at her skeptically.

"I thought I'd start by interviewing the medics and firemen he trained and worked with here in New York—maybe some of the people who spoke at his memorial—and then trace back to the time he spent in Africa. That is where it all began, he said. 'What happened in Tanzania made me who I am.'" Erica purposefully pushed the omnipresent box of tissues further from her chair. "It will be like bringing him back to life." She quickly read the doubt on Elizabeth's face. "Okay, not to life of course, not really." Erica felt her cheeks redden. "But the story will bring me closer to him, give me that closure you're always talking about. Maybe that's the best I can hope for."

"Do you think that this might be a little... precipitous?" Elizabeth asked, her eyebrows raised in a way that irritated the hell out of Erica.

"Precipitous? Really? I've been working at finding some way to make sense of this nightmare for two years and you call the first idea that actually makes me feel something other than complete despair precipitous?" Now she was fuming.

Elizabeth quickly backpedaled.

"I'm not trying to belittle your plan, Erica, just to test it. Maybe you want to take a few more months to work out the details. And, by the way, I hope you know that even after you leave here, you can always come back if you need to talk."

Erica allowed herself be mollified.

"I appreciate that. But I think I've found a way forward." She began to gather up her things to leave. "You know, one of the last things I ever said to Cal was that we've got time. And I was wrong. It's now or never."

Elizabeth still looked less than convinced, but hugged Erica and wished her luck. Erica left the office with a sense of purpose and clarity. She hoped that one day Paul would do the same.

Now, lying in her hotel bed in the heat of Africa, staring past the revolving fan blades, Erica pictured the once-dreaded tape. It sat in her apartment in a drawer that had once held Cal's things. At first when he left, she was going to pitch the items she found in there—two thick paperback books on emergency medicine, a deck of playing cards from United Airlines, and another of his many plaid flannel shirts with torn elbows, along with the stupid rock from the bathroom, into a trash bag and consign them to landfill hell. After his death, she believed that some force in the universe had made her keep those things for a reason. Night after night she touched them one by one like sacred artifacts, trying to absorb some leftover essence of him through her fingertips.

Within a month of going through the prescribed process of de-sensitization, Erica was able to donate the books to the fire department to be given to student medics. She brought the shirt and the cards to a thrift shop with a bag of her old clothes. Only the rock remained, holding open the wonky door. One night she tripped over it on her way to the bathroom and cut two of her toes. They bled for such a long time she wondered if they needed stitches. Cal would have been able to tell her.

A rap on Erica's hotel room door jarred her awake the morning after her meeting with Drew, and for a moment she hung in that no-man's-land that separates states of consciousness like the rabbit-proof fence across the Australian desert.

"*Jambo, jambo.* Car for you, Miss," sang out a voice.

Of course. Sammy. Africa. Cal. She swung out of bed and began to dress hurriedly.

"Please tell him I'll be right there," she called, wriggling into a t-shirt and zipping up her shorts. She took a swig from the bottle of water on her nightstand and grabbed one of the emergency granola bars she had packed in her tote. A quick trip to the bathroom, speed-brushing of teeth and hair, and she was out the door.

Now Erica rested heavily against the back seat of the cab and let her eyes close a moment. Most of the morning, she and Sammy had driven through the town of Moshi and the area around Mount Kilimanjaro, and now they sat parked in a precious oasis of shade outside a trading center where Sammy had taken Erica to shop. Although she hadn't intended to bring back much in the way of souvenirs or gifts, she found herself buying an assortment of beaded bracelets and bowls and small woodcarvings of animals, mainly to establish good faith with Sammy.

Sammy, the very image of the tall, gaunt Maasai tribesman depicted by many of the paintings and carved ebony artifacts she had handled that morning, sat folded into the small front seat of the cab like origami. When he picked her up at the hotel this morning, he had been sipping a Coke through a straw, an image the soft drink company should snag for a future ad campaign. Now, they each had an icy bottle of the same beer Drew had served her. Erica pressed hers against the exposed skin of her throat and chest.

In the noonday heat, the air in the cab reflected the accumulated history of many bodies over a long period of time, like cabs everywhere. She opened her eyes and cranked the window as low as it would go to encourage the meager breeze and returned to the conversation they had been having on and off all morning.

"Then what in God's name *was* he doing here?" Erica heard the shrillness in her voice, but was helpless to alter it. She wondered what this man who seemed to know so much could be making of her agitation. Earlier that morning, when she told Sammy of Cal's death, he gasped and pulled the car over to the side of the road precipitously. He shook his head from side to side as he silently absorbed the facts. Then he grilled her for details. Even after she'd laid bare the awful events of that day, she heard him repeating, "Mr. Calvin, dead?" in a soft, disbelieving voice. Calvin certainly made an impression on people, she thought.

"Well, I can't say for sure about making buildings for the Peace Corps, but Mr. Calvin he was making many things," Sammy was now saying in an odd tone she couldn't quite read. "Money, sometimes. Sometimes not." Sammy snapped the caps off a couple of bottles of Kilimanjaro Lager. He passed another one back to Erica.

"And how was he doing that?" Erica demanded as she grasped the moist, cool glass in her palm. At this point, she might not be surprised if he told her Cal was counterfeiting currency, or trafficking in human beings.

"Tanzanite, for one thing. You know tanzanite?"

Erica shook her head mutely as she watched Sammy's glistening face in the rearview mirror.

"I can't believe it! You've been here how long? Usually they grab the tourists first thing. AfGem, Tanzanite One, the big boys. Got most of the market sewn up, they have. They take groups through a model cutting facility and then sell them all the worst crappy stones. Boy George, that's a racket for you."

He rummaged under his seat and tossed a brochure into Erica's lap. On the cover, a sapphire blue gem the size of her fingertip was ringed by a belt of diamonds. Gaudy. Nothing Erica would ever wear. "The Story of Tanzanite," the cover read.

"I can take you to visit a real tanzanite cutter, if you like. Get you a good price, too. I have friends." He stared at her, lifting his chest proudly. "I have worked the mines."

Catching his eye in the rearview mirror, she shook her head. She had come to Tanzania with what she thought was a jewel. That it was being trampled into the mud was regenerating the grief she had carried for so many months. She didn't think a shiny brooch would restore anything of value to her.

"There was money to be made and Mr. Calvin wanted some of it," Sammy continued. "Got some, from what I heard. And more than that. He was one of a kind, Mr. Calvin." Again that rueful tone that she couldn't understand. Then he let out a low whistle. "But I can't believe you don't know tanzanite! A very beautiful jewel and only from our country."

"Okay then, tell me about tanzanite," Erica sighed. So far, Sammy had gotten her to buy gas for the taxi, breakfast and lunch for them both and a crazy assortment of trinkets from three different shops. She would draw the line at jewelry, however. But while she was expecting the sales pitch, she wasn't expecting the lesson in geology.

Tanzanite is actually blue zoisite, Sammy told her. Discovered by a Maasai herdsman at the tail end of the Sixties. Once the Tiffany Company in New York City started selling it, they changed its name because they were afraid that people would pronounce it Blue Suicide. "Anyway, tanzanite is a much better name, don't you think so?" He twisted around to face Erica, and she found herself nodding in agreement, although she had only been half-listening. Satisfied with her response, he settled himself comfortably again and took a big swig of beer before he continued.

"Tanzanite—technically hydrous calcium aluminum silicate—$Ca_2Al_3(SiO_4)(Si_2O_7)O(OH)$," he rattled off, the way she and her friends used to race each other through the spelling of antidisestablishmentarianism—"is hundreds of times rarer than diamonds."

"I'm not really that into jewelry," she said wearily. Erica wondered how Sammy had acquired his technical acumen.

"Do you know what *pleochroic* is?" he continued, as if she had never spoken. Without waiting for a reply, he told her, "It's when you look at a crystal and it looks blue from one side, red from another and violet from a third. That's what tanzanite is like. After it's heated, that is. When you first find the crystals stuck in a rock—they call it boudin—they're usually as dull as this beer bottle." He clanked the empty against the steering wheel to be sure he had her attention. "It was only after lightning struck some of the stones that they were noticed at all."

"I'm sure it's very pretty, but I didn't come here to shop," she said. Sammy seemed undeterred.

"You should buy some. Most of it has already been dug out. It took almost six hundred million years for the gems to form and in another fifty years, it will all be gone."

Where was all this information coming from? A taxi driver who hadn't even finished eighth grade, as he'd told her, with the working knowledge of a trained geologist. She sighed, hoping he was finished with the sales pitch.

"You're thinking I'm pulling at your leg." Erica felt the blush rise from her neck to her hairline.

"I was assistant chief engineer at a mine once. Owned by my father," Sammy said proudly. "It's the truth, I swear before God. Now I drive this cab. All things considered, I like this better. I'll live longer. You get too close to tanzanite, sometimes you don't live long. Some people will cut your throat as soon as look at you." He looked in the rearview mirror and took both hands off the wheel for a quick moment to pantomime a slicing gesture across his throat. "I have a wife. Children. Cows."

"Sammy," Erica began again, "I'm sorry if I seemed rude. I'm just tired and upset. I came here to learn about Cal but what I've learned is not what I expected. Do you understand?"

"Sure I understand. People are like tanzanite," he said, as if that put an end to it. Erica was rendered silent by confusion. He looked into her eyes in the mirror, then explained, slowly and softly, as if to a child, "*Pleochroic*. You look at them from one side and they look one way, from another side they look another, and from a third side, some other way still, no?"

Yes, thought Erica sadly. But the more sides of Cal being exposed, the less she understood any of them.

"I'd like to go back to the hotel now," she sighed. "Thank you for this morning."

"Are you sure you wouldn't like to see where the tanzanite is cut?"

"No, I'm pretty tired. I'd just like to go back now."

"Tomorrow?"

"Thank you, but that won't be possible. I'm going to Arusha tomorrow."

Sammy was silent as he steered the car through traffic on the narrow streets. "Are you going on safari then?" he finally asked.

"I don't know yet. I'm trying to find some other friends of Cal's—Anna Marie and Billy. Perhaps you knew them?"

"There were several others who lived with Mr. Drew and Mr. Calvin. I didn't know any of them well."

"I would love to see more of Tanzania. I was hoping for a couple of short trips while I'm here, but I didn't know if there would be time for a full-blown safari." Just saying this made Erica feel foolish. Maybe she had acted, as Elizabeth had broadly hinted, on a rash, emotional impulse. She had tried repeatedly to reach Anna Marie and Billy, without success. She had called Peace Corps headquarters and left messages at the numbers in Cal's book. Either they were no longer in the country or had no interest in talking to her. And yet she had flown halfway across the globe, hoping that once in the country, she would find them, as she had Drew. And now Sammy. Pleochroic? Cal? Anna Marie and Billy might be her key to finding out. Her skin prickled with sweat and frustration.

Meanwhile, Sammy's furrowed brow was reflected in the rearview mirror. "No, no, no," he insisted finally. "You must see Tanzania. I know the best safari guides in all of Africa. I will get you on a tour that will show you more of the country and our wonderful animals than anyone else. A special tour. VIP."

"Please, don't go to any trouble," she began.

"No trouble, no trouble at all. For a special friend of Mr. Calvin and Mr. Drew. *Tafadhali*, please, accept this insignificant gift of assistance. I will have the company call you at your hotel."

Erica wasn't sure what to make of this offer. Sammy had proved a surprising cab driver, with his intimate knowledge of geology and mining, but could she trust his judgment on safari tours? She considered the offer all the way back to the hotel.

"*Asante*, Sammy, for everything," she told him as she stepped from the cab, her bag of trinkets forgotten on the floor.

"And the safari? I will have someone call you?"

He looked so earnest. Erica imagined herself sitting around the Arusha hotel for the next two weeks getting more depressed by the day. Screw it! She would go on safari—the trip she and Cal dreamed of taking—even if she had to do it alone. If nothing else, she could see what Cal had seen, and it could only add to the biography. She'd make one more round of calls to Cal's friends and leave the number of the safari company office for messages.

"Yes, please. This is very kind of you." She wrote down the name of her hotel on a slip of paper. She hoped she had made a wise choice.

ROSE

*T*he mines weren't always as they are now—angry veins drilled to the very heart of the earth. That's what I wanted my babies to know and to remember. It was important to me that they see things the way they were in the earliest days as well as the way they are today. With that hope in mind, I sought to nourish their spirits with my stories.

My daughter's favorite story was about the day my baba found his first piece of stone; it was lying loose on the ground in the grasslands of the Merelani hills. In the night, a big storm had burst the clouds and pocked the dusty earth like the face of Mbiraru whose skin bore the scars of an exploding river stone tossed stupidly into the fire. My mama pointed to Mbiraru when she taught me to dig the fire pit: Never use stones from the river, she said, or you could turn out like that. My skin, like hers, was as smooth and dark as the heart of the ebony tree and we wore it proudly. But as I said, that morning the earth was pitted with the memory of rain, and my baba walked with my little brother, gathering up our cows, who had wandered out, browsing greedily. Overnight, the yellow grasses had turned as green as the sunny backs of the masked lovebirds and my little brother ran along, letting them tickle his chubby legs.

Baba's rock had been waiting for him on a patch of bare earth. Of all the stones that were scattered there, it was the one that glinted red in the sunrise that my father stooped to pick up. Embedded in its belly was the shining jiwe, and he dug it out with the point of his spear. It rested in his hand as warm and large as the heart of a dik-dik. The stone that it had nested in was as ordinary looking as dried antelope dung. But as he turned the jiwe in his palm, it shone purple, cobalt, blood red as the flowers of the Flamboyant Tree, and he slipped it into his pouch and returned home, where he made a gift of it to our mother. I could not take my eyes off it, wishing it for my own. She knotted it in a thin strip of hide that had already been strung with blue glass beads, and tied it around her neck. I never knew her to take it off until the day she died. Then she gave it to me. And in turn, I gave it to my daughter. It rests near her heart still.

The next day baba went back and he found more, mainly smaller crystals but these were bright bright blue. Later, we learned from the white men who came to buy the stones that it was probably the lightning that had turned the jiwes their bright colors. And the plain gray stone in which they slept. Carrying a pouch of the jewels, some still embedded in the boudin, my father walked half a day to Arusha, where he braved the streets full of automobiles to find buyers for such stones.

Soon the other men of our village followed. They went out to the place where the jiwe stones were found, and at first it was as though the stones were growing from the ground. The men hauled home sacks of stone and sold them to the white men who had begun to descend on our village as quick and as sure as marabou birds to a kill. When the earth stopped spitting up the stones on its own, the men began to dig. Shallow pits made the land look like the pictures of the moon that we were shown at school. When they weren't moving the cows across the savannah in search of water, some of the boys came, too, to scratch away at the dry earth. Soon the pits were so deep the heads of even the tallest boys disappeared as they stood in the bottoms.

The men carried the stones to Arusha and came home with all kinds of things. One time, my baba came home with sacks stuffed full to bursting but as light as air. Peel-lows, he told us. The white men sleep with them under their heads. We, of course, slept on dried cow hides, slick and easily wiped down and hung outside each morning. My *brother and I grabbed one of the peel-lows and began rolling around with it. I imagined it would feel like trying to sleep on a sack of birds and made bird noises until we shrieked with laughter. But our mother said the peel-lows would smother us in the night and she took her knife and tore them apart. White stuff like inside the seed pods of the sausage tree filled the air and blew across the plains; for days I found it trapped against the rough grasses and in the thorny branches of the fever trees. All summer, you could see bits of it sticking out of the nests of the weaver birds. My baba was angry and stayed away at the mines for several days without coming to see us. The next week he returned to Arusha with new stones, but this time he brought home the beautiful purple and red cloth my mother loved best, and they stayed together for a long time in the new* nyumba *my mother had built in his absence.*

By the time my babies were born—the girl and then the boy chasing quickly behind—I had left my village and lived with their father at the edge of Arusha in a house that was nothing like the round nyumbas *of my childhood. This house had several rooms, all with flat walls that met in sharp lines, and windows so large the sun poured in like hot oil if I forgot to pull the shades. Instead of a dung fire, I used a stove to cook our meals. That is a story all on its own, though. And by the time my babies were born, I had learned to sleep in a soft bed like white people and to rest my head on a pillow. My children accepted this as easily as they accepted the heat of the sun on their backs.*

My son's favorite story was the one about how I found my first stone, and this one I gave to him.

Each day, from the first hour after the sun rose until it was almost directly over our village, I drove my family's cattle. Our great god, Enkai, had been good to my family. He had given us many many cows for safekeeping, and they shared with us their milk and their blood for food and their dung to plaster our nyumbas. *We had goats as well, and a couple of donkeys, but as the eldest, I tended most to the cows, even though I wasn't a boy. We enjoyed great good fortune and, most years, sufficient water that we did not have to leave our village to pasture the cattle. And because of that, I was soon able to go to school, another kind of treasure.*

My first stone, I pried from the hoof of one our cows. She went lame one morning, walking across the heat-shimmering yellow plain, and because she was my favorite, I stopped in the shadow of a wait-a-while bush to look at her feet. Sure enough, there in the cleft between her hooves was a bit of stone. I took my stick and dug it out. It shone in my hand like a dark star.

The day I found that first jiwe, *I carried it to school with me, but I showed it to no one. Each time I thought of it, I reached into my school bag and squeezed it hard in my palm so that I could look at its shape pressed into my skin and know that it was really mine. That night I gave it to my father, but he and my mother said Enkai had sent it to me to show his favor.*

From that day to my last, I was a miner. Everywhere I went I looked for the stones. Flaming red, purple as the sky in the moment before night, blue as the feathers of the starlings. My entire life was a gift from Enkai, powerful god of the rains, and the end of my life would arrive at his discretion as well.

Often, my babies begged for the story of how I got my name, Lucky Rose, and I would gather them onto my lap and breathe in their warm, grassy smell as I told them the tale.

Each day, as the sun raced up toward the middle of the sky, my cousins took the cattle from me and left me to walk the dusty miles to the tin-roofed school manyatta *alone. By the time I arrived, the sun was over the tops of the fever trees down by the river. But what was there was worth the walk. I loved the courtyard swept bare, where we assembled in our uniforms and from which we marched, singing, into our classrooms. Every day began with singing and stories in our native Swahili. But soon we were learning to sing and to speak in English like the Sisters who had come to teach us. After only a year I could read the books that told tales from places where other children lived in ways that were as strange as if they lived in the sky.*

In a place called New York City, children live in nyumbas *stacked one atop the other into villages that reach the heavens. In France, they ride bicycles through fields of flowers of the sun. In Egypt, which our teachers told us was close to our part of the Earth, a dead child king was found wrapped inside a stone box hidden under a mound of stones twice as large around as our village and higher than the tallest baobab tree. Some of the children snickered with disbelief and distrust for the teachers, who were surely tricksters. But I loved these tales, although I sometimes thought they must be stretching the truth as thin as the filaments of Anansi's web.*

When I started school, there were three other girls with my same name—Semayan. At home, I was mainly called kerai, *child. Our teachers asked us to choose "school names" to make life easier for them. Some children chose a new English word they had learned—there were a Piety and a Unity among my classmates. Others selected from the saints' names. I quickly selected Rose. I don't know why. It was the name of a flower that my father brought home from Arusha one time. The petals of that rose felt like calm lips pressed to my cheeks. I kept the flower close while I slept and thought it would cool me on my walks across the grasslands. Instead, I woke the next morning to find it bruised and crumpled and no use to me at all. I buried it at the edge of our encampment. Still, once I chose that name I kept it—for school and for home.*

One day I was chased home by black clouds and winds that blew the thorns from the acacia trees. I wrapped my apron around my face and ran blind until I could run no more. Then I hid in a shallow pit. My pit filled with rain and I splashed in it like the child I was. Soon, the storm passed and blue sky cut through the clouds like a knife. With my fingers and a stick, I dug deep into the cool mud and pried out a heavy stone the size of my fist and with a knuckle of the deepest blue on one side.

This stone sucked the color from the heavens, threw it into my eyes like a spell. I ran the rest of the way home and presented it to my father in front of the entire village.

People began to call me Lucky. Lucky Rose, the elders called when I returned home from the school each day. Often I came home and emptied a stone or two from the sack I carried on my back to hold the books they gave me at school. I thought I was lucky, too.

Often, after school I walked first to the mines and if I didn't find any stones, I sat inside in the shade of the pit and read the books my teacher let me take home. I am not ashamed to say that I soon became the best reader in the class. And in my second year, I was made to read to the smallest children and help them write the letters in their names. My favorite teacher, Sister Marina, told me that I could grow up to be a teacher like her. She came to my village and said the same to my parents, who were very proud, but I told her that I had already decided that I would be a miner like my father.

It was a silly boast. How was I to know that the best of the mines would soon be snatched from our people and given to the white men, men as overstuffed with false promises as their peel-lows?

5

On either side of the concrete path that led through the Arusha hotel grounds, plants—spiny and desiccated and as familiar to Erica as her own name—struggled up from parched yellow earth. Euphorbias with their false spines, aloes and sanseverias, the ubiquitous snake plants that survived equally well in both the brutal glare of their native climate and the merciless environment of a New York City apartment. In the midday sun, heat radiated upward, searing even through the soles of her sandals. The band of her hat was sticky with sweat. Dried shoots, leafless in the heat, forced themselves through cracks in the earth. If she had come in the wet season, she knew, each shoot would be topped with its flower in eye-popping color. There were places in Africa where the very stones themselves appeared to burst into bloom each year in celebration of the rains. When they came. And when they didn't, the vegetation, the animals, the people suffered the scorching heat as nowhere else.

This hotel, the jumping off site for several safari trips, billed itself as the image of a small Maasai village. Searching for the individual round hut-like structure that was her room, Erica felt as if she'd been walking along that pathway for miles. Erica had to examine each identical faux-*ngoma* hut she passed for its number.

She was looking for 103, which was nowhere to be found near 102 or 104. The path was about to come to an abrupt end. There was only one more hut tucked just out of sight, and there, finally, was a sign for number 103 and an arrow pointing to the left. Gratefully, she fingered the room key and hurried along.

The first thing she did upon entering the room was to turn on the air conditioner. It rattled and hummed and sent tepid air eddying through the heat ineffectually. In another moment, she was stretched across the queen-sized bed that took up most of the space in the room, the mosquito netting loosed from pull-back hooks in the wall so that it surrounded her like a frothy cloud. Her eyelids, singed from the sun and the dry persistent wind, began their slow, delicious descent and she drifted off to sleep even before they were completely shut. When she woke, later in the afternoon, Erica lay there, looking around at the bare walls of the room daubed with ochre and gray paint to resemble the inside of a mud hut. Beyond the small windows, the scene shimmered like the air over a charcoal grill, *ngomas* receding along the pathway like a string of gray pearls.

She had spent the morning by the small pool, reading a mystery she had found in her room. She hoped the intricate plot would hold her attention and keep her from replaying, again and again, the discomfiting scene with Drew. She had mishandled that situation, of that she was certain. There was something Drew was holding back and she should have insisted on hearing it. Or she should have confronted him as a liar and demanded to know why he would slander an old friend. And what was all that business about Cal and money that Sammy was telling her? Cal never appeared to be someone who chased the almighty dollar. His salary as a paramedic was enough to live on comfortably, but not much more than that.

She was sure he could have pursued any number of higher paying careers. Except that he said he was happiest on the front lines. Erica found herself seeing Cal in a strange, almost incorporeal light, more like smoke than flesh and blood. He was one thing, and then another. A galloping horse and then a fire-breathing dragon. Maybe she had been in the sun too long. She left the pool and stopped at the bar for a cold beer before heading for her room.

Despite some earlier hesitation, she had decided to go with the safari recommended by Sammy. She'd been convinced when Makinde, the head tour guide, telephoned her personally to describe the wildlife that had been spied on the previous trip into the bush. On that trip, they had shot (*on film*, he stressed) four out of Africa's famous "Big Five" animals—the ones most difficult to bag in the old days. His enthusiastic description of the lions, water buffalo, leopards and elephants, not to mention hippos, warthogs (*little baby warthogs!* he crooned) and baboons, pushed her over the precipice of desire. When she mentioned the name of the tour outfit at dinner last night, two of the women at her table excitedly told her they'd be among her fellow travelers. They brought out the glossy brochure and detailed itinerary from the tour company for her to see. Each day was packed with intriguing details about the terrain and the wildlife that could be expected. Erica had already decided that Jane and Marcie seemed well-traveled and discriminating, which added some assurance that her choice was a good one.

Now Erica had a couple of hours until the minibus would ferry them to the safari departure point. She felt eager and anxious in equal measures. It was billed as a "tented safari," but Marcie assured her that their tents would be nothing like the Boy Scout pup tents of her childhood; the tents would have actual cots and individual camp showers. By signing onto a trip with a company she'd never even heard of, she had put her wellbeing into the hands of strangers. Not my usual M.O., Erica thought, but no one lives forever. She winced and thought again of Cal. People did live as if they'd go on forever. As if we could trust that the next moment and the next will be like the last. And then, just once, they are wrong. She was about to embark on a magnificent adventure. To see plants and animals she had dreamed of all her life. Instead of torturing herself with existential questions, she'd stick to the more practical challenge of preparing herself for two weeks of reduced personal hygiene.

Camp showers, as she knew from summer experiences, consisted of nothing more than a giant plastic bag of water suspended over the roof of the tent piped down into an area set up with a hole in the floor and maybe a wooden palette to stand on. Eager for one last real shower, she rose from the bed and slipped out of her clothes, leaving them where they fell. As she brushed through the mosquito netting, it slid over her bare body like the rough skin of a hand.

In the bathroom, Erica adjusted the temperature of the water before stepping into the shower. Oh, the simple pleasure of water rushing over her scalp, neck, shoulders, back, butt. She turned her face up to the torrent as the water crept up around her ankles above the slow drain. She shampooed her hair thoroughly, rinsed and added an extra measure of conditioner—she suspected that the camp shower would run out of hot water long before she got that far. Even after she was soaped and rinsed, she continued to stand under the hard spray until she began to feel guilty about wasting water in this arid land.

She turned off the taps and wrapped herself in the threadbare towel she'd been given at the reception desk. There was no need to rub dry—the air would suck the moisture from her skin in moments. Instead, she bent from the waist and hung upside down to comb out her hair. She took the time to comb detangler through the strands and clip her nails carefully, letting them fall into the toilet. Erica filed her nails as short as she could and then twisted her hair into a tight bun to keep it off her neck and discourage frizz. She rewrapped the towel around her torso and stepped out of the bathroom.

Something felt different. The smell of Africa—that burnt cork smell to which she had not yet grown accustomed—had been swept aside by something cooler and more floral, as if a finger of icy, perfumed air had crept, snakelike, into the room. Or rather, not floral, but more of a vegetative tang, like the scent of crushed thyme. The door, which she knew she had locked, was still shut tight. Her damp skin prickled with chill. She looked around the room furtively. Although there was no place for anyone to hide in the simple wide-open space, she felt watched, exposed. She wrapped the towel more securely and tried to convince herself it was all in her imagination. Her clothes lay where she dropped them by the side of the bed. But the netting, which she had left encircling the bed, was now wide open on one side.

And on the bed, its spread still rumpled from her earlier nap, lay four white roses arranged fanlike on the pillow.

Erica gasped and spun around, expecting to meet the gaze of the interloper, but there was no one in the room. She rushed to the door; it was still locked. In a panic she pulled it open and stepped onto the pathway, ready to cry out for help. But there was nobody out in the flaming heat. Everyone was still at the bar, or taking a siesta. Suddenly aware she was in nothing but a towel, Erica crept back into her hut. The door hung slightly ajar, and Erica realized that she was lucky it hadn't swung closed, locking her out in near nakedness. She made another circuit of the room, checking the one shallow closet and the bathroom. No one. She yanked the roses off the pillow, crying out as a thorn pricked her finger. But she was no Sleeping Beauty. She crammed the flowers upside down into the wastepaper basket and quickly put on her clothes.

Could this be a Tanzanian custom for bidding farewell to guests? Maybe a chambermaid had let herself in using a passkey, not realizing that Erica was in the room, and arranged the flowers for her to find on her return. Tanzania had developed a thriving international trade in growing roses for the European market. It made sense, sort of. Certainly, there had been other customs here that surprised her. Like the fact that each hotel offered her a glass of juice upon arrival. Maybe the roses were another Tanzanian notion of hospitality. The idea of this calmed her racing heart and the cold sweat dried on her neck. She was overreacting. Later, she'd ask the others if they liked their roses. With a little cringe of embarrassment, she lifted the stems from the wastepaper basket and set them into one of the glasses in the bathroom. She filled it with water and propped it on the vanity. The flowers glowed in the fluorescent light but gave off no fragrance, typical for the super-cultivated hybrids that grew quickly and travelled best. Erica herself preferred the older species roses, even the wildly rampant Rosa rugosa, with its sweet-spicy aroma. What, after all, was a rose without its fragrance? A ghost of its former self.

6

Four guides stood waiting for the travelers as they got off the bus in front of the lodge. Three of the guides were men, and the last was a striking young woman with skin like the polished heartwood of the mahogany tree. She appeared to be the youngest of the leaders, but would soon prove to have the sharpest vision and the keenest sense for where the most elusive animals rested in the midday heat. Nothing escaped her sweeping gaze. It was she who would detect the leopard lazily slung across the high branches of the sausage tree no more than fifty yards from the road on their second day out. And that same day, she would spot a pair of female lions about to lunge from the tall grass for their kill—a still-wobbly wildebeest foal whose unwary mother had wandered off, nibbling at the dry grass.

"*Tafadhali*, please, call me Nini," she told the group as they all shook hands. Erica was struck by Nini's piercing gray-green eyes. Strapped to her waist was a long, brightly hued leather sheath, and around her neck she wore a leather band, knotted with a handful of beads and anchored in the center with a jagged crystal that resembled a raw, uncut ruby, but Erica guessed might be tanzanite. Although Erica had seen similar beadwork necklaces in Moshi when Sammy dragged her from trading post to trading post, none of them were graced with such a striking and beautiful stone. She made up her mind to ask the girl about it before the trip was over. Now *there* was the sort of piece worth splurging on and taking home as a memento, Erica thought.

Four Land Rovers would be used by the group of fifteen travelers, each of them driven by one of the naturalist guides: Hassam, Leni, Makinde, and, of course, Nini. As each of the three others stood and introduced himself, Erica searched for a way to associate the names with the faces. Hassam was short and thickly built with the doe eyes and teak-colored skin of an Arab. Erica had no trouble linking his name with his face. Despite her rational refusal to blame all Muslims for what a radical few had done, she found the idea of putting herself in the hands of Hassam mildly distressing. Even though she had read that Tanzania considered itself a Muslim country, despite its many tribal peoples, she had managed to overlook the ramifications of that. She was embarrassed by her gut-level reaction and determined to see this as an opportunity to work through her prejudices. In contrast to Hassam, Leni was tall, darker and extraordinarily thin—lean, leanie, Leni—no problem. Makinde, dark as ebony, was as powerfully built as his name and might be a strong leader, and it was he who led the greeting at the camp. Nini was soft spoken but by far the most amusing of the group.

"I am Maasai," she explained. "We Maasai own all of the cows in the world—a generous gift from our god, Enkai—and I am here because I am tired of walking behind them in the noonday sun and would rather drive." The travelers all laughed politely. "I am happy to show you my country and its many noble creatures. I hope you will return home with a deep love and understanding of our great land." The sincerity behind her words showed in her eyes, which peered searchingly from one guest to the next. Her intense gaze raised goose bumps along Erica's arms. She wished yet again that Cal was beside her. She imagined that with a few words of Swahili, he could have established a deeper relationship with their guides.

After the brief introduction, the escorts waved everyone through the camp lobby and into an open-air bar covered by a tall thatched roof and amply furnished with deep leather chairs clustered into groups. Erica was taken aback by the opulence of the place after the inexpensive hotels she had suffered in Moshi and Arusha. Sammy was right—this was going to be a more lavish tour than she had imagined. She wondered for a moment how he had managed to get her such a reasonable price.

The tour company had suggested that she might prefer to share a tent with another single woman, but Erica protested. The idea was anathema to her. And it wasn't merely the prospect of sleeping inches from a stranger—her breath, her dreams, intermingled with Erica's own—that led her to reject the idea. In the past year, Erica had painstakingly built around herself a shell as fragile and brittle as the thin layer of sepal cells that surround and protect each developing bud, and the idea of bumping up against another human being threatened that delicate barrier. Rocked by unpredictable moments of grief, she imagined how the mildest intimacy might leave her weeping at the knees of a stranger, her story spilling drop by precious drop. The kindness of strangers was no kindness to her. She didn't want to explain to anyone her real reason for being in Africa. She wanted to appear, insofar as possible, a simple tourist. She'd gladly pay a premium for the privilege.

"Don't worry about your luggage," Makinde announced as he handed out the tent numbers on their way into the bar. "As long as your bag is marked with your name, it will arrive at your room or your tent each night, even before you do." And while this was being accomplished today, he noted, they would all enjoy a brief orientation and a chance to get to know one another. He had a broad face and a wide, inclusive smile, but deeply serious eyes. He walked to a raised platform at one end of the room purposefully, although with a pronounced limp, and as soon as everyone was seated, he began his orientation.

"*Jambo, jambo bwana,*" he began, "*wageni, wakari bishwa!*" Hello and welcome, esteemed ladies and gentlemen. We are looking forward to sharing our beautiful nation of Tanzania with you. We hope you will learn much not only about our wonderful animals, but about our wonderful people." As he spoke, Nini handed out safari journals, each with a checklist of animals and birds the traveler could expect to see and many blank pages for recording his or her impressions. Erica noticed, though, that there was no matching list of flora. She thought she might assemble one of her own.

A sudden shriek echoed through the space, and eighteen heads jerked nervously to and fro. Makinde, though, merely chuckled and pointed into the canopy of trees.

"Ah, so your welcome has been seconded by my good friend, the blue monkey. Watch out for that one, he's a sneak-thief of abundant talent. Be certain not to leave your tents unzipped even for a moment if you don't want to see your undies on the heads of every member of his large family." Everyone giggled nervously and a couple of cameras clicked.

"But have no fear for your safety. Our experienced guides are all expert marksmen with their rifles and my friend Nini here once slit a hyena's throat with her Maasai knife before the beast could tear into one of her family's calves." Erica thought Nini shot him a quick glare, but he continued to move on, extolling the virtues of Tanzania, a peace-loving country and one that had taken the lead in nurturing and protecting its precious natural resources. As he spoke of the many places on their itinerary and what they might hope to see, a pair of waiters came around offering juice, bottled water or Kili. No one chose anything other than beer.

Makinde raised both his arms to the assembly and proposed a toast. "I wish us all *Safari njema!* Good travels!"

The group members turned in their seats, from side to side, clinking bottles with their neighbors and introducing themselves. As soon as one bottle of beer was empty, a silent waiter came and replaced it with a full, cold one. Before long, most of the other guests were laughing like old friends and wishing each other *Safari njema,* and *Hakuna matata!* No worries!—parroting Makinde, who beamed at them all like a proud papa as they tried out his mother tongue. He called them to attention once more.

"Each morning I would like you to choose a different guide's car and a different grouping of passengers," he instructed. "This will help you get to know all your fellow travelers and also to take advantage of the particular expertise of each of our excellent guides. They have the eyes of the tawny eagle when it comes to spotting animals. And they have battery chargers on board so that your cameras can stay at the ready. They also have rifles, although I trust we will not need them."

Erica looked around at the people with whom she would share this journey. On first glance, they all appeared coupled up, including one obvious team of four sporting University of Wisconsin t-shirts (*Go Badgers!*). But then she picked out a few solo exceptions besides herself. An older woman wearing a broad-brimmed straw hat introduced herself as Bea. A man in his early forties fiddled nervously with a pair of black-framed Wayfarers. On and off, off and on, he kept repositioning the glasses as if he were deciding whether or not to buy them. While they were off, Erica noticed that he was quite good-looking with slightly graying eyebrows set at a quizzical angle over deep-set brown eyes. Bedroom eyes, her friend Karen would have called them. If Karen were here, she would have nudged Erica in the ribs and given her a little head tilt that said, *check him out!* It was Karen's considered and vocal opinion that Erica needed to push herself back into the world, and particularly into the world of datable men. How did you convince your best friend that your heart was about as numb as a crutch, Erica often wondered. Whenever Erica imagined herself with a man other than Cal, she experienced a cold sick feeling that radiated from the pit of her stomach like a case of bad clams. She had resigned herself to it and tried to move on. There was more to life than sex and romance. The only problem was, she didn't quite believe that. In the sweltering shade of the African afternoon, Erica continued to listen to Makinde's orientation while watching the man's unconscious sleight of hand with his eyewear. He glanced up, caught her looking and broke into a shy smile. Erica turned quickly and began to search her bag for her own sunglasses, which she then realized were on her face. Although he had already looked away, Erica withdrew a tube of lip gloss with sunscreen and applied some to cover her embarrassment.

While most of the guests were paired off, two were so blatantly affectionate that Erica (correctly) guessed they were on their honeymoon. They kissed between sips of beer and sat shoulder-to-shoulder, never breaking physical contact. It made Erica twinge with longing. Suddenly, she found the alcohol-fueled joviality disagreeable.

How could she have thought this magical trip would be the same in Cal's eternal absence? How could she explain herself to these happy vacationers? Erica wondered if it was too late to cancel and get at least some of her money back. She could stay in Tanzania just long enough to determine whether Billy and Anna Marie were available to interview and then book a flight home. But this idea seemed even more discouraging. The prospect of being alone in a dark womblike tent suddenly held appeal. Instead of joining in the enthusiastic patter peculiar to strangers becoming instant friends, Erica feigned a headache and promised to meet them all at dinner. In fact, her heart was aching more than her head, but who could explain such a thing to strangers?

"I think I'll just check out the tent and maybe read until dinner," she muttered, standing. The others made room for her to leave, murmuring their *hakuna matatas* at her as she passed. No worries. Erica wished this were the case. Jane and Marcie caught up with her as she was about to leave the bar.

"You're okay, right?" Marcie asked. "Not feeling ill? Because Jane was feeling a little queasy this afternoon. We think it might have been something she ate for breakfast. Those sausages seemed a bit suspect, I thought." Marcie's face was screwed up into a look of deep concern one might have for a child or an injured pet. She put one arm around Jane and gave a squeeze. Jane responded by rolling her eyes good naturedly and leaning back into Marcie. From this, Erica read the story of their lives together. A tight and happy couple with clearly defined roles: the nurturer and the nurtured. Clearly, though, they were making space in their circle for her. Erica was warmed by this, but also a little wary. *Not too close*, piped up her squeaky internal warning system.

"No, I'm fine. I just need a little alone time. I'm not a natural mingler. Anyway, I want to finish that mystery before we head out on safari. I need to know whodunit and why." Erica surprised even herself with the inanities she could come up with in a pinch. But the two women seemed satisfied.

"We're in tent six," Jane said. "If there's anything you need, just come by. We're prepared for almost anything, from cramps to trypanosomiasis. Marcie's mother is an epidemiologist who sent us out here with a medicine kit that would make Doctors Without Borders envious. In fact, we're planning to offer it to the school out in the Serengeti that we'll visit on the tour. In the meantime, though, just yell if you need anything."

Erica smiled gratefully. In truth, she had brought almost nothing that could be useful in a medical emergency. The only thing she had plenty of was toothpaste, ibuprofen and Ambien.

She headed alone into the encampment. The path to the tents paralleled a steep drop-off to the Tarangire River valley where a threadlike stream serpentined its way between clumps of gray-green vegetation and thorny stay-awhile trees. The overall palette ranged from ochre to taupe. Most of the trees were leafless, although there were occasional clumps of gray-green foliage. A stone wall kept the unwary from tumbling over the edge. Erica strayed from the path and pressed her palms into the warm stones of the barrier. The haze and the miniature aspect of the plant life down there made it impossible to guess how far above it she was and how far the valley stretched. It was like staring into a giant terrarium—only yellow and sere instead of moist and green. There was no sign of man as far as the eye could see. Suddenly a slow, rolling movement caught Erica's eye. There, walking along the river, was a lone elephant. *An elephant.* Taking his late afternoon stroll down by the water. Not in a circus, not in a zoo, not in a movie starring Meryl Streep, just an animal in search of water and food rolling his slow, majestic girth down the dusty valley to satisfy his needs.

Erica's neck prickled with excitement. Unconsciously, she reached both arms out toward the great beast until she could see the curve of her fingers hugging it like a pair of parentheses. My first great African creature, she thought. Mine and mine alone. She stood without moving until the majestic monster moved beyond her ability to see.

She reached into her backpack and pulled out a small pair of binoculars. Unused to them, she took some time to focus, but when she did she was amazed by what she saw. Rather than an empty plain, the valley before her held small groups of zebras, clustered tightly to share the meager shade thrown by the leafless thorn trees. Scattered about were pairs of great birds—some kind of buzzard—that she had mistaken for tufts of grass. The elephant slowly made his way down the valley; now he was wading in the narrow rivulet, his tusks standing out in relief against the pale earth. How cool the water must feel against his leathery soles; Erica wished she could wade along with him. After a while, he left the stream and made his way to a jutting bank—an indication of the depth the water would reach in the rainy season. He swung his great head from side to side and rubbed his trunk in the rough grass at the top of the bank. Then he turned around and did the same thing with the side of his head and finally his hind end. Although she had never thought of an elephant having an itch, Erica could almost feel his relief. Finally, he lumbered off and eventually moved out of Erica's sight, even aided with the binoculars.

It was already growing dark when she returned to the path. Here at the equator, dawn and dusk were brief moments compared to the lengthy transitions they represented back home. She walked briskly, not eager to be out as night crept up. Around her head whined a mosquito. Erica swiped at it and hurried on. The insect repellent was in her duffel. She'd have to remember to keep it with her from now on.

As opposed to the chaotic placement of the rooms in her Arusha hotel, the tents were in proper numerical order and she found hers easily. It was larger than she'd expected and had been erected on a wooden platform, part of which formed a front porch set with a small table and folding camp chair. Very civilized, indeed. She stepped onto the platform and crouched to open the pair of heavy duty zippers that closed, first a net screen, and then the heavy tent canvas. Erica stepped through the opening into a cozy room furnished with two fully made up cots, each flanked by a night table. A small folding stand at the foot of one bed held her bag. Part of the floor was covered by a bright hand-woven rug and the rest was swept clean, and the cots were freshly made up with purple and red plaid blankets folded back to reveal crisp white sheets and a pair of pillows on each bed. A beautifully carved wooden bowl sat on each nightstand along with a small reading lamp. Overhead, a light had been created from a beaded bowl suspended upside down over a tiny cluster of LED bulbs. A switch on the wall turned the energy-sparing lamp on and off.

Toward the back of the tent was another zippered-off area and Erica went to explore this. Beyond that canvas wall was a private bath, complete with a pair of sinks set into a long, narrow wooden table. There were no taps for running water, but two large pitchers held water for washing. A note warned occupants that this was not meant for drinking, and four new bottles of water had been left nearby for that purpose. Behind the sink, more canvas provided privacy for a chemical toilet on one side, and a camp shower on the other. The entire setup was as ingenious as it was ecological, and Erica was charmed. If all the camps were this well planned, she would be comfortable indeed in the bush. She was particularly glad to see that she wouldn't have to venture out of the tent late at night to use the bathroom.

The main room of the tent had a number of screened windows with canvas tied back to let the light in. Through one of them she now watched as the rest of the group sauntered down the path and turned off to their separate tents. The sky had grown darker, the deep valley below now hidden in purple dusk. Erica took a moment to relish her secret knowledge. Where was the elephant now, she wondered. Had it found its herd, or was it, like her, a solitary creature, wandering alone on this great expanse of earth? She thought of the little drawing that set the stage for Saint-Exupery's story of *The Little Prince*. A drawing that grownups saw as a hat, but children recognized as an elephant that had been eaten by a boa constrictor. *The Little Prince*. Cal's favorite book. She'd reread it after he mentioned it. With a resonant sigh, Erica began to unpack the items she would need for the night. They had been allowed only one medium sized duffel bag, weighing no more than twenty five pounds, fully loaded. She had packed her nightclothes and bathroom supplies right on top, and now she laid these out on one of the cots. Underneath them was the notebook she had brought to fill with the memories of Cal's friends here. She reached for it and let it fall open to a page at random as she perched on the other cot. It was the interview with Cal's partner, Frank, and she closed the book without reading the entry and placed it back in her bag. It wasn't so much what he said about Cal, but what he said about her that disturbed her fragile sense of peace. Even now, she couldn't think about it without a creeping sense of humiliation.

The bus ride from Port Authority Terminal to the small Catskills village where Frank lived had been slow and fume-ridden. Again and again, Erica reached into her purse with its precious cargo as if to reassure herself of its safety. In the past month the notebook she carried everywhere had been filled with the reminiscences of half a dozen people who had been part of Cal's life. A college roommate, a childhood friend who turned out to live around the corner from Erica, one of his teachers from his EMT training, a few of the guys from the bike club. Each was eager to share a memory. Erica tape recorded the participants telling their stories—how he and Cal spent a night lost in the woods when they wandered off from Camp Housatonic, how Cal bailed him out when he was arrested for having two joints in his backpack, how Cal came up with an improvement for evacuating a disabled person from a walkup apartment while he was still a trainee. Some even offered her photos of Cal at various ages. Her favorite was one of him peering down from the branches of a pine tree at summer camp. His impish grin clearly said, *just try and catch me!* She imagined him shinnying up higher and higher as his counselor pleaded with him to be sensible and return to the ground.

Erica had anticipated the interview with Cal's partner with both trepidation and anticipation. This was the man with whom Cal had spent up to ten hours a day, side by side in the ambulance or at the stationhouse, sharing just about everything in their lives, and side by side on the front lines of emergency medicine, sometimes literally up to their elbows in the lifeblood of the people they treated. Erica had met Frank only once, when she had dropped by the station at the end of Cal's shift. Her main impression at that time was of a tall, bookish man with slightly receding curly reddish hair. She would have taken him for a librarian had she passed him on the street. But when he shook her hand, his physical strength became clear. Her hand felt as frail as a newly hatched sparrow in his grip. He smiled at her warmly and looked straight into her eyes with a palpable curiosity. Erica wondered what Cal had told Frank about her. She and Cal left before she could have much of a conversation with the man, though.

Cal hadn't said a lot about Frank except that he knew he could count on him. That was high praise from Cal, who treated self-reliance as an art form. Erica had no illusion that he had relied on her when they were together, at least not in any ordinary way. Unlike some of the husbands of her friends, who might possibly starve if someone didn't put cooked food on the table, Cal would actually start preparing dinner if she didn't arrive home on time, and he almost never asked her to do any of the mundane chores—make his dentist appointments or replace his worn socks—that so many men asked of their spouses and partners. He took care of his own dry cleaning (what little he had), did laundry and bought himself every item of clothing he wore. He bragged that he could live like a solitary hermit in a cave if he had to, but if pressed by Erica, tempered that enough to grin and admit he was glad he didn't have to. Erica liked to believe that Cal relied on her in a deeper, more emotional way. She read it in his touch. In the way his lower lip trembled slightly when he looked at her as they made love. In the way he would reach for her hand in the middle of the night when he couldn't sleep.

Erica hoped that once she assembled all of the recollections reading the notebook would be like watching a photograph develop, a human figure distinguishing itself from the background, the individual details emerging, hazy at first and then with greater and greater clarity, fleshing out the form and giving solidity to a life cut short.

Frank's interview, however, would be the hardest. In the weeks following the attack, when the names of the dead were appearing on list after list, Erica had searched daily, expecting to find his. Frank Kavanagh. Surely he was there when the unthinkable happened, when the towers imploded and everything and everyone left inside slid sickeningly into the abyss. But his name did not show up.

At first, Erica was too shell-shocked to take any additional steps to locate Frank. Since the memorial, most of Cal's family had closed ranks and treated her like an outsider, so she couldn't ask them about him. Obviously, he hadn't shared his plans to return to their life together, although that didn't surprise her. He hadn't shared much with them, as far as she could tell; it was unlikely they knew much more than she did about Frank. Which was almost nothing. She didn't know where he'd lived, or even if he lived in the city. In the end, Erica took her quest online, sobbing as she read once again the long lists of those who had perished in the attack. Day after day, the *Times* published biographies of the dead, the office workers, business people, merchants, policemen, chaplains, firemen and paramedics whose lives ended that morning. Cal's name appeared on the very first day and once she could go on reading, Erica looked once more for any reference to Frank that she might have missed. There was none. She looked in the next day's paper and the one after that. Nothing.

Finally, she forced herself to visit the stationhouse and ask about Frank. At first, no one would give her information. Why should they? She introduced herself as Cal's girlfriend. Anyone could make a claim like that, and none of them had met her when Cal was alive. Just as she was about to give up, the captain admitted that Frank had gone to recover from health issues at his family's farm upstate.

All this time she had assumed the pair of them had perished the same way they had eaten their meals—side by side. A Web search unearthed a short article in an upstate paper about the native son of a small Delaware County farm family whose life was spared that day because he paused in his dash up the stairs to help a dazed and choking building worker back through the smoke-filled lobby to safety. In the process, he gave the man his respirator, leaving him to "take a feed" as the firemen called it—to suck in lungfuls of the toxic smoke. By the time Frank headed back into the building there was no visible lobby to return to, and he spent the next six months in the hole that remained, working with the teams that searched for remains. Along the way, he contracted pneumonia and had been in and out of an Oneonta hospital undergoing treatment for complications and lung tissue scarring.

Only after several long, pleading phone calls would the man consent to see her. She took the bus to the tiny hamlet of Margaretville and interviewed him on the porch of his family's home. His red hair was sparse and gray, and he sat stooped and shrunken on a peeling wicker settee. The hand that shook hers was boney and dry. He indicated with a nod the worn porch glider across from him, and Erica sat down and took up her pen and notebook. Frank stared at her without warmth. When he spoke it was with effort, and his words came between wheezing breaths.

"What are you looking for?" he asked.

"I want to know about Cal's life. The things that made him unique. Stories from the people he knew best."

"I don't think I can help you," he said flatly.

"But you were his partner. You two must have shared a great deal in your time together. You could help people come to know him."

"What if Cal didn't want to be known?"

Erica looked at him, confused.

"He was one of the most outgoing guys I've ever met," she said. "Everyone who knew him, loved him. I could read you some wonderful stories." She started to thumb through the notebook.

"Those stories are not about Cal," he wheezed. She looked up blankly. "Stories are just stories. Distorted memories of the people who tell them. Cal in a funhouse mirror."

Erica tried to reframe her request a way that might make her less of an adversary. "I feel like you knew Cal better than most," she began. "And if that's true, how can you help me understand him better?"

"I had a dog once," he said, looking directly into her eyes. "Brought him to the vet to have him fixed. For days afterward, he would jump up and scurry away, startled, like someone was goosing him. But he was running from his own hind end. Cal was like that dog. Whatever was chasing him was a part of himself." After that, he didn't say anything for a long while.

Erica didn't know how to respond. Did he know that Cal was seeing a therapist? She considered whether telling him would constitute a breach of confidence. In any case, Frank was clearly impaired by his own illness. Were his words a reflection of deep emotional wounds? Was he angry at Cal? Or at her?

"I knew as soon as we approached the doorway that there would be no exit," he said finally in a flat monotone. "We all knew. Smoke and grit turned the famous light-filled lobby into a spookhouse and we ran in as one body, silent and grim behind our masks, through the murk and toward the stairs. Cal was the last to put on his mask. He was smiling."

Again, neither of them spoke for several minutes. Inside, the ordinary sound of a meal being prepared seemed to belong to some other world entirely.

"You're stalking him. You know that, don't you?"

The word shook her. At first Erica was too stunned to reply. Her cheeks burned, first with anger, then shame.

"How can you say that?" she finally managed to get out. "We loved each other deeply. He was working on whatever issues had driven us apart. I'm only trying to keep his memory alive. Let others know the Cal we both loved."

"What you're doing is scavenging through other people's memories and feeding off them. He can't stop you. But you can't honestly believe that he would have wanted you to pursue him this way, can you?"

It was so cruel, so gratuitously wounding. Erica was completely unable to respond.

Later, recounting the interview to Karen, Erica felt her cheeks burning again. Although Karen was her closest friend—the one she spoke to at least five nights a week—she was unwilling to repeat to Karen the ugly words that Frank had uttered.

"Frank seemed really damaged," she told Karen, instead. "He was skin and bones, and he had a lot of trouble breathing. But mainly, he looked like a walking case of survivor's guilt. At one point he said it outright—*I should have been there. I should have died alongside my team.* After that, he didn't have much to say." Not trusting herself to look into Karen's eyes, Erica busied herself clearing their coffee cups from the table.

Now, searching the duffel for her insect repellent, Erica came across the gift that Karen had given her when she dropped her off at Kennedy Airport.

"Don't open it until you see your first zebra," Karen had said mysteriously, unzipping an outside pocket of Erica's duffel as she yanked it from the trunk of the car and depositing the small package inside. She re-zipped and handed the bag over to Erica.

She gave Erica a final hug and returned to the driver's seat as the traffic security guard glared and waved her on impatiently. Ever since the attack on the Trade Center, dropping someone at the airport had become an act that elicited an attitude of suspicion on the part of airport security and could only be accomplished at breakneck speed. No more long goodbyes. Erica stood a moment at the curb and watched until the car disappeared from view. She had the most awful feeling that she would never see Karen again. That something horrible would happen in her absence and her friend would be gone when she returned. Vaporized into thin air. What her therapist Elizabeth called a *phantom feeling* and Erica called *the way the world rolls now.*

Just recalling the moment, Erica's heart began to beat an awkward tattoo in her chest. It fluttered and flopped like a fish dropped on the deck of a boat. Like the phantom feeling, the sensation was not at all unfamiliar: she experienced it recurrently throughout the day for several days running and then not at all for weeks at a time. When it first started, over a year prior, her doctor had given her a Holter monitor to wear for a week. The results showed nothing significantly amiss and the doctor suggested that the symptoms were merely hormonal, which Erica interpreted as "hysterical." He offered her beta blockers, which confirmed her suspicions. But she didn't want drugs. The feeling was not at all painful and didn't seem to affect either her breathing or her strength. At work, she could still hoist forty pound bags of compost and till them into the soil without breaking a sweat. In some ways, in fact, the sensation was pleasurable—at least it reminded her that she still had a heart and that it continued to beat, albeit with its own eccentric—or perhaps compromised—rhythm.

Karen's package, about the size and shape of a deck of cards, was wrapped in silver foil printed with pink tea roses. Erica turned it over in her hands a few times, trying to guess what might be inside. *Not until you see your first zebra,* Karen had insisted. Erica had, in fact, seen her first zebras only moments after they drove through the tall wooden gates that marked the entrance to Tarangire National Park. Like a welcoming committee, the five animals stood to the side of the road, their chiaroscuro hides dappled by the shade of a low tamarind tree, camouflaged by their stripes. *Disruptive coloration,* Cal had explained to Erica. *Extremely effective at dawn and dusk when most predators are at large.* Seeing their shapes emerge from the stippled shadows gave Erica new appreciation for this. She was the first of the passengers to spot them and she gasped, audibly. Almost immediately, the cameras starting whirring and clicking, but Erica could only stare. Three decades of nature shows had left her completely unprepared for the sudden realization that such creatures actually walked the same Earth as she did and existed completely unaware and uncaring of her presence. Not fed huge rashers of hay in a zoo or theme park, but freely wandering the same land where they had evolved. The enormity of this made Erica tearful with joy. Funny, she thought, that tears were the paramount expression of both sadness and bliss.

The sweat from her fingers had dampened the wrapping paper, and the pink roses were bleeding into the silver paper. Inside was a framed photograph—one of her, Karen, and Cal at the Bronx Zoo, taken shortly after Cal had moved into her apartment. In the picture, they stood at the African Plains exhibit while a herd of zebra grazed just behind them. A trick of perspective made it look as if a couple of zebra had joined them, the heads of the animals appearing in the space between the shoulders of Erica and Karen. Erica had given the picture to Karen as a birthday present, and now Karen had sent it along with Erica on this journey. In some small way, she felt that this image brought Cal full circle back to Africa.

She was zipping the photo back into her bag for safe keeping when a noise outside the tent made her jump. A rhythmic snuffling and grunting was coming from just outside one of the back windows. Now the tent wall shuddered a tiny bit, followed by a solid bump. Erica sat frozen to her cot. Lion? Leopard? Should she yell, or stay silent until the beast decided to move on? Could she quietly unzip the front door and slip out unnoticed? The guttural snorts continued from behind the tent, joined by a rhythmic swish. But this sound she recognized for the animal it was. Someone was walking toward the tent, his or her footsteps growing closer, nylon pant legs brushing each other in rhythm.

As quietly as she could, Erica worked her way toward a window on the side from which the steps were coming. She rolled up the shade. It was that tall man with the cameras—Mike, she thought his name was—and he was only a few yards away.

"Psst!" Erica hissed out the window. "Psst! Mike!" He looked toward the tent, startled.

"Who is that?" he called. "Bea? Is that you? Are you okay?"

"No," she called back in a stage whisper. "It's Erica. Be careful. There's some animal behind my tent."

Mike stopped walking and looked all around him.

"An animal? What kind of animal?"

"I wish I knew. Sounded large. I think it's lying against the back of my tent. Can you see it? Be careful!"

Mike looked unsure of whether he should move. Then he began walking backward.

"I'll get one of the guides," he told her. "I'll be right back." He scurried quickly down the path, looking left and right as he departed, leaving Erica alone again. She snatched up one of the wooden bowls in case the animal attacked.

Maybe this was a big mistake, she thought. Maybe I should never have come here. She felt under siege yet again. It was like those early months after 9/11, when everyone worked so hard at trying to act normal, but scratch the surface even lightly—a train stalled a moment too long between stations, a power outage or blown fuse, a steam pipe burst or unexpected fireworks—and the slumbering beast of terror roused and shook itself, and people's carefully cultivated sense of wellbeing shattered like the windows of a greenhouse hit by a falling tree limb.

Erica heard the approach of the crowd before she saw it. Half a dozen of her fellow travelers had followed Leni, Nini, and Hassam to see what great creature had taken up residence behind her tent. The aggregate of hushed voices was loud enough to block the raspy breath of whatever was lurking there. Hassam, leading the way, carried a rifle perched on his shoulder, and behind him, Nini had her knife ready in her hand, the long blade glinting in the sun. But as he got closer Hassam started to laugh.

"Come out and see, Miss Erica. Come see what we have found," he called, jovially. The rest of the group had gathered in a semi-circle behind him. By the time Erica joined them, the inevitable photo equipment was clicking away. Basking in the sun at the base of the canvas structure were not one, but half a dozen warthogs of varying sizes, from adults as large as collies, with formidable-looking tusks and mustaches of coarse bristles, to diminutive babies, frolicking like pups.

"You must have been calling to them," Hassam said, grinning. "They seem to enjoy your company very much." The heat of her embarrassment was hotter on her cheeks than the scorching sun. "Everyone, we should thank Miss Erica for bringing us the wart-hogs." A smattering of applause broke out from those not engaged in filming the event. Erica felt torn between bowing to acknowledge it and bolting back into her tent. In the end, she managed an embarrassed curtsy, the bowl hidden behind her back.

Leni said, "Be careful not to crowd them, or they could give chase." Erica was sure she wouldn't be crowding a warthog any time soon. Those tusks looked sharp as sabers.

"I think it's time for a celebratory drink," Robert said. After snapping a few last shots, everyone but Erica followed him back down the path.

"Aren't you coming Erica?" asked Nini. "It is always safest to stay close with the herd."

ROSE

*I*n my village, people believe that stories are like the fruits of the wild mango trees—bright and sweet treasures that nurture and support us through the dry seasons. Every family cherishes its stories. Our family story, the most important one for my babies, my husband and me, at least in the beginning, is that of the biggest jiwe I ever found.

Habari, dada?

How are you, sister? Those are the first words he spoke to me. This was just outside the school compound, and I was hurrying, because I was late to class. I was so wrapped up in my own thoughts at that moment that I didn't even notice the man until we were only steps apart. I was so surprised to hear my language come out of his white face that at first it was as though he had spoken in a foreign tongue. I stared stupidly, I'm sure. He must have thought I was mute or slow. Finally, I managed to croak a simple, Mzuri sana, asante. *Very well, thank you. And I made to brush past.*

How had he gotten there? There was no sign of a jeep or even a donkey. Surely he could not have walked from Moshi? For one moment I thought that maybe he was a spirit come to take me young to Enkai. But he smelled like any other white man, of tobacco smoke and exhaust fumes, and my thoughts of death vanished.

"Unazungumza kiIngereza?" *he continued, not stepping aside.*

"Yes, I do speak English. Do you?" *I stared into his face.*

He laughed at that, and my face burned to think I had said something so silly. He was small for a grown man. No bigger than my brother, who was then fourteen. Young and smooth-skinned, but with an older man's eyes. Shrewd eyes, colored like the wings of the olive parakeet, with wrinkles stretching from their corners. He wore no hat over his dark, straight hair, bound behind his head in a thin strip of fabric, and his skin was going to burn from the sun, like that of all white people. Despite my embarrassment, I started to feel sorry for him.

He came from America, he told me, where he was a college student and was visiting our country for his studies. He wanted to know if I was a student at the school and what my grade was. Of course, by this time I was one of the oldest girls, and more of a teacher. My brother had taken over herding the cows, which left me to divide my time between school and the mines, where I had begun to work one of the claims that my father had registered. A young giraffe could still poke his head out of the pit at that point, and the mine had given up many dozens of nice stones. This not only made me a miner, but also a very eligible bride, something that both amused and horrified me. In the dance circles, the iloran, the young warriors, jumped their highest in front of me, trying to catch my favor, but I kept my eyes lowered and favored no one. My mother told me not to be so shy. I was not shy at all, but wary. I did not want an iloran whose true regard was for my mines rather than for me. In fact, I was less and less certain that I wanted any iloran at all, or that my future life would follow the shape my mother and my friends were content to trace with theirs.

In another moment, Sister Marina came out of the classroom, and saw us. "Jambo, jambo! Karibu!" she called in greeting, and as he turned toward her voice, I slipped past him into the compound.

"Nakutakia siku njema," he called after me. Have a nice day! I kept my head tall and refused to look around as I walked into my classroom, but I knew his shrewd eyes were on me.

I did not see him for the rest of the afternoon, although I could hear the foreign melody of his voice from a couple of classrooms away. I could not make out his words, but the children—first graders—were laughing uproariously, as if he were telling the funniest stories. I was certain they couldn't understand a single word he said. But children are good readers of the soul, and if they accepted him I would bear him no ill will.

Sister Marina came to me as I was getting ready to leave for the day. It was a long walk home, and at that time of year the sun descended quickly. I had little time to spare.

"Would you be willing to teach our guest to speak Kiswahili?" she asked me. I thought of his shrewd eyes and knew he would be an able student, but I felt a nagging concern.

"He seems to speak already," I answered.

"Yes, he has a few words, but he is very interested in learning more. And of course, it is our duty in the world to give to those less fortunate than ourselves. If he remains in our country"—by this time she had grown to think of Tanzania as her country as well as mine—"it will be a sort of poverty not to be able to speak, don't you agree?"

How could I refuse? I told her I would have to ask my mother for permission, and left quickly. Although it was getting late, I went first to the mines, where I could think without the bustle of people around me. Everyone had left for the day, and I sifted through the stones at our claim with only the sound of the wind sighing in the grasses and the occasional grunt of a lion far in the distance. In each stone I turned over, I sought an answer. I should teach him; I shouldn't; I should. None of them spoke to me. I wasn't certain why the question troubled me so deeply. He was just another iloran from another country. He would be my student, and then he would be gone. But something in my heart knew better.

Stone after stone turned up gray and mute. And then one didn't. I dislodged a rock so large it took both my hands to roll it on its side, and a tiny spot of deep green, as bright as a bee-eater, caught my eye. I poured water from my canteen onto the stone to clean away the dust and then stared in disbelief. Hiding in that rock were more jiwes than I had ever seen before. In the wet stone, they winked at me like the eyes of panthers, all but invisible. They were not as bright as some of the jiwes I had found, but flashed darkly as if waiting for lightning to strike and bring them to life. As the stone dried, the panthers closed their eyes and the jiwes disappeared almost completely—all but one that echoed the color of the stranger's eyes. I sat staring at it in amazement. This was the largest jiwe rock I had ever seen. I wasn't even sure I could *carry it the distance home. But I had no more time to think about it. If the sun dropped any further I would be stranded in the dark, prey for the cheetahs and hyenas. I hoisted the stone into my arms and set off, breathing as quietly as I could and listening intently for the sound of danger. Little did I realize that I was cradling the greatest danger in my arms. The sun was sinking behind the fever trees as I gratefully approached the thorny fence surrounding our* manyatta. *My brother had already gone out to search, carrying his spear and his bow. My mother said I was lucky to be alive. They had heard a lion close by. Although my father wanted to take my treasure to the white men, my mother said it would offend Enkai, who had spared my life, and I was warned to keep it close by and guard it.*

Later, although the individual stones were too small to bring much money, I meant the rock to go to my children for their protection. "This stone represents our family's love," I told them. "It is our past and your future." Even after the stone had been taken from us, I told them again and again of how it foretold of our lives as a family and remained our dearest treasure, no matter how far away it dwelled.

The next week, our lessons began. As it turned out, I was to be both teacher and student.

Jina lako ni nani?

Sielawi. *I don't understand.*

Jina langu ni Rose. *I tapped my chest with both palms and repeated myself pronouncing each syllable clearly as you would to a child.* Jina lako ni nani? *I pointed to him and tried to look questioning.*

He nodded slowly. Jina langu ni Calvin, *he pronounced slowly.*

It was funny to me what odd things he knew how to say in Kiswahili and what things he didn't know at all. For example, he knew to ask for siagi *to butter his bread, but not how to ask,* choo ni wapi, *where is the bathroom? I wondered how he had been learning until now.*

He arrived at the school just before lunch by jeep. Whoever drove him there left immediately and did not come back until the end of the school day. This happened almost every day. I never did find out what the driver did in the hours in between. We held our lessons in an empty classroom while the children ate their lunch under an acacia tree and played soccer in the dusty courtyard. Occasionally, we had to shout to hear ourselves over their screeching laughter, like the cry of vultures squabbling over the carcass of a wildebeest.

I taught him to count—moja, mbili, tatu—*and to say* tafadhali *and* asante *when asking for and receiving something. Every now and then one of the children would peek into the window and fall back in laughter at the grownup who didn't know such simple things. He was a quick student, though, and before long he was able to speak fairly well.*

To thank me for my teaching, he brought me books. The poetry of Emily Dickinson, Walt Whitman, Elizabeth Bishop. A book of one-act plays and one of short stories. These I loved, even when I didn't wholly understand them. He also brought me the book about a young lord who fell to Earth from the sky. At first, I thought it was silly for a grown man to be so attached to a story written for children. But later I understand that, like Calvin, the little prince had journeyed to Africa. He, too, loved a rose and she had tamed him, which made her unique to him, and him to her.

It took a fox to teach him:

To you, I am nothing more than a fox, like a hundred thousand other foxes. But if you tame me, then we shall need each other. To me, you will be unique in all the world. To you, I shall be unique in all the world.

And it was the fox who told him the greatest secret of all:

It is only with the heart that one can see rightly;
what is essential is invisible to the eye.

The look in his eyes that day, I will never forget it. I turned away toward the window as if I had heard a sound from that direction. He had gained my favor. It was as though he had jumped higher than the boldest of the iloran. *When I turned back to him, our lips met—briefly but with the lightning heat that would turn boudin to* jiwe. *After that, we divided our time between speaking Kiswahili and reading aloud to each other. The hour passed more quickly every day. Sometimes we continued our lesson at the end of the school day, after the children had filed out the doors and dispersed across the dusty plain.*

7

Erica picked her way up the broad, rocky slope trying to avoid the freshest piles of dung as best as possible. The sweeping parade of animal life that made this part of the globe a treasure of the natural world also covered just about every square inch of the terrain with its soil-enriching waste. Behind her, the sun was slipping quickly down the broad reach of the plain, igniting the sky into a blaze of super-heated copper and gold. She paused for a moment and turned to see the scattered acacia trees transformed into black, flat-topped silhouettes against the conflagration. Nesting high in their thorny branches, a flock of marabou storks stood out as hulking portents.

This morning the group had broken camp and set forth on the long drive from the Tarangire River National park through the Great Rift Valley to Lake Manyanara National Park, where their next campsite awaited them. Earlier in the afternoon, Makinde had halted the jeep along the track so that they could watch as a trio of the long-legged storks, plus a number of vultures, picked the carcass of a wildebeest clean. By the time they'd arrived on the scene, lions and hyenas had already made off with most of the animal's flesh, but in minutes the ravenous birds turned what was left of the body into a death's harp before their eyes—the spine stretched sinuously along the ground and bare, pale ribs reached for the sky. For all their graceful flight, these carrion-eaters, with their bald red heads and long, hairy necks, gave Erica the creeps. Although a couple of the other travelers were disappointed to have missed the drama of the kill, Erica found herself more distressed by the post-mortem.

They had been on safari for three days, leaving the campsite early each morning to drive along the bumpy tracks in search of wildlife, which had been plentiful. The sight of Erica's first bao-bab tree – its massive trunk the girth of a small house, ending in what looked like a gargantuan tangle of roots at its top – moved her to tears. The upside down tree, some called it, branches sunk in the earth, roots reaching for the sky. Each time she spotted one of these she thought about the quest of *The Little Prince*, whose miniscule planet was beset by the colossal trees. The tiny monarch had gone on a journey through the heavens for a sheep to eat the baobab seedlings, never realizing, until he fell to Earth, that this would endanger his most precious, if demanding, rose bush as well.

All roads lead to the abodes of men, he mused, as he wandered lost on the Earth. But as far as she could tell, here in Africa all roads just twisted and turned back on themselves and if she were to follow one it would likely end in the jaws of a predator.

Erica shivered despite the heat and hurried on. She trailed behind the rest of the group after stopping to examine some unusual seed pods. She snapped a few photos she could use later to help identify the plant. For a moment, she was tempted to slit the dried pod and slip a few of the seeds into her pocket—her friends back at the gardens would love to have a chance to grow these—but she fought the urge (they'd been sternly warned to take nothing) and hurried on.

For all the power of the sun by day—and sunshine was clearly the most violent weather on this continent—nighttime came quick and certain. Erica picked up her pace. She did not want to be left behind without protection. All night long the camp—a crescent of bulky canvas tents roofed with thatch to foil the sun—was circled by local tribal warriors toting spears or bows and arrows—once even an AK-47—who were hired to guard the *bwana* travelers. Even so, this morning the sand around one of the tents was marked by what Bea identified as leopard tracks. Priscilla had spotted them first and called to Erica as she headed to breakfast.

Priscilla was squatting over the space between their two tents. Her husband, Big Mike as she called him, stood about six feet away, training his camera lens on her compact body.

"Smile!" The shutter whirred. He came in for a close-up. Erica stepped back to give him a clear view.

"Stop!" Priscilla finally demanded as the photo op went on and on. "It's enough already. I want to show Erica."

Erica bent to see what Priscilla was looking at. There were the distinct paw prints of a cat in the dirt. A central pad roughly in the shape of a VW beetle, topped by a quartet of little pear-shaped indentations. They were exact replicas of the tidy ones her childhood pet Snowball used to make padding across a fresh blanket of snow, except these were at least four times the size.

"Leopard," Bea said, peering over Erica's shoulder. This was Bea's third safari; she'd trekked in Kenya and searched for great apes in Uganda. A retired middle school science teacher, she was practiced in identifying spoor and tracks. Even Nini consulted her when they came across something curious. Erica herself couldn't tell a warthog's print from a wildebeest's, and all poop was merely poop to her. And although she was quick to point out the difference between a flat top acacia, *acacia abyssinica*, and an umbrella thorn, *acacia tortilis*, her skill as the resident horticultural expert was not nearly as much in demand.

By this time they had been joined by Jane and Marcie and the newlyweds, Paul and Denise, looking sleepy and disheveled as they did every morning.

"What's going on?" Paul asked.

"A leopard checked us out in the middle of the night," Priscilla said with a shiver. "Did anyone hear anything?" Paul and Denise looked at each other and actually giggled a little. Erica was glad her tent was separated from theirs by several others.

"I think leopards are masters of the stealthy silence," Marcie said.

The prints were clear and therefore recent. How had it escaped the notice of the guards? While everyone took turns bending low to get a good look at the prints, Erica and Priscilla followed the tracks, which wandered between the tents and then circled Erica's. She pictured herself standing outside the night before and the uncomfortable feeling she'd had of being watched. Perhaps the leopard had been there, crouched in the whispering grasses.

"We could have been his dinner!" Erica gasped.

"Nah, leopards are pretty shy of people," Bea laughed. "Mainly they go for smaller prey. This one was probably more curious than hungry, or maybe looking for our leftovers."

Erica liked Bea's intrepid attitude but thought the woman was being overly cavalier. "How do you know it was a leopard? Maybe it was a lion."

"No, see how the tracks are wider than they are long? Lion prints are usually taller than they are wide and a little more crowded in the toes." Mike had begun photographing the tracks again, his lens inches from the ground. Erica felt sorry for those friends back home who were doomed to view every single one of his vacation photos.

Now Nini appeared in the center of the group.

"Is there a problem?" she asked. Then, looking down, she noticed the tracks. "Ah, leopards."

"Should we be worried? Will they bring back their big brothers the lions?" Mike looked gleeful as he spoke.

Nini just shrugged and continued toward breakfast, apparently unconcerned. One by one, the rest of the safari travelers followed her like khaki-clad ducklings.

Now, walking up the hill, Erica remembered a story Cal had told her about the first time he saw one of the great cats. He had been on his way home from the school where he'd been teaching and was tutored in Swahili, when he was forced to stop the car while a large herd of wildebeest and their attendant zebras stampeded across the road.

"Why attendant?" she asked him.

"Because wildebeest are almost blind, but the zebra have incredibly sharp eyesight. And likewise, the zebras rely on the wildebeests for their keen sense of smell." In any case, he said, he noticed the meaty odor of flesh and entrails and foolishly, he left the vehicle to look for what he assumed would be the remains of a kill. "Don't ask why I did such a stupid thing," He had just reached a hill of bare boulders—not unlike the one Erica was climbing now—when he heard a deep growl. A moment later, a leopard came slinking down the rocks, heading not for him, but in the direction of the same kill he was tracking. Cal said he didn't know whether to scramble back to the car or continue to stand like a statue, but it didn't matter, because he realized he couldn't run if he tried. He completely understood the phrase *rooted to the spot*. He held his breath and waited for the cat to notice him, but in another moment, the leopard had apparently located the kill and dove in for his share. There was a quick shriek, followed by a flurry of birds that rose up from behind the boulder. The scream broke the spell, and Cal found himself able to make a dash for the car. He rolled up the windows and waited until his hands had stopped shaking before he drove home. But when he told a Maasai friend the story the next day, the friend just shrugged.

"If that happens again, shake your arms over your head and laugh like a hyena. That sends most leopards on their way. Hyenas are crazy fierce. Even leopards back down from them."

Erica could hardly imagine Cal so frightened he couldn't move. She knew him as a man of action, someone who dove into the fray to do what was needed. Against her will, she pictured him once again in the burning tower. So many times she had pondered what feelings must have gripped him as he realized there was no way out. Now, oddly, she wondered if, at the last moment, he might have raised his arms and laughed as death bore down on him. Frank had said that he'd smiled as he put on his mask. She pushed the thought away and climbed faster, until she noticed that she was out of breath. She hadn't had much exercise in the week she'd been in Tanzania. It wasn't as if you could go for a walk. As Makinde wasted no time in explaining, people were all merely another type of prey on the plain. Even walking up this hill was not without danger, although the guides had checked the area carefully.

At the top of the hill, a magical scene awaited: a circle of trees was hung with oil lamps that twinkled and swayed from the thin branches, and a long table was set for dinner. Having performed their by-now-habitual ablutions, the other guests were moving slowly around the table, jockeying for positions next to the people whose company they had come to enjoy over the past three days. Erica looked for Jane and Marcie, whom she found smart and funny and possibly the happiest pair on the trip; certainly more so than Helena and Don, who often glared at each other in silence in the Land Rover, or Honey and Jerry, who volleyed thinly veiled insults over meals. There was an empty place at their table, but it was next to Robert. She had nothing against the man personally, but she had been somewhat taken aback to learn that he lived in Bethpage, only one town over from Cal's family on Long Island. For reasons that she knew were highly irrational, this made her uncomfortable. In addition, given that they were the only two single travelers of similar age, she had the nagging feeling that people were watching for them to start up something akin to a summer camp romance.

Aside from Jane and Marcie, Erica most enjoyed spending time with their guide, Leni, who told stories of growing up Maasai. He, too, was seated at that table. Erica found Leni something of an enigma. He told them that before he got the job as a guide he worked in a tanzanite mine, but like Sammy the cab driver, he appeared awfully well educated for someone who had had spent his youth sweating underground. She was determined to learn more about him. She also had to admit she found him a strikingly handsome man, with his chiseled cheekbones, lean, muscled physique and striking green-flecked eyes. If Michelangelo had worked in ebony, Erica thought, his David might have been a Leni.

She who hesitates is lost. Now the only empty seats left her a choice between Robert and the newlyweds. Jane looked up and waved, and the decision was made. Leni stood as she approached the table and pulled out her chair. He had been in the midst of a story about the first time he went to *the city*—Dar es Salaam—with his uncle, in an ancient Ford pickup loaded with goats, and he picked up where he had left off as the rest of them dove into grilled lamb chops and vegetables.

"When the axle of the truck came apart, the gate bounced open and the goats leaped free and it was my job to chase down each and every one. I was down to the final goat when I ran smack into a beautiful woman walking on the street carrying her load of firewood high on her head, as is our custom. The wood fell, and I fell in love. And that's how I met my first wife!"

"What number wife are you on now?" Jerry asked with an exaggerated grimace.

Honey rolled her eyes. Leni just laughed and didn't answer.

Erica thought she saw Nini shoot Leni a critical look from across the table. Nini, she noticed, maintained a much more decorous relationship with the travelers, helpful and friendly, but aloof. Erica found Nini's abilities as a guide and naturalist awe-inspiring. It was as if she could creep into the mind of the animals they were tracking and anticipate their next moves. Nini seemed like someone who didn't form attachments easily and did not suffer fools gladly, but would be a loyal friend if you managed to rise that high in her regard. Did she find Leni's garrulousness undignified, or was there some more personal meaning to that censorious glance? Perhaps their relationship was more than professional. They would make a handsome couple, Erica thought, with their regal bearing and graceful movement. Their eyes, flecked amber and green, were riveting.

Robert nudged her elbow, bringing her back to the more concrete matter of dinner.

"I noticed you came up the hill last this evening. In another minute I was going to organize a search party. But since you're alive and well, would you care to join a few of us for a game of cards after dinner?" he asked.

Erica smiled weakly and pushed her chair back.

Standing, she said, "No, I'm not much for card games. Except maybe solitaire." She needed to steer clear of Robert.

Erica stood in front of her tent and turned her face up to a sky frosted with stars. Out of habit, she tried to orient herself by searching for the Big Dipper and for the stretched W of Queen Cassiopeia, recognizable from a string of summers at Camp Sheldrake where she never failed to receive the astronomer's badge. At the annual Naming Ceremony, her counselors bestowed on her the Indian appellation Head-in-the-Stars for her obsession with recording the number of shooting stars she'd seen in the course of the annual two-night Perseid meteor shower. Erica left her bunk each of those August nights after everyone was asleep and stole out to the volleyball court, where she was found every morning, lying wrapped in two blankets and clutching a notebook full of checkmarks—one for each flash across the firmament. Her best friend, Aileen, who spent most of her nights hunched under the covers with a flashlight and a book, marveled at Erica's courage.

"Isn't it scary, lying out there in the dark all alone? Don't you worry about something coming by and eating you?" she asked.

And it was scary, but not in the way Aileen supposed. What was scary, once you discounted the faint squeals of the bats swooping out of the trees to snatch bugs from the air and the general snuffling of small creatures in the weeds, was the sheer depth of the sky itself as Erica's eyes scanned in loopy circles, waiting for sudden streaks of distant fire triggered by bits of space dirt, most no larger than a grain of sand. Erica peered further and further into the thick web of stars. Numb from lying on the hard ground, she lost all sense of gravity and mass. Instead, she began to feel as if she were on a limitless rubber bungee cord, now vaulting deep into the starry depths, now falling farther and farther away. It wasn't her body that was on the cord, she felt, but merely her.... what? Her brain? Her self. What were the odds, she asked herself on those long rebounds through the universe. What are the odds that I am here, that I am *I*, surrounded by all these other *Is*? And what are the odds that we're the only *Is* in all this endless excess? Her pulse would begin to slow at the notion, and the next thing she'd know someone's sneakered toe would be shoving her awake in the dewy morning, the stars withdrawn behind a watery sun.

But this was Africa, and overhead the constellations, cloaked in velvet, refused to reveal their identities. Like Africa itself, full of stories and riddles beyond the visible. It made her feel unrooted, uneasy. Something moaned out in the grass and something behind her shuffled. Erica spun around, but it was only one of the Maasai warriors patrolling the camp.

"Jambo," he muttered, striding past her.

"Jambo, jambo," she replied, stepping toward her tent. The man disappeared into the dark. As Erica felt around for the zipper, something furry brushed her hand and rushed from inside the tent. Erica squealed and jumped back, stumbling and almost falling off the platform, which made her cry out again. She jerked her head around, trying to catch a glimpse of whatever it was in the beam of her headlamp. A flashlight clicked on in the next tent and its beam through the screen window picked up a small furry gray head that vanished toward the grass.

"Are you okay?" someone called.

Erica heard the buzz of half a dozen zippers, like a hive of angry bees, and a moment later she was surrounded by a clutch of her fellow travelers clad in their pajamas. She laughed, despite herself. Through their midst an almost blinding light approached Erica at eye level: Makinde, whose long-ago injured leg gave the beam of his headlamp a rolling gait.

"What's going on?" he demanded, blinking like an owl in the play of half a dozen flashlights across his face. "Is everyone alright?"

"Something was in my tent," Erica stammered, breathlessly. "I was feeling around for the zipper and something furry jumped out."

Makinde pushed the tent flap aside and played his flashlight around the walls. He stamped on the wooden platform. Nothing moved.

By now Erica's heart had slowed and she was calm enough to feel a little self-conscious. "Blue monkey, I guess, like you warned us about, although I can't imagine how it got in there," she said. They had all been repeatedly cautioned to guard against leaving their tent flaps open even the tiniest bit lest the resourceful little thieves break in and filch any sweet or shiny goods. But Erica felt certain she'd pulled the heavy zipper to the ground when she left for dinner.

"Do you want me to come inside and make sure there aren't any more unexpected guests?" Makinde asked. Embarrassed by all the fuss and her part in causing it, Erica assured him she'd be fine on her own.

"We'll just consider it a life lesson," she said. "I won't be caught with my zipper down—or rather up—again."

He turned to address the crowd that had gathered. "Okay then, get some sleep; tomorrow is going to be a long day." Excitement over, the group around her broke up almost as quickly as it had formed.

Erica entered the tent and looked around in consternation. How could such a small creature have created such chaos? Her duffel had been completely ransacked—underwear, tank tops, socks, pants and shorts were strewn everywhere. Even her nylon bags of lotions and soaps were emptied and scattered around the small space. It looked like a crime scene.

She began picking up the items strewn about, shaking and re-folding each piece of clothing before laying it neatly back into her bag. Nothing was obviously missing. She did notice that a half-empty tin of ginger Altoids had disappeared from the nightstand and imagined the errant monkey returning to his tribe and passing the tin around like a theatergoer before the rise of the curtain.

In the bathroom area of the tent, Erica carefully poured some bottled water into a small glass and used it to brush her teeth and then to clean both her toothbrush and the glass itself. She was vigilant about not letting a drop of the local water near her mouth. A bout of stomach trouble could put an end to her whole purpose here. And she still hadn't gotten a reply to her messages to Billy and Anna Marie. She was counting on them to resolve the questions raised by her meeting with Drew.

According to Cal's address book, both Anna Marie and Billy both lived in the Arusha area. Although the entries were old, she called the numbers on her first day in Africa and again after she booked the safari. An answering machine picked up at the number for Billy with a brief outgoing message left in a gruff male voice—no identification. She left what she thought was a persuasive invitation to get in touch and talk about Cal and the telephone number and email address of the safari company where a message could be left. The booking agent there assured her that she would definitely be able to get word if any messages came in. At the number for Anna Marie, a woman answered who spoke only a few words of rudimentary English. Erica left the same message, though it was impossible to tell whether the woman understood. Afterward, she realized she might not even have reached the right people. Even if she had, would they know about Cal's death? She rehearsed what she would tell them. No matter what Drew said, Cal had died a hero.

She plumped up her tired pillow and wriggled between the blankets on the camp bed. The blankets smelled sharp, like something between dusk and smoke. *Smusk. Doke.* It was a scent that characterized Tanzania for her. The smell that had greeted her as she left the plane in Kilimanjaro Airport. Now her eyes were heavy with many hours of sun and dust and she closed them and waited patiently for sleep. Like an instant replay, the evening's surprising events passed before her: the unfamiliar stars, the brush of fur against her knuckles, the gray-blue head and back of the little thief as he scampered off in the night. And something else. In the moment that the tiny head raced through the flashlight beam, something else skittered through her vision, a tiny pale scrap of cloth or paper. Erica sat up in bed, her heart thudding. Something else was missing. Something much more vital than a tin of breath mints. She fought her way out of the constricting blankets and flicked on the solar-powered bulb that hung overhead. In the near-dark she began rifling through her bag, disrupting all the order she had restored. She brushed through each of the inside pockets, ran her fingers under the cardboard base. Nothing. She returned to the bathroom and dumped out each of the zipped nylon bags. It wasn't there, either. The precious address book she had carried like a reliquary—her link to Cal's history—was gone, borne into the night by a simian thief. Now she was totally at the mercy of Billy and Anna Marie to return her messages. And if they didn't? All she had was Drew's cryptic account. Useless at best; insulting at worst. She looked up and blinked in the dim LED light.

On the shelf above the tiny camp sink sat something she had failed to notice in her earlier confusion—a Kili bottle, which she hadn't put there, and in it a single white rose. Under it, a scrap of paper with an inkblot that, as she stared, resolved itself into the shape of the leopard's paw they had seen earlier. Erica gripped the sink, feeling as if the floor had tilted abruptly. Surely she was imagining this, but she looked again, and the shape was clearly the track of a large cat. A track that ended at her tent.

8

From a great distance, the lumbering bull elephant approached like a dream, silent and shimmering in the hot, damp atmosphere that separated him from the jeep. "Just look at the length of his tusks," whispered Nini. Indeed, the animal's tusks were as long as Nini was tall and easily as big around as her legs. Five pairs of binoculars rose to the challenge and in another moment were replaced by five cameras clicking and whirring.

The elephant moved with an easy rhythm through the pale wheat-colored grass, neither hurrying nor hanging back, but following its own intentions. All conversation in the car ceased as the travelers chronicled his journey. After several minutes, the outsized quadruped had come so close—maybe a dozen yards from the jeep—that they were moved to abandon their electronic gear and face him with bare eyes. Concentric arcs of wrinkles—like aboriginal tattoos—marked the beast's wide forehead, on either side of which was a concavity deep enough to cradle a house cat. His skin was like the cracked earth of a sun baked riverbed, a mosaic in shades of gray. Up close, the ivory tusks were glossy white in some places, rubbed and worn in others—Erica could easily imagine their formidable efficiency as weapons. They tapered, uninterrupted, to tips that were pointed and almost delicate.

"Unbroken. Undefeated," Nini whispered.

But Erica knew that despite his strength, the giant remained as vulnerable as a naked chick in the wider world. Those same tusks that marked him as alpha among his kind made him a priceless trophy. Size and strength were no match for man's greed and his genius for murder. Erica had seen evidence of that genius firsthand the morning the Towers were brought down by hatred and a pair of ordinary airplanes. Hubris had given way to ruins.

The elephant's leathery ears, ragged around the edges, had been flattened back against his massive head, but now one and then the other flared forward. Like the floating leaves of the giant Amazonian water lily, each stretched the length of Erica's own height across. Bracketed by the tusks, his enormous trunk bore the grizzled texture of an armadillo's back. At its end, the nostrils twitched and tilted delicately, tasting the air for news.

"Shhhh," Nini cautioned. "We don't want to anger him at this close range. If he feels threatened, he will charge. Don't let his size fool you; he could overtake us in seconds."

The beast swung his massive head side to side for a moment and stared at the vehicle and its passengers with cool disregard through one fringed eye. Then, without a sound, he pivoted on great flat feet and began a long, slow trek back cross the plain. Erica was surprised to find herself on the edge of tears at the sight of his solitary retreat through the stark landscape. Loneliness crashed over her like a wave.

Meanwhile, the rest of the passengers in the jeep erupted in muffled applause and amazed conversation. Don high-fived Mike. Mike hugged Priscilla. Robert raised two thumbs to Nini in a victory salute. Everyone agreed that this had been the highlight of the day, maybe even the trip, thus far. No one breached Erica's silence as she kept her head lowered and her hands busy cleaning the camera lens.

Erica wondered again if this safari had been a mistake. She felt increasingly cut off from the burgeoning fellowship, even as she was stirred by the landscape and the wildlife it sustained. Without a doubt, every day had its crowning moment: The congress of baboons that swept past their car like a tide, carrying babies on their backs and clutched against their bellies; the sleeping jaguar stretched along a branch of a red thorn tree, his dangling tail twitching as he dreamed in the midday heat; the female lions who lay napping by the riverbank with their young one moment and in the next, rose to make a bloody kill of a foolhardy young giraffe. This was the Africa Cal had described to her so affectionately. The swish of the grass, the rapid snort and pant of creatures only yards away; it was a miracle. But sometimes it was also a punch to the gut.

One afternoon, a male lion with full golden mane and deep scars on his brow came down to the river to drink, and Erica, in the jeep, captured the instant in a photo that caught droplets of water glinting as they fell from the great cat's flushed tongue and back into the muddy stream. Nearby, a female lion—presumably his mate—lay on the baked red clay, flicking her tail. He left the stream and crossed closely in front of her, once and then again. The lioness growled softly. Without warning, she rose and arched her back as he turned and mounted her. It was over in an instant. Anyone who had looked away missed it entirely. To Erica, it spoke to the fleeting nature of joy in this world. As the great lion disappeared into the tall grasses, he reminded her of Cal—there and then completely gone. The way love so often ended.

Each day brought fresh wonders. She spied ostriches flushed pink with the readiness to mate and lion cubs scuffling like toddlers in tall grass. Giraffes led their young, perfect miniatures of themselves, to graze among the thorny trees. Gazelles and zebras crossed the road within yards of their vehicle. One day, a flock of crested herons rose and flew alongside the Land Rovers, their bellies lit up pink by the low sun. Later, a dozen secretary birds performed their insane earth-pecking dance of joy for the travelers. Yet for Erica, the spectacle was undercut by a mounting sense of isolation and unease. All these animals—and her fellow travelers— were in plural, while she remained singular. A dangerous state on the savannah.

Each evening, the guides built a campfire and the travelers dragged chairs into a large circle to review the wonders of their day. Nini often took on the role of official storyteller, as she related a series of traditional Maasai tales extolling the cleverness and bravery of her ancestors in their quest to accumulate wealth, mainly in the form of cattle. The Maasai, she noted, were not a warlike tribe, but had always been respected for their cleverness, bravery and fierce protection of what was theirs. One night, she told the tale of a caterpillar who falsely occupied the home of a hare and kept at bay a jackal, a leopard, a rhino and even an elephant who had come to help, by shouting, "It is I! Yes, I, who crushes rhinos to the earth, and tramples elephants into dust!" In the end, the lowly usurper was undone by a frog who, by claiming to be "the one who crushes the crusher of the rhinos of the earth and trampler of elephants" flushed the terrified intruder from the den and then gobbled him up. The tale teaches, she explained, that lies and false pretenses will always be vanquished in the end. And that storytellers—liars—end up at the mercy of their tales. Tonight Nini had finished her tale early and said goodnight to the others.

Only Erica, Bea, Marcie, Jane, and Robert were left around the campfire, which had burned down to embers and ash, and offered dwindling warmth in the chill of the high-altitude camp. Marcie commandeered a long branch and poked through the cinders with it, stirring up a few more flames and steering in bits of wood that had escaped the blaze.

"She can keep this up all night," Jane said. "It's her personal quest never to let a single bit of fuel go unburned. It's a point of pride with her."

"Jane's just jealous because she couldn't start a campfire with a flame thrower and a quart of lighter fluid," Marcie countered. The two of them looked at each other and grinned.

"Are you okay?" Robert asked, turning to Erica.

"Mm-hmm. Just thinking." He drew his chair a little closer to hers. On the other side of her, Bea did the same. They were closing ranks around her, sheltering her. It felt good. Maybe she had friends here after all. If she could loosen up enough to accept them.

"Everyone has a story, Erica," Marcie said, turning to face her in the flickering light. "Jane and I have told ours and Bea has shared hers. *Tafadhali*, please, won't you reveal an epic tale from the life and times of Erica?"

Erica sighed deeply. Maybe she could, indeed, tell them something of the life and times of Erica.

The heat of the sun had all but evaporated from the bare rocky soil and the cold was flowing into the darkness, building from the ground up. Faces appeared and disappeared as flames caught the last bits of uncharred wood. Marcie and Jane bent their heads toward one another and rested against each other's skulls. Bea curled her feet up under herself and was as compact as a folding cot. Robert's eyes were closed. Erica imagined Cal walking into the scene.

These are my friends here in Africa, she would tell him. Where are yours?

A muffled chuffing came from the distant grasses. A lion on the hunt. Female lion, Nini had explained to them, the real killers on the savannah. The males don't generally make the effort, she said. They just wait for the kill and then move in, chasing the females and cubs away. Yesterday the travelers had seen the body of a dead cub, a limp furry little Halloween costume of a creature, about ten feet away from the picked-clean bones of a Thompson's gazelle.

"What would have killed a lion?" Mike asked. "Aren't they pretty much the top dog in these parts?"

Nini told them, "That's what happens to a cub who doesn't relinquish what is not rightfully his." The males would destroy a cub just for standing too close to a kill or even too close to a female in heat that the male had chosen for his own. "Most cubs know enough to get out of the way and wait their turn. It's the law of the bush." As she spoke, a marabou stork landed and began to pluck at the tiny body. The bird, so graceful circling in the sky, was as ugly as a vulture up close. Nini paused another moment and then revved the engine, which sent the bird flapping into a nearby acacia. As they drove away, Erica saw the stork dive down to land on the body and begin picking it clean.

"Erica?" It was Robert. He was fanning the blowing campfire smoke away with one hand and holding out a bottle of Kili, foam escaping from its newly snapped neck, with the other.

"Thanks, no, I'm already over my limit," she said. He pulled his chair closer and took a swig from the bottle.

"Can't have too much of a good thing," he said.

Erica jumped. That was exactly what Cal used to say as he finished up the last bits of a meal she'd prepared, the last bite of dessert at a restaurant. Or turned to make love to her one more time.

"What? Did a tsetse fly get you? You flinched," Robert whispered.

At first, Erica thought she'd just ignore him. But then she said, "I had a friend who used to say that all the time. He's gone now. He died on September 11."

For a long moment no one spoke.

Finally, Bea said, "As a teacher, I always tried to emphasize the human side of history, but I have to admit that I can't even imagine what it must have been like to have been so close to that awful event."

Erica's jaw clenched. She had become acutely sensitive to people's responses to 9/11.

"How far from *Ground Zero* do you live?" Mike had asked when he first learned she was from New York City.

Ground Zero, Erica had thought with disgust, for about the millionth time. Why did people—especially tourists—insist upon using that term? In her mind, it simultaneously turned the awful events of that day into a made-for-TV movie in which they fancied they had a part, and depersonalized the whole experience with a glib moniker. It was almost impossible to walk anywhere below 14th Street in Manhattan without having some visitor come up and ask, "Which way to Ground Zero?" At first, Erica gave them directions and answered their questions about that day, but after a while she began to sense when sightseers were approaching, and turn away. The very idea that a mass grave had morphed into a tourist attraction—she had seen hundreds of people on the platform surrounding the pit snapping pictures and taking video exactly as she and her fellow safari travelers did—made her queasy with anger.

Now she emphasized the words. "The World Trade Center was just a mile from my apartment. The police barricades were a few blocks down Sixth Avenue. No one could pass without authorization. I guess I was lucky to be above Canal Street, or I might have had to move out of my place. As it was, the smoke and the ash—some of it human ash—coated my windowsills for weeks." She stopped suddenly, unsure how much of her history to share.

Robert jumped in before she could decide.

"So many people from my town worked in the area," he said. "Two families on my block alone lost family members, and some friends of my parents in the next town lost their only son. He and I had gone to the same high school, although he was a couple years ahead of me. He was a first responder. EMT. Those guys were total fucking heroes. Pardon my French," he said, turning to Bea.

Erica's heart leaped to her throat. She stared at Robert with something approaching terror. Could he be talking about Cal? But there were so many first responders who lived in that area, she told herself.

"How awful," Jane said. "They must have been devastated. All those poor families. We read the obituaries in the *Times* for months."

Robert was looking at Erica intently. She tried to recompose her face and knew she was failing miserably.

"Are you okay? You look like you've seen a ghost."

Erica cleared her throat to buy herself time.

"My friend who died that day," she finally managed to say. "He was more than that. He was my lover. For life, I hoped." She couldn't manage another word. Even in the dark, she knew that every face was staring at her with concern. Jane reached out and squeezed her hand gently. And then Erica broke down and told them her story. The story of Erica and Cal. Of Cal's death. She hadn't really meant to say as much as she did. She noticed Robert sitting forward attentively as she spoke. Was it attraction, or curiosity? He had been polite and amusing since they met, but now she definitely felt an extra element of scrutiny.

"I'm so, so sorry." Marcie reached for her other hand. Erica felt pinned to the spot by their attempt at comfort. "I don't mean to press you, but if you want to talk, we're here for you." Erica nodded.

Robert was still staring at her with what Erica thought was an odd look. His parents' friends' son was a first responder? Is that why he'd been so keen on getting to know her? Could he be the source of the cryptic notes and the flowers? Erica disengaged from Marcie and Jane and stood to leave the circle. But her legs buckled and she found herself clumsily reseated. Robert moved to help her up.

"Yes," he said, "we're all here for you." He reached for her arm and Erica slowly stood.

"Thank you. I appreciate your kindness." As soon as she established that her legs would hold her, she fled to the relative safety of her tent. Under the covers, she lay awake, torn between relief at shedding the weight of her solitary existence and fear that she had said too much. Something was chasing her. Or maybe, like Frank's dog, she was running from herself. She could no longer tell.

In the morning, after having spent several days deep in the bush, everyone was particularly excited about the plan to visit a nearby Maasai village. No one mentioned the conversation of the night before and Erica was grateful. At breakfast, the guides briefed them on what to expect.

"They are very eager for your visit," Makinde told them. "They are a proud people and delighted to educate you in their ways. In your honor they have prepared a traditional dance, in which the *iloran*, the young warriors, compete to see who can jump the highest. This is typically how they seek to impress their future brides and it is a very serious rivalry indeed."

Not only had they prepared this exhibition, he went on, but the tribal elders had offered to show the travelers around the village itself and some of the women would likely invite them, as honored guests, into their *ngomas*.

"It is a little like crawling into a snail's shell," he warned. "There is no door, but the winding entrance prevents large predators—lions or leopards—from entering as the family sleeps. Also, once inside, it can be more than a little smoky. But I urge you take advantage of their hospitality. You will get to see the typical beds on which they sleep, which are nothing more than well-dried cow hides. If any of you would prefer to trade your camp cot for one of these, I'm sure that Leni or Hassam would be happy to make the arrangements."

The travelers groaned on cue.

"Will we be able to buy any traditional beadwork?" Priscilla asked.

"Absolutely. They are as eager for you to do this as you are," Makinde said, laughing. "This is their chief way of acquiring currency, since they almost never sell their cattle."

Mike raised his hand and Makinde acknowledged him.

"I heard from a friend who was here a few years back that the men really admire American goods like sneakers and sandals. I brought some extras. If anyone asks for anything of ours, is it alright to give it to him?"

Makinde looked serious as he thought a moment.

"As I have said, these are a proud people and will never abase themselves by asking you directly for anything, although sporting a pair of American sandals would have roughly the same cachet you might attach to driving to the market in a Porsche." Again, the group laughed on cue, and Erica wondered where Makinde had picked up his facility for the nuances of first world culture. Mike, she noticed, was blushing, and she wondered if he did, indeed, drive a status car. She wouldn't be surprised. He certainly carried enough high-end camera equipment.

"On the other hand," Makinde continued, "some of the men with greater command of English may make rather obvious hints and compliments about your footwear. If this occurs, you can either ignore it, or make a gift of the item. You could also offer to trade for some of their beadwork. It is entirely up to you."

When they arrived at the village, which perched at the flat top of a mesa that offered an astonishing view of the plain below, the entire tribe had gathered in a huge circle. Men and women alike stood tall and rail thin, toga-wrapped from neck to slender ankle in layers of fabric in shades of blue, purple and red. Both sexes sported shaved heads and closely cropped hair. Men held their wooden staffs, while many of the women were adorned with beaded necklaces that looked like wide, flat, doughnut-shaped plates. Complex beaded earrings hung from the cartilage around their ears almost to their shoulders.

"My granddaughter would kill for some of those," whispered Bea, who stood on one side of Erica. Marcie and Jane flanked her on the other side. They had stuck close to her all morning. It was like being enveloped by a protective herd. Erica was relieved to see Robert standing with Mike and Leni on the opposite side of the circle. He waved casually when he saw her looking.

"I hope they have some of those earrings at the market," Bea continued. "Half the fun of bringing them home will be how ticked off it makes her mother!" Erica thought that she had underestimated Bea—the woman definitely had a roguish streak. Her own grandmother had had a similar sense of mischief.

One older tribeswoman wore a simple string of red seeds that ended in a well-polished brass key that looked just like the one to Erica's apartment. When she noticed Erica looking at it, she smiled and lifted it proudly, displaying the pendant as if it were an amulet or a precious jewel. Erica was surprised to feel a pang of homesickness at the sight. She wondered if Karen had been picking up the mail regularly and if anything had shown up regarding the inquiries she'd made to the fire department about starting a paramedic training scholarship in Cal's name. The Hero Fund, she proposed calling it. She tried to push away the thought of Drew scoffing at the idea of Cal as a hero. But Erica believed. She had to believe.

The tribe began the performance with a great shout that yanked her back into the present, and the dancing commenced. The entire group took up a rhythmic chant and continued for at least half an hour, the men taking turns to see who could leap highest and the young women laughing admiringly. Outside the circle, children crouched or sat on the dusty earth, clapping out rhythms.

When the demonstration ended, the woman with the shiny key approached Erica and Bea with a wide grin and shepherded them into the center of village. The Maasai woman stopped at one of the round *ngomas* and gestured to the other two to enter. Erica bent low and crept slowly and carefully through the winding passage. It went on a lot longer than she would have guessed, and passing through it felt as she imagined reentering the womb would. Finally, they arrived into a domed space just tall enough for Bea to stand. Erica, who was taller, stooped. As Makinde had warned, it was smoky, and the three women sat on the dried cowhides that served as both couch and bed. Erica, who struggled with insomnia in the best of circumstances, could not imagine how she might sleep on the unforgiving dirt floor. She wondered if anyone had thought to introduce the Maasai to the concept of pillows.

The woman set a small kettle over the fire and prepared bush tea for her guests. When she offered the cups to the visitors, Bea waved her hands in front of her in a universal gesture of refusal, but on a whim, Erica accepted the refreshment and took a small sip. It tasted like pure distilled smoke, and Erica struggled not to spit it out for fear she would wound the woman's pride. What would Cal do? Erica was sure he would be more gracious, and aspiring to his courteousness, Erica blew gently on the steaming liquid and then took another small sip. This time, it didn't taste quite so bad. A bit sweet, in fact. A third sip finished the cup and she handed it back to her smiling hostess.

"*Asante sana*, that was delicious," Erica said. The woman's smile widened and she nodded happily. Erica decided that Cal would have been proud of both her tea drinking and her halting Swahili.

In another minute, the three women rewound their way through the nautilus passageway and emerged, stretching, into the now-blinding sunlight.

The market was in full swing, with the rest of their party working their way around a ring of stalls displaying colorful beadwork and haggling happily with craftswomen. Erica and Bea joined the parade. At a number of stalls, Erica bought bracelets and necklaces that weren't really so different from the ones she'd seen at craft sales back home. Bea, however, was clutching a handful of absurdly long earrings and several of the broad beaded collars. She held up her purchases and winked at Erica.

Back on the rutted road, Erica was so tired she thought she might be able to sleep on those bare cowhides after all. The regular breathing and occasional soft snorts told Erica that almost everyone else in the car had drifted off. She rested her head against the seat back and tried to join them, but found herself contemplating yesterday's encounter with the elephant. Nini had warned them that if he felt threatened, the elephant would attack. That's the way it was in the wild, she noted, even an animal that seemed placid could launch a lethal confrontation under the right circumstances. Like Cal, Erica surprised herself by thinking. Warm, compassionate, kind so much of the time, but she had seen another side of him emerge when he felt under attack.

She had been moving a stack of his books into a bookcase they'd picked up at a stoop sale when a thin, airmail envelope fluttered to the floor at her feet. The handwriting was almost childlike in its precision—like the prototype cursive writing alphabet that had ringed the walls in her third grade classroom. The letter was addressed to Cal, but it bore no indication of the sender, other than a Tanzanian postmark. It was dated four years earlier. Erica laid it carefully in the middle of the kitchen counter so that Cal would find it when he came in from work, late that night. But after a short time, she found herself drawn back to it. When she opened it, a small piece of onionskin dropped out. All that was written on it were the words, *Tafadhali—kuweka jiwe yangu salama*. She played with saying the words out loud again and again – they were musical, like a poem. Then she put the paper back in the envelope. The next morning it was gone.

"So what does *Tafadhali kuweka jiwe yangu salama* mean?" she asked, as she got ready to leave for work.

Instead of answering, he walked into the kitchen. Then he returned with a glass of juice. She tried once again, expecting him to laugh or correct her pronunciation.

"That note. Very cryptic. Was it from one of your old Peace Corps friends?"

Without warning, Cal turned on her.

"What do you mean by picking through my things?" he demanded, his eyes narrowing to knife-edged slits. He slammed the juice glass down on the table. "Do I go sneaking around through your stuff and then demanding explanations?" Erica was stunned into silence. Cal had always seemed so pleased to share his stories about Africa. "Well, do I?" he shouted, both his hands balled into fists at his side and trembling as if physically restraining himself from lashing out. Erica would have been frightened if she hadn't been so shocked. She reached out a hand to try and calm him, but then she pulled back. He was snarling like a cornered animal. Touching him would have been like trying to pet a coiled cobra.

"I don't appreciate being grilled by you about my life. If you can't respect my privacy, then maybe I've made a mistake moving in here!" And with that, he grabbed his keys and stormed out the door. Erica automatically jumped up from her chair and began to follow him, then stopped just short of the door.

What just happened, she wondered. Less than a minute had passed between the time they'd sat down to eat and his infuriated exit. In a daze, Erica began to clear the table, methodically putting away each object, trying to reclaim the skewed balance of her world.

When Cal had not returned by 10:00 p.m., Erica went to bed and fell into a deep, druglike sleep. When she woke, Cal was in bed beside her, snoring deeply. She stared at his now-peaceful face, hardly daring to move. Seeming to sense her gaze, he opened his eyes, and then they made love slowly and wordlessly. Afterward they both drifted back into sleep. Eventually, Erica's alarm rang, and she dressed quietly and went off to work. When they returned home that evening, it was as if nothing had ever happened. Neither of them ever brought up the subject again.

Bouncing along in the dusty African heat, Erica wondered about the relationship between that letter and Drew's mocking derision about Cal's time in the Peace Corps. Both hinted at the existence of a shadow Cal—someone who would remain unknown to her. Maybe even someone she didn't want to know.

Now the jeep turned into the parking area at the camp. Her fellow passengers awoke, stretching and feeling around the seats for their belongings. They'd stayed out longer than usual, and they were told that dinner was already prepared and would be served immediately. Erica had been looking forward to a few hours on her own. Robert had been her seatmate in the back of the Land Rover this afternoon and tried his best to convince her to meet for an after dinner drink. Marcie invited her and Bea to their tent for a game of cards. But as soon as dinner was finished, she fled for the sanctuary of her own tent.

What was taken must be returned.

The note on her pillow was written in awkward block letters using what appeared to be charcoal. Erica turned it over, as if expecting it to say *Just Kidding* on the back. But who would play such a ridiculous prank? Was this a safari game of some sort? She certainly hadn't taken anything from camp or from any of the other guests. They had been invited to borrow books from the small camp library, but she hadn't even visited it. Erica unzipped the door of her tent and stepped outside to see if anyone else was emerging from a tent with a similar square of paper and puzzled expression. In the gathering dark, the camp was completely quiet; all the tents were zipped up tight. Bluish light glowed from behind a few of the screen windows. Not even the Maasai guards were in sight—probably working their way around the back, Erica thought.

Again, she had the distinct feeling that she was being watched. That rustle in the grass. She zipped her fleece jacket higher around her neck and dipped back through the screen door, zipping both the screen and the canvas doors firmly down to the very bottom. The tiny LED lights strung over the bed left most of the tent in shadow. Feeling a bit paranoid, Erica reached for the flashlight on her nightstand and played it across the walls and into all the corners. She was alone. She crumpled the paper and dropped it into her duffle. Then she got into bed—fully dressed. The roses, the leopard print, the note. Was this malicious or merely her own paranoia? Was she the butt of a joke? Something more malicious? Back and forth she debated the points all night, her eyes refusing to close for more than a moment. This would never have happened if Cal were here, she thought.

At the thought of Cal, her breath caught in her throat and she felt submerged in guilt: how could she be here reveling in the sights and sounds of his beloved Tanzania when he could never do so again? She writhed with the familiar ache of loss that she hoped she had left behind in the closet with the tape of her memories. Maybe there was no escaping that pain after all, no matter what Doctor Elizabeth claimed. And no matter what doubts were planted in her mind by someone who clearly had his own murky agenda.

What was taken must be returned. She'd like to issue the same demand to the world at large.

Erica liked to think of herself as stringently honest—a person who would never take what didn't belong to her. But she knew the truth was a bit more ambiguous.

The charm bracelet had glinted warmly against the midnight velvet of the little box. An unfathomable treasure to a ten-year-old Erica. A row of tiny gold hearts linked together and lying flat along the fabric like a furrow of freshly planted marigolds. And dangling from the bracelet an array of pre-teen fantasies: A golden four-leaf clover with I LUV U incised in its center, a laughing green jade Buddha on a gold throne, an old-fashioned telephone with a miniscule dial that could actually be turned. The best charm of all was a tiny three-dimensional gold tree, each branch tipped with a perfectly round gem—a ruby, a sapphire, an emerald—as petite as the white nonpareils that paved the top of her favorite chocolate candy.

Erica had seen the bracelet for the first time when she was home from school with chicken pox. To distract her from the itching, her mother had invited Erica into the bedroom and set the two of them the project of sorting through her nightstand drawer and its boxes of old jewelry—much of it costume—throwing out what was no longer wanted.

The image of the charm bracelet never faded. Left at home alone, Erica often rifled through the drawer until she found the long, narrow box. She clasped the bracelet around her wrist until it was time for her parents to return.

And then, one night when she was thirteen, she didn't put the bracelet back. She wrapped her booty in a pair of socks that she kept in her backpack and put it on each morning as she walked to school. Content to be its sole admirer, she kept it tucked up her sleeve so no one would ask about it. On the way home, she reversed the process. Often, during the day, she pressed it against her skin;

the sharp gold edges against her wrist made her feel mysterious and joyous.

Until the day the bracelet disappeared. A block from home, Erica reached up her sleeve as usual to remove it, and found nothing there. Frantic, she tried over and over like a failed magician, each time coming up empty. The bracelet was gone.

To make matters worse, the tension she had begun to sense between her parents had escalated until it filled the house with the electric hum of overt hostility. Waking late at night, she heard whispered arguments, and once her mother's muffled sobs.

"You gave it to that slut at work, didn't you?" she made out through the bedroom walls. "I've had enough. I won't take it anymore." Erica's guilty conscience assumed the missing bracelet was the source of the conflict.

A week later, Erica's father took her out for dinner, and over a pepperoni and mushroom pizza told her that he would be moving to an apartment a few blocks away.

"Just for a while, I hope," he said, holding both of Erica's hands on the tabletop as though he were inviting her to join a séance. "Sometimes people disagree about important things and they need some time apart, but if there is one thing we agree on, it's how much we love you." Against the checkered tablecloth, Erica's bare, pale wrist gleamed like a beacon. Her stomach churned and the pepperoni turned greasy and cloying in her mouth. She fought back the tears but then realized her cheeks were wet in spite of her struggle. Her father watched with a hangdog expression of guilt.

"I'm sorry," he said. His eyes were rimed with red and he suddenly looked like her grandfather, jowly and old.

All of this was her fault. It was up to her to make things right.

He moved out the next weekend, the car piled high with cardboard boxes. On Wednesday night Erica finally got up the nerve to face her mother. She found her sitting bolt upright in the middle of the couch in a darkened living room, the glow from the TV lighting her profile. Erica took a seat in the big recliner that had been her father's spot.

"Mom," she began. The rest of the words dried on her tongue. They sat in silence until Erica finally gave up and went back to her room.

In the end, she resorted to writing a note of confession.

Dear Mom, I took your charm bracelet. I'm really, really sorry. Don't hate me. Love, Erica. P.S. Can Dad come home? She left the note, scented with a little Charlie perfume, on her mother's pillow.

The next morning at breakfast her mother walked into the kitchen, hugged her hard and sat down opposite her at the table.

"Why did you take my bracelet without asking?"

Erica just hung her head.

"Haven't we taught you the difference between right and wrong? We didn't raise you to be a thief! "

Erica's desolation knew no bounds. She was worse than a thief. She was someone who ruined the lives of everyone around her. She looked up at her mother, miserable.

"I'm sorry," she finally choked out. "I was just borrowing it. I planned to put it back." That last part might have been true. Erica wasn't certain. "Can we call Daddy now?" Erica put her head face down on her folded arms, like a kindergartner taking a nap.

"I know you're sorry. I'm sorry, too. But this thing with your father..." Her mother paused for so long that Erica thought she might have left the room. Erica looked up. Her mother was staring, her eyes unfocused on something that hovered in the air between Erica and the calendar hanging on the wall. As if she had just thought of something new, she started again.

"Erica. Where is the bracelet now? I would like it back."

Erica had known the dreaded question was coming. She hung her head and whispered to the placemat in front of her, "I don't know. I lost it."

"What?"

"I lost it. I put it on when I left for school one day and it must have fallen off. I've looked everywhere. Please. You can punish me. This is all my fault!" She put her head down again and burst into tears. When she finally stopped, her breath shuddering with the aftershocks, her mother was looking at her with pained confusion.

"Listen to me," her mother said, lifting Erica's chin firmly and turning her face up as Erica struggled to look anywhere but in her mother's terrible eyes. "The trouble between your father and me is not your fault. You did a very bad thing by taking the bracelet, *if you really did take it*, but your father has had girlfriends before and he probably has one now and he will never be moving back into this house. Never. Do you understand me?"

At first, all that Erica heard were the words if you really did take it. In her mother's eyes she was either a thief or a liar. And then the word *never*. Never is a long, long time, her grandmother used to tell her. And she would never feel the same about herself again. Things would never be the same and it was her fault, one way or the other.

As an adult, of course, Erica knew that taking the bracelet was not the event that precipitated her parents' divorce. But the child within still smarted with guilt. *Never*, she swore to herself, never would she take something that was not her own.

But in fact, she had taken something.

What was taken must be returned.

It was inconceivable that anyone would know about her theft of the address book. And yet, someone clearly did, and that person wanted it back.

That day in Cal's apartment, while his sister Margy went into the bedroom to get the package with Erica's name on it, she saw his beat-up leather address book pushed to the back of the desk, half hidden by the usual workaday detritus. Almost before she knew what she was doing, she reached out and extricated it from the pile of envelopes and a couple of old *New Yorker* magazines and slipped it into her purse. The curled leather felt warm and alive in her hand. Like calloused and sun-warmed skin. The way Cal's hands used to feel.

Put it back, she told herself. Still gripping the book deep inside the bag, she massaged the leather between thumb and fingertips. *You did a very bad thing,* she heard her mother's voice warn. But Cal was gone. The address book didn't belong to his sister, or even his mother. It certainly didn't belong in the trash. In the awful interim between his leaving and his promised return, Cal had left her with so little. A few used books and a stupid rock. A couple of shirts barely good enough to send to Goodwill. She was heir to nothing but his memory. Erica longed for something that had been close to him, something that had been touched by his hand. If she asked for the book and her request were denied, it would be lost to her. These people acted as if she had been nothing to Cal. Just another cast-off girlfriend. They knew nothing of his true feelings. But she knew better. She was his next of kin—*next of skin,* he had said one night as they lay in bed.

Cal was gone, he had no further use for the book, and maybe she could put it to some good use. Yes, she thought. She could, at the very least, get in touch with his faraway friends and let them know what had happened. Let them know the wonderful person he'd become and how he had kept them in his thoughts. So this wasn't really stealing, but making good use of something that would probably be tossed away. In the end, she could send the book back, she promised herself. She knew, though, that she never would.

Cal's sister swept back into the room, holding a small express mail parcel in front of her. In a flash, Erica's hand released the book inside her bag.

"I looked for you at the memorial service," Margy said, handing her the package.

"I was there."

"There were so many people. So many grieving souls. I can hardly even remember what I said at the service. Did you speak?"

"There were too many people ahead of me."

"I'm sorry."

Put back the address book, Erica commanded herself. But Margy was holding out the package, waiting for Erica to move. She accepted it with a wan smile but didn't open it. Cal's sister remained standing. There was nothing more to be said. Erica had no choice but to get up and leave.

Erica made herself get all the way home before opening the package, which also turned out to hold a book. *The Little Prince. Happy Birthday*, he had written on the inside front cover. *Sleep Tight, Love Cal.* She traced the words with one fingertip.

She had never thought to ask him when they were together, but the question returned again and again after he was gone: Why *The Little Prince*? Why was that book important enough to live in his nightstand? It was worn and stained and the dust jacket was held together by tape along the spine. One night, after she woke

him with her tossing and turning, he pulled it out and offered to
read to her.

"Do you want me to start at the beginning, or just pick a place
at random and jump in?" he asked. In a few minutes, she felt herself drifting into a warm, resilient sleep.

After that, whenever she couldn't sleep, he read to her from it.
She assumed that he thought she'd like it because of the baobab
trees. The first time she took him to the Botanic Gardens, she told
him that she had been fascinated by them since she was a child—
their bare branches like knobbed roots flailing upward. At the gardens, there were a number of baobab seedlings in the cactus house,
none of them thicker than her thumb or taller than her knees, all
of them hiding the secret of their eventual gigantism. She told him
she was sad that the prince had to pull every last seedling from
his diminutive home planet in order to keep them from splitting
it apart with their massive roots. But more than the baobabs, he
seemed to love the book for the tale of the fox, who taught the
tiny traveler the sacred relationship between yourself and the special creature you tamed. "People have forgotten this truth," the fox
said. "But you mustn't forget it. You become responsible forever
for what you've tamed. You are responsible for your rose." The line
was underscored and starred in his copy. She thought of it often
after Cal moved out. It offered one more piece of evidence that he
would eventually return.

Or else.

About a month after Erica had taken the address book Margy
called and asked if Erica had seen it anywhere when she was at
the apartment. She was looking for the phone number of a friend
of theirs from high school. With hard-won coolness, Erica denied
having seen it at all. Now she shuddered with a chill in the African

heat. Just as she had with the bracelet, she'd lost the very item that needed to be returned. History repeating itself. Original sin. Proof of her true unworthiness, no matter how many good deeds she did in the interim. Erica sat on the camp bed in shock and wondered what to do next. Could Robert be behind this? Might he have been in touch with someone in Cal's family and mentioned that he'd met her? They could have asked him to avenge the theft. It seemed beyond absurd—almost insane—to think this, and yet someone was clearly targeting her with these demands. She thought about how she might broach the subject without sounding like a crazy woman. In truth, there probably was no way. She would wait, then. Maybe the whole thing would blow over. Maybe it was all in her head.

On the table next to her lay a wilting white rose, its petals bruised and limp.

ROSE

O ne day, Calvin arrived in the jeep alone. And only a short time after the lesson began, he looked up and said, "Twende." Let's go.

"Wapi?" I asked him. I was not about to get in an automobile without even knowing where we were going. As it turned out, he wanted to take me to meet his friends, who lived in the outskirts of Moshi, only a few miles east of the school. He told Sister that he would drive me home to my village well before the sun set. I thought I caught a flash of concern, but in the next instant it was gone. After all, I was old enough to make decisions for myself. I opened the car door.

I had never been in one of those things before, but it seemed import-ant to look worldly in his eyes, so I climbed inside as if I rode every day. I settled onto the scratchy fabric seat and pressed my feet into the floor, hoping they could anchor me. I slapped at a tsetse that entered the car and brushed the body from my arm. It came to land on the round globe that topped the sturdy stick between our seats. As Calvin climbed in, he reached over and flicked the fly to the floor. He smiled widely and reached across to lock my door. His elbow brushed against me and his face turned a deep rose as he quickly brought both hands to the wheel. Staring out the window, I sat as tall and as still as a heron focused on spearing her next meal from the rushing water, and I hoped that he would see me as the strong Maasai woman I was, almost.

Perhaps, though, he found me out when I jumped at the sound of the revving motor—from inside, a sound more alarming than the trumpeting of an enraged elephant. As the jeep leapt forward I couldn't help myself—I clutched at my chest and let out a tiny shriek that sailed away on the wind. He laughed, but not in an unkind way, and squeezed my arm briefly with assurance. The pressure of his hand on my arm faded, but slowly, like an echo.

My babies both rode in a car the very day they were born. They always rolled their eyes when I told them this story, as though they couldn't believe anyone had ever been so naive. Once, though, my daughter asked if I was afraid that he might have done me some harm. Then it was my turn to laugh. I, who wrung the necks of chickens with my hands, who had killed a black-backed jackal with my knife when it threatened our goat kids, was not worried that this small white man could take my life or do me physical harm. What I should have been worried about, the danger I really faced, never crossed my mind. It was many, many years of stories later that my children learned of this.

We drove for what seemed like a moment but put miles between us and the school. The town, which I had never before visited, rose up suddenly on the side of the road like a mongoose popping up from his den. Calvin's house, shared with friends, was at the very edge, separated from the rest of the village by a large garden surrounded by a thorny boma fence. When I stepped from the jeep, I had to pause for a moment to stop the trembling in my legs. I could still feel the vibrations through my veins, and I thought I might stumble and embarrass myself. The house was not much larger than the shacks our own people built out at the mines or on the edge of Arusha when they were forced to work for wages. The walls were scraps of metal and planks of wood painted bright red and blue. The roof, also metal, was rusted and dark. A basket of flowering thorn rose hung from one corner; bees and a hummingbird dove in and out.

"Jambo, jambo," they called as we walked up to the door. Calvin's friends—two young men and a girl not much older than me—introduced themselves loudly and with exaggerated clarity, as if they feared I was hard of hearing or slow. I responded in English and my softest voice, the one I would use to soothe a fretful child. To their credit, they understood what I was telling them in this way and they began to speak to me in more normal tones.

Inside, it smelled foreign and a little bland, without the comforting tang of a cooking fire or the sweet grasses cemented into walls with cows' dung, or even the dusty chalkboard smell of the school that had begun to feel like another home to me. The flat walls were covered with pictures, like the pages of a children's book, and a long wooden table took up most of the center of the main room. Calvin walked me through the other two rooms, each with a wide, soft bed and shelves of books. Peel-lows, I noted to myself, and almost laughed. I would have to remember to tell my brother that I had now visited the very people who slept in this foreign way. For a moment, I imagined lying down on one *of the large beds, just so I could tell him how that might feel.*

"Sit, sit," they begged me as we came back to the large room, and we all perched on chairs as if a lesson were about to begin. The girl, Anna, brought out a tray of glasses and a large pitcher of juice, so cold it made my throat ache. And Calvin opened a tin of biscuits and passed them around. Everyone seemed to relax after that. From this I decided that people were the same everywhere—if you shared food with them, they seemed more like friends. They asked polite questions about me and my family and they murmured approvingly when I told them about our many cows and our good fortune in finding the jiwes. Anna admired my bracelets, which my mother had beaded. Still, I could feel their eyes flick over me and back to Calvin as if asking secret questions.

We didn't remain long—they invited me to stay for the evening meal they had been preparing, but Calvin declined, saying that he had to get me home before sunset, which was true. I was never really sure why he brought me there, although I have had many ideas. On more generous days, I have believed that he was proud of me and of our friendship. On less generous days I think that he was showing off his prowess, either as a man, or as the sort of man he turned out to be.

After that we were rarely apart, so that when he left, I was like the fox who, once tamed, grieved to find himself again living the lonely life of the wild.

9

"**A**s you will see, every animal in the park is either predator or prey," Makinde had told the group that morning as they prepared to embark on the day's foray into the savannah. "You eat, or you are eaten." A white-backed vulture swooped low overhead and then veered sharply away, a black dart slicing across brilliant blue. Makinde pointed upward. "Or you clean up after those who have eaten." A couple of travelers chuckled.

The group had gathered in the parking area as the other guides loaded cases of bottled water and the ever present rifles into the Land Rovers. Priscilla followed Erica's gaze to the rifles, then turned toward her and made a face. Priscilla, Erica thought, was one of those people who came to Africa, looking for the Disney version of *The Jungle Book*. She'd already announced that she would greatly prefer not to see a kill in progress, since she had been known to cry watching *Nature* on PBS. Erica tried to look less judgmental about that remark than she felt, although she thought this was somewhat disingenuous for a person on safari. Cal had long ago disabused her of such sentimentality.

"I used to root for the underdog," he told her one day when they were poring over some travel brochures. "I was a fanatical Mets fan as a kid, which pretty much says it all, right? When I first arrived in the bush, I saw a pair of lionesses cut a young wildebeest from the pack and toy with him until they ran him down. The whole time I cheered for the little 'beest. He was still screaming as they ripped him open and began feasting. Their mouths dripped with his blood and gore. Another time, I saw a pair of lion cubs starving to death in their den. Limp bodies as soft as kittens. They could barely raise their heads. I had a fucking emotional meltdown. I couldn't say who the underdog was any more. So I decided the answer was to stay out of it, emotionally speaking. One day the lions would win and their cubs would eat. The next day, the wildebeest would make it back to the safety of the herd. I'm content to let life be a crapshoot."

Life was, indeed, a crapshoot, Erica now realized, and not just for the wildlife. Members of the human herd she lived within back home felt they were safe in the hub of the city's glass and steel towers. They never saw the predators coming. A sudden buzzing made Erica bat at the air near her neck, but too late. In one motion, the tsetse fly landed on her shoulder and bit hard. With a little yelp of pain, she slapped the insect dead. Predator or prey, she wondered about herself.

"If you had to choose," she had asked Cal that day, "which would you rather be: the lion or the wildebeest?"

"Personally, I'd be a hippopotamus," he said.

She looked at him blankly.

"Neither predator nor prey be, to badly misquote Polonius. Hippos are vegetarian—they eat about a hundred pounds of grass a day—so they don't hunt or kill other animals for food, but they're so huge and also so lethal when angry—much more dangerous than practically any other animal out there—that nothing dares to prey on them. In fact, I'm kind of hoping to come back as one in my next life."

Today, the group had driven to Lake Manyara for the express purpose of watching the hippos wallow in the muddy pools there. They parked the cars and gathered on one side of the enormous lake, shallow in this dry season, Bea and Marcie making space for Erica between them.

"The hippopotamus, or *kiboko*, in Swahili, is the third largest land mammal, weighing in at anywhere from four to six thousand pounds. That would be, oh, say, the same weight as our Land Rover with all of you inside," Makinde told the travelers. "They spend about sixteen hours a day submerged in water to stay cool." He pointed to a narrow trampled pathway through the tall scrub on the far side of the river. "At sunset, they walk single file for hours in search of their grazing grounds. You don't want to cross paths with them either in water or on land. They are easily angered and faster than their massive size would have you believe." Cal had told her about a guide he'd met who had come upon a hippo in the high grasses and only managed to outrun the charging beast by seconds because he had been an Olympic level sprinter.

Across the lake, a herd of wildebeest wandered by, large geese pecked at the muddy ground and a line of red-billed ducks waddled into the water, which was thick with water hyacinths. It occurred to Erica that these animals no longer triggered the awe-driven rush to photography that they had only a week earlier. In the eight days they'd been traveling, the voyagers had gotten as jaded as children kept too long at the zoo. But hippos were something new. Everyone jockeyed for a place at the protective fence that had been built to separate the tourists from the beasts. At first, Erica saw nothing but vegetation, greenish water and slick, mossy rocks—what time do the hippos arrive, she wanted to ask—and then the object of their quest came into focus: masses of leather-backed giants that bobbed like boulders and then rose from the water to yawn with mouths as tall and wide as cellar doors. The lake, which at first appeared lifeless, was awash in hippos. Beady eyes and blunt snouts peeked up from the water's surface. Domed backs, slick with mud, followed a foot or two behind. Cameras began to click and whir. She gazed at the hippos with love and admiration, searching, praying that somewhere in that great gathering she would find Cal, returned to Tanzania as he'd wished, his spirit infusing one of those mammoth bodies.

In the months following the attacks, Erica continued to see the mirage of Cal at every turn. Hunched over a newspaper on the crosstown bus, stepping into the revolving doors at Macy's, disappearing around corner after corner after corner. Later, he began to appear only in fragments—a shock of unruly hair, calloused knuckles, a full lower lip, a slightly hairy ankle bared between jeans and beat-up leather moccasins. She felt him coming apart, disintegrating. The pain of it was like walking over ground glass. Soon, she feared, there would be less and less of him, and then—nothing. But here, in this gathering of giants, he might reemerge. She scanned the lake and its far shoreline, crowded with the massive, lolling bodies of hippos and the sinuous white egrets that tiptoed, unmolested, among them. Next to her, Robert waited with his camera poised, trying to get a shot of one of the beasts mid-yawn.

"I'm prepared to wait forever," he whispered, giving her a wink.

All of a sudden, in the muddy water not thirty feet in front of Erica, one of the largest of the pack mounted the nearest female, submerging her almost completely. The water around them churned gently. A moment or two later, that same male complied with Robert's wish for a gaping yawn. It was all Erica could do not to applaud. The hippo considered the tourists and their cameras with a smug leer, even as a tiny bird alit on his head. That one, she was sure, had at least a little of Cal's spirit.

Erica had just reached down to unzip the tent screen when she heard her name being called. Turning, she saw Makinde heading in her direction backlit by the deepening purple sunset. He waved, and a piece of paper fluttered in his hand. She waited on the porch patiently while he approached with his slow, uneven gait.

"Miss Erica," he said, touching his hand to his baseball cap, emblazoned with the name of the tour company and a long-horned gazelle of some sort. "There was a letter for you at the office in Arusha where I drove yesterday to pick up the permits for our next camp." It was all Erica could do not to snatch the paper from his fingers.

"*Asante sana*, thank you so much for bringing this to me," she said, breathing deeply to try and effect a look of calm. "That was very kind of you. I have been expecting word from…." How would she describe the people from whom she awaited word? Not friends, at least, not her friends. Not even acquaintances. Erica let the rest of the sentence float away on the tepid breeze. She reached out and the guide placed the envelope gently in her hand. It was hot and slightly wrinkled, as if it had been wet and then dried in the sun.

"Are you waiting for anything else? One of the cooks will be going back soon for supplies and I can alert him to check for you."

"That would be great."

"I will tell him then." Again, Makinde touched the brim of the hat. Erica wondered whether a tip was in order, but Makinde turned and left before she could consider it further. Clutching the envelope, she bent again to unzip the tent door and noticed that her fingers were trembling. She slipped inside and sank gratefully onto the camp cot.

The envelope was almost weightless in her hands and as thin as if there were nothing inside it at all. The handwriting on the front was in heavy letters, all capitals, the initial caps slightly larger than the rest. There was no return address. Erica slid her thumbnail under the sealed flap and slit it until it was wide open. Inside rested two small sheets of paper. The first was a typed note from Billy.

Dear Erica,

I was sorry to hear of Cal's death. I understand that you are in country looking for material for his biography. Although we were buddies here in Tanzania, and I helped him out when he needed me, we hadn't been in touch in the intervening years. I thought of him often, though. I am still teaching in Africa—Kenya—but I'm about to leave for vacation in Australia with my family. I searched around and found this old letter from Cal, which arrived shortly after he left Africa. I hope it can be of some use.

Best of luck,
Bill.

Erica's heart quickened. A letter from Cal! The second letter was on onionskin stationery that had apparently been wet at some point, whether before or after Billy posted it, she couldn't tell. It was crinkled and smelled slightly of mildew. Erica opened it carefully and pressed it flat. The dried paper had taken on the texture of seersucker. The ink had smeared and faded in several places, but most of the words were still legible.

just wanted to thank you for getting me the ticket back to the States. Here's a check   fare and a little more for your generosity and speed. My father died three days   arrived. My mother and sisters are so grateful I made it   truth is, the old man never opened his eyes the whole time I was there. So now

I'm left in the supposed bosom of my family while my heart beats
7,500 miles away. There was no other choice; I have to believe that
        You know as well   that there are no idle threats among
the Maasai. I did what had to be done to make sure my loves would
live, even if just to hate me. Still, I feel their judgment. Theft, betray-
al, desertion: Guilty as charged. People say life is long.   someday
I can make amends.

   Again, my thanks to you for your help.

   C

Erica picked up Billy's note and reread it. She turned it over
and thumbed it, looking for a second page with some explanation.
How was she supposed to take this? Cal had told her he returned
to the States when his father was dying. He had told her about
pacing at his bedside for hours on end without any assurance that
the man knew he had come. Cal said he kissed his father's forehead
every night before leaving. And then one morning, his mother got
the call. It was over. But who remained alive *to hate me? My loves,*
he called them. With no way to reach Billy, she was left with little
more than gloomy confusion. *Betrayal, desertion*: not words anyone
would associate with Cal. *Idle threats*—against whom?

   People are like tanzanite, Sammy had said. *Pleochroic. You look*
at them from one side and they look one way, from another side they
look another, and from a third side, some other way still. But no matter how Erica looked back at Cal, she couldn't see him as anything
approaching a thief or a deserter. If he were, he might still be alive.
So many words were missing in the letter. Had Cal been the victim
of threats? Had he uncovered a plot involving betrayal? *My loves*
would live. Erica stood up and exhaled deeply.

   Outside the tent, the upper reaches of the sky had turned a
bruised, smoky purple. Below that, a distant line of trees was sil-

houetted against a setting sun and looked like a flaming mushroom cloud surrounded by deepening shades of orange and fuchsia. Although the scene was magnificent, Erica found it unsettling, a portent of something tragic or evil. She shook her head to clear it of such nonsense. Here in Africa, the sunsets were often dramatic, the clouds morphing and shape-shifting in a thousand blazing colors before settling into the ebony night.

Erica touched Cal's water-damaged letter. She brought it up to her nose and breathed deeply. Of course, after so many years, nothing of Cal remained. Just as nothing remained of him after he ran into the Trade Center. So many dead with no remains. Her throat swelled with despair. As in the first days after the attack, she tried to convince herself that it was all some kind of frustrating dream—and once again she failed miserably.

10

Erica came upon the pair by mistake. All of the safari travelers had been warned not to walk outside of camp alone, not to wander beyond the mown and trampled grassy areas that were patrolled by the young warriors. But no one had ever said anything about taking a stroll behind the double parentheses of the tents, and that was where Erica decided to go. Too many days sitting in jouncing vehicles and too little exercise had made her restless and irritable, and she thought a brisk walk in the rapidly cooling evening was the logical cure.

She left the table while everyone was still eating dessert. Tonight it was gingerbread bathed in a caramel sauce spiked with Amorula, a local liquor made from the fruit of the Amorula tree. Even elephants appreciated the buzz they got off the fermenting fruits, the travelers were told.

When Erica left the tent tonight, no one asked where she was going, and she did not seek company. The evening sky was amethyst directly overhead, while flames of gold licked at the horizon. The safari staff, who earlier had manned portable sinks for the travelers to wash their hands before eating, had all disappeared—gone to their own dinners, Erica assumed. She stretched her arms toward the sky and then swept them down to her toes, popping the kinks that bound her lower back. Then she set out at a brisk pace for the farthest of the tents and slipped around the back. It was like falling off the edge of the known world. Behind the guests' tents was another cluster of somewhat shabbier dwellings. She headed to those. But before she had gone more than a dozen paces, she was startled by the sound of voices from the parking area, hushed but clearly engaged in heated disagreement.

Erica paused to listen. She had never heard Swahili spoken in such rapid-fire tones, consonants like sticks hurled against glass. Until now, all she had heard were individual words and phrases the guides had imparted. *Hibari?* How are you. *Mazuri sana*, very well. *Karibu!* Welcome. And finally, as they became more familiar, *tafadhali*, please. *Uhaligani?* How's it going? *Labda*, maybe, and *quinoco*, go away (in no uncertain terms), useful for putting off pushy salesmen in the market. But what Erica was hearing now was clearly a bitter argument and she listened, rapt, as the syllables flew, not feeling ashamed for eavesdropping because she had no idea what was being said. A man's deep voice growled some words, then a woman spoke, shrill with anger, and cut him short. In English, she spat out, "Coward! Let the hyenas take care of it and leave the rest for the jackals then!" And all conversation ceased. A moment later, Nini stalked out from behind a jeep, followed by Leni.

They stopped cold when they saw her and stared for a long moment. Then, instead of acknowledging her, each turned sharply and headed in a different direction. Erica, alarmed at the look of anger on their faces, turned hastily to walk back to the safety of the campsite. What could have inspired such ferocity? Before this, she had never even seen more than a passing conversation between the two. Was this a lovers' quarrel? But the resentment in their eyes seemed directed more at her than at each other.

Erica backed down the path slowly for several steps before

she turned and sped away, her cheeks burning with shame—over what, she didn't know.

That night, for the first time in many, many months, she was visited by the dream that had plagued her after 9/11. At first, the dream had threatened her regularly. While she could drift off at any given moment in a day—reading, watching television, even talking on the phone—the specter of the dream kept her wakeful and terrified each night. After a while, the dream visited less often. But each time she thought it had disappeared for good, it came back with some variation on the theme.

This time, she was standing at the edge of the pool at the Arusha hotel. The sun—hot, bright—beat painfully on her sunburnt shoulders. Suntan lotion sizzled and snapped like the sound of her dad frying eggs on Sunday morning. She smelled burning toast. The longer she stood, the worse the heat became until it seemed unendurable, but so did the idea of the deep, icy water that was her only alternative. Through the calloused skin of her soles, she could feel every grain of sand and crack in the concrete, and the tiny sugar ants burrowed for passage beneath her toes. Somewhere behind her, kids were shrieking as they raced back and forth. The blue of the noon sky was so intense it was leeching the color from her eyes. Soon she would be blinded by it. But not before the sun burned through her skin and the narrow bones of her shoulders. The wind, hot as the breath of an oven, crackled threats and warnings through the leaves. An enormous insect with wings like lace helicopter rotors and a giant stinger for a tail buzzed past her ear and she jumped. The concrete disappeared from underfoot. She hung suspended and waited for the icy water to bite and suck her under. But there was nothing. Just falling. And more falling. Dark, light, dark, light, she opened her eyes and looked down. The ground was a million miles away, the people were smaller than sugar ants and still she was falling.

As always, she woke slick and stinking of fear right before the sidewalk struck. Erica blinked until she was certain where in time and space she was, and then she padded to the sink in the back of her tent and poured some water from the pitcher onto a towel. She scrubbed her face and neck, then her arms and chest. The rough cloth scoured away the last wisps of the dream and evaporation cooled her skin. Her breath grew slower and her heart stopped beating itself senseless against her ribs like a bird trapped on a screen porch.

Erica's therapist, Elizabeth, had suggested that she try and think about something pleasant after one of these dream incidents. Not to force the thought, but merely to allow a new subject to float up in her mind. Now Erica thought about the hippos. Peaceful vegetarians, short-tempered destroyers—it struck her that this was a strange animal for Cal to have identified with.

But just as she was about to return to bed, Erica looked up and saw the wilted rose, drooped over the side of a Kili bottle. She was certain she had thrown it in the waste paper basket below the sink. Perhaps one of the staff thought she had dropped it there accidentally and replaced it in the bottle? But that made no sense. Surely they didn't go through people's trash each day. Once more, she dropped the bottle into the basket. It hit the bottom with a satisfying crack.

She looked at her watch. It was only 10:00. She knew that unless sleep was as fleet as a charging hippo, it was unlikely to overtake her tonight, if it bothered to come after her at all. What she wanted more than anything was someone to talk to. A few days ago, a second note had appeared in her tent. This one was sticking out of her makeup bag: *What was stolen will become the stone around your neck.* She had crushed it and thrown it as hard as she could against the wall of the tent, but it bounced ineffectually. Who was pursuing her like this? Again, she thought of the address book with creeping shame. There was no rational explanation for anyone on this trip to have any connection to that. With the possible exception of Robert. She pushed the idea away. He was a nice guy. Almost a friend. The other night he had bought her an Amorula. They sat in the dining tent and talked for an hour about nothing in particular. If he had been sent to get back the address book, he could have just said so, damn it.

Now Erica slipped into sandals and the day's dusty clothes that rested at the foot of her bed, put the two notes in her pocket and stepped out into the night. The night settled around her skin like velvet and only the soft glow of LED lights told her where the tents were arrayed. She should have grabbed her headlamp, she realized, but now that she was outside, she just wanted to keep moving forward. Gulping the cool air, she gaped uselessly in one direction and then another, unsure which way to go. Bea's tent was in one direction, Jane and Marcie's in the other. Her decision was made when she heard the crunch of footsteps coming from her left. Without another moment's hesitation, she raced to the right and in seconds was on the front porch of Jane and Marcie's tent, where she froze, pressed up against the canvas.

Inside, the occasional rustle of a page indicated that someone was awake, which was all Erica wanted in the world. She raised her hand to knock and then realized there was nothing to knock on. Instead, she coughed and tapped one foot against the wooden floorboards.

"Jane? Marcie? Are you there? It's Erica? Can I come in?"

"Erica? What are you doing out there?" came a hoarse whisper. Bare feet shuffled against the tent floor and in another second the tent was unzipped and Jane emerged from between the screen halves. She flicked on a flashlight and Erica winced in the blinding light. Jane backed quickly into the tent, drawing Erica after her. She flicked on another LED light that hung from the tent ceiling.

"Erica, you look awful! Are you ill? Marcie's fast asleep, but come in." She held the screen aside and retrieved a book from the floor—Hemingway's *Green Hills of Africa*—and motioned to the bed. Marcie mumbled in her sleep, but her eyes remained closed.

"Sit. You look like you're about to fall down. What's going on?"

Erica sank gratefully onto the bed, Jane sitting beside her. Marcie stirred.

"Hmm? Jane? What's the matter? Who's here?"

"It's Erica. Something's wrong."

Marcie sat bolt upright. "Another leopard? A lion?" She threw her legs off the bed, her feet searching for her sandals.

Now Erica didn't know what to say. It seemed so humiliating. What if they thought she was crazy? She took one deep breath and spilled the entire story—roses, notes and all.

Jane and Marcie looked at each other in silence when Erica had finished.

"I'm not sure how to put this in any kind of delicate way," Jane finally said, taking Erica's icy hand in both of hers, "but in my humble opinion, you have yourself a stalker."

Erica let out a little laugh and tried to look unconcerned as she shook off Jane's hand.

Marcie said, "Clearly, someone is deliberately following you and trying to frighten you with these messages."

A stalker? Erica could hear the world ringing in her head—

not Jane's voice, but that of Cal's partner Frank, accusing her of stalking Cal, *scavenging through other people's memories and feeding off them.* When Erica looked up, she practically expected to find Frank's face staring at her, but of course, it was Jane's face she saw, and Jane's eyes were full of concern rather than anger. Misreading the look of fear on Erica's face, Jane grabbed her hand.

"Oh, Erica, I know how that must sound," she continued. "I'm worried for you. Do you have any idea who could be doing this? Or why? There are only a couple of dozen of us out here. I hate the idea that it's one of the other guests, and even worse if it's one of the guides or the kitchen staff."

Erica hadn't thought at all of the kitchen staff, a small handful of workers who were essentially invisible, but who had been briefly introduced when the travelers arrived at the first camp. Tucked away behind the campsite, these people worked hard to produce and clean up three meals a day. But why on earth would any of them, much less the guides, be stalking her, and what did they expect her to *return?* She had nothing of value. Her luggage consisted entirely of clothing—now filthy—photo equipment, shoes, books. All well-used and of little real value. She had only about three hundred dollars in traveler's checks and the same in cash, reserved mainly for tips. The only thing she'd brought of value, if she thought about it, was Cal's address book—and that had been lost to a simian thief.

"Erica? Erica?" Jane was peering into her face with concern.

"Sorry. What did you say?"

"I was suggesting that you talk to Makinde about this. He is responsible for us, after all."

Makinde. Yes. But what if it was Makinde who was behind it all? How was she to know? Didn't he have the most access to their tents? And knowledge of where the travelers were at any given time? Hadn't he arrived almost immediately when the monkey escaped from her tent? Crazy thought, but everything suddenly felt a little insane. Suddenly she remembered: Makinde was the one who had persuaded her to join this trip. In her mind, he loomed larger and larger as her nemesis.

"I don't want to bother Makinde," she said quickly. "I was just thinking I'd talk to Nini instead. She knows so much; maybe she could help." Erica hadn't thought of talking to Nini until that precise second, but the notion seemed to satisfy Jane.

"Good idea. She seems kind. Quiet and thoughtful. And everyone trusts her. I bet she'd have some ideas." Jane had been as flushed as Erica was pale, but now both of them returned to a more relaxed state.

"I want you to know that I haven't got anything that belongs to anyone but me," Erica told her friends. She felt a twinge of conscience as she said this, but in truth, the address book was no longer with her. "And if I could think of anything, I'd be more than happy to return it." Yes, more than happy, but—and this new idea made her suck in her breath—what if it was something she didn't even know she possessed? She didn't dare mention this to the women, who looked relieved to have gotten over the hump of this difficult conversation.

Jane and Marcie invited her to stay for the night, but Erica insisted on going back to her tent. They walked her there and made her promise to shout if anything untoward happened in the dark.

It wasn't until a few days later that Erica caught up with Nini along the path to the camp kitchen.

"Nini," Erica called.

Nini stopped mid-step as still and wary as a gazelle. She did not turn her head.

"It's Erica."

Now Nini turned and although Erica couldn't see her face with the sun behind her, she felt herself swept from head to toes by the girl's cool gaze. Silhouetted against the bright sky, Nini looked more than ever like a carved figurine, the long bones of her legs from ankles to knees, knees to hips and the equally lanky proportions of her arms marking her as Maasai, and almost identical in form to Leni. Erica had seen them together several times since the argument. Nini covered the distance between them with a few long strides.

"*Hibari dada?*" she asked.

"Very well, I mean *mzuri sana*," Erica stammered.

"Is there anything you need? I believe Makinde is still in camp," she said.

Erica was about to thank her and turn away, when another idea struck her.

"I came out just for some exercise, but I need, well, I need something else that I'm not sure Makinde can supply." Nini looked puzzled but curious. "I need someone to talk to. Are you in a hurry? Do you have a few minutes?" Erica was losing resolve even as she spoke. Everything she said was bound to seem ridiculous to this woman. "But you're probably tired after driving all day. Maybe we could talk another time." Erica made as if to turn away.

"I would be happy to talk. We could sit on the wall by the car park. There is usually a breeze there at this time of day."

Erica looked at her, grateful for Nini's generosity. She must be worn out with pointing out wildlife to tourists, not to mention anticipating their every need. The two women walked to the parking area, meeting no one along the way.

But when they sat down, Erica found herself confused about where to start. Finally, she pulled the notes from her pocket where she had been keeping them. There were now three altogether, the last one received only the previous day.

What was taken must be returned.

What was stolen will become the stone around your neck.

And the most upsetting one of all: *The mate of a jackal is hunted for a jackal.* Jackals, she had learned, were scorned by most tribes as even lower than other carrion eaters, for their thieving ways, and could be shot, trapped or poisoned with impunity.

"Do you have any idea where these came from?" Nini asked, with a deep frown of concern.

"They've been appearing in my tent, along with white roses, one every few nights," Erica said. "I can't imagine why, and if they're meant to frighten me, they're doing a damned good job. Do you have any idea who could be doing such a thing? Is it some kind of ugly joke?"

Nini continued to stare down at the papers in her hands. After several moments she said quietly, "I don't think this person is joking. You may be in danger. Can you think of nothing that you have come by in a dishonest way? No one who might feel you possess something that is not truly yours?"

Erica was a little offended. Was this girl, probably not much more than half her age, questioning her honesty? "Nothing. I've taken nothing that did not belong to me."

Nini touched the rough stone around her neck that Erica had admired on the first day of the safari. She stood and took a few steps toward a nearby acacia tree, where a pair of bearded vultures had settled. The enormous birds raised their wings and rose heavily into the air. Nini returned to the wall and folded her lanky body back into repose.

"Why are you in our country?"

This seemed completely unrelated to the subject at hand, and nothing Erica wished to discuss. Her reasons for being there had nothing to do with this situation, and anyway, how could she possibly describe her loss to this stranger?

"Why are you here?" Nini asked again, more sharply. "You are not here just to see the lions, no?"

"No," Erica admitted.

"Maybe Africa is more dangerous than you knew."

Erica was beginning to form the same conclusion, although she wondered what prompted Nini to say such a thing.

"I came to learn more about someone I loved and lost," she finally admitted. "My friend. My lover. We were like one person, he and I, and since he is gone, I have been only half a person." Having begun the telling, the story seemed to slip from her lips of its own accord. At the end she said, "He lived here many years ago and I wanted to talk to his friends who had remained in Tanzania. To interview them about his life. It may seem strange, but doing this is helping me to become whole again." The vultures returned to the tree, watching the women through hooded eyes.

"Possibly he has no friends in Africa. Maybe you should not have come." She shrugged. "But it's your life."

Erica was stunned into silence. What could this young woman know about such things?

Nini stood once more, and waved her arms to startle the birds. "The vultures seem to think there will be a feast for them," she said. "When I was a girl we used to sing songs to them. We promised them that if they left our cows alone to die a natural death they could then have their bodies for a feast. We believe vultures can see into the future. Maybe these vultures foresee a tasty meal ahead."

Then she turned toward Erica, and with that swift movement, her dark mood appeared to dissolve. A peaceable smile spread across her face.

"I have work to do, but I am glad you came to me with your concerns. I will give it more thought and let you know if I have any idea about who could be behind these notes. And the roses, of course. Could it be an admirer? Robert, perhaps?" she said, smiling coyly.

Erica was startled. More confused than ever. Frightened and then icily irritated at the notion that her concerns were being dismissed. A tightness crept up her neck and around her temples, the first sign of the pounding headache to come.

11

The sun had risen high by the time Erica awoke, and her tent was hotter than the cactus greenhouse on a sunny day. Had she actually slept through the calls of *Jambo, jambo?* She got up from her cot and pulled on the pair of gray nylon capris she had washed in the shower the night before. After days on safari, her clothes had acquired a copper patina of red clay dust. Washing them had little effect, other than to make the fabric stiffen as if starched. Erica decided she'd be leaving most of her clothing behind when she went home. Which would be in only one week. And still, she hadn't had any further messages from Cal's friends, nor had she come any closer to understanding Drew's scornful words. She despaired that she ever would. More upsetting, those words had worked their way, into the deeper recesses of her mind, like worms through an apple, eating away at her memories of Cal and riddling them with holes.

Lately, when she tried to picture Cal's face, she found it blurry and generic—two hazel eyes, a straight nose, a full mouth that could belong to almost any attractive man. Worse, her memory of Cal as a hero had gone from solid marble to something closer in texture to a cork tree—spongy and pliant. She was ashamed at how malleable her belief in him was proving.

Erica layered a shirt over a tank top and listened for the voices of her nearest neighbors, at this campsite Honey and Jerry. The bickering Bickersons, Erica's mother would have called them, and normally their voices were inescapable, but now the only sounds she heard were the squawk and response of distant birds and the susurrus wind through the grasses.

At first, she assumed that everyone else had already gone to breakfast. Then she remembered that, in fact, the other travelers had been awakened well before dawn for their hot air balloon ride over the plains—the reputed jewel in the crown of this trip. She was, apparently, the only one who had opted out. No one could quite believe that she would turn down such an opportunity, but the four hundred dollar fee was more than Erica could afford, and, more to the point, heights made her sick to her stomach. She imagined spending the entire flight crouched at the bottom of the rattan basket or hanging over its edge, heaving her breakfast onto some unsuspecting warthog. Even Marcie's offer of Dramamine and a loan didn't tempt her. Erica said she'd be happy to stick around camp and read or catch up on documenting the animals and plants they'd seen in the safari journal they'd each been given. Her journal was still as blank as the look on a baboon's face.

"*Jambo, jambo!*" came a booming male voice from the tent porch. Erica put down her book and came outside.

"*Jambo*, Leni. Didn't you go on the balloon trip?"

"Good morning, Miss Erica, No, as you see, I got left behind. Makinde told me I might find you here. I hope I didn't take you away from anything important?"

"Not at all. The book I was reading was so boring it was putting me to sleep."

"Well then, why not come with me for a drive? I have to pick up some supplies at a village not far away, and you might enjoy seeing the kopjes along the way."

Erica hadn't spoken to him at all since the night when she stumbled on the argument between him and Nini. His face bore no trace of the rancor it had displayed that evening. He looked genuinely eager for her to accept his offer.

"I'd love to. Give me ten minutes to get ready. I'll meet you at the car."

"Excellent. You will enjoy the ride and I will enjoy the company." He turned and walked down the path.

When Erica got to the parking lot, Leni was moving some boxes and the ever-present rifle from the floor of the passenger side to the back seat.

"Here, I brought some sandwiches and cookies for your lunch." He handed her an insulated bag, which she stowed by her feet next to several bottles of water.

"Asante sana."

"Do you wish for me to charge your camera batteries while we drive?"

"No, I think today I just want to look and not photograph. Sometimes I get the feeling that we're all so busy taking pictures and videos, we end up missing everything that's happening in the present moment."

Leni nodded. "Yes, we guides have thought this, too. The tourists and their cameras are a great source of amusement to us. I do not believe I have ever seen Mike, for example, without a camera around his neck. Even at dinner."

They drove for almost an hour across red clay roads, where the Land Rover's wheels kicked up spinning dust devils like miniature tornadoes. At first, Erica tried to make conversation, but with the wind and dust flying through the open vehicle, that proved impossible. She fell silent and enjoyed the view. When they finally reached the town, the fine clay powder had turned her and Leni practically the same ruddy color.

"I would be better if you would wait in the car. I will only be a few minutes," he said.

Erica was taken aback by this request, but Leni was already on his way into the small tin-roofed shop with the word Magazeti painted in blue over the door and what looked like bags of soil, or maybe cement, piled high against the walls. It took Erica a moment to realize what was strange about the scene—no women. Only men were wandering around the town and lounging against the wooden buildings, hands in the pockets of their baggy pants. At first Erica was confused, but then she realized that this must be a Muslim village and its women would spend most of their time behind closed doors. Leni returned quickly. He loaded several large boxes into the back of the jeep and then handed her a bottle of Kili through the window before climbing into the car.

He said "Now I will show you something beautiful." The car backfired once before the engine caught and every head in the street turned.

Leni took a different route back to camp. This time, the faint track wound through tall grasslands and eventually emerged into a barren, rocky landscape. The sun had baked deep fissures into the soil. The landscape looked like the badlands of Utah, where Erica had gone on a summer course in adaptive plant growth. The grass was short and sparse, an ochre lawn bent stiffly in the scorching breeze.

Leni drove more slowly now, stopping every few minutes to survey the scene.

Erica said, "Strange, we haven't seen a single animal."

"It's the migration. In a couple of days we will catch up with it in the North, but the drought pushed the herds from here weeks ago. And with them, the predators. Only the rocks and the wind remain behind."

Erica noticed that even the piles of dung ubiquitous everywhere else were absent here.

"More than two million animals follow their food and water in a clockwise circle almost two thousand miles long. Meanwhile, the country behind them gets a chance to recover and regrow in their absence," Leni said.

The flat ground was punctuated occasionally by candelabra-shaped euphorbia and twisted, man-sized termite mounds. Staring at the watery waves of heat radiating up from the terrain as she sat in the stultifying heat of the car lulled Erica into a half-sleep.

As they came around a bend, however, all that changed. On the horizon were a series of rocky outcroppings that looked like islands in the sea of grass or discarded playthings scattered by the children of giants. Erica shook herself awake. As they got closer, she noticed that some islands were made up of mammoth boulders balanced on clusters of smaller ones, while others were like angular granite plinths, thrust dramatically up through the soil. Bare and knobby or thick with vegetation, they looked as if they defied gravity, with egg-shaped boulders poised atilt against the cobalt sky. Erica was enthralled.

"Kopjes?" she asked, turning to Leni.

"Yes, you know the kopjes? They're very ancient stones—hundreds of millions of years old—that worked their way from deep underground to the surface and then survived as the softer soil was worn away. They are the bones of Africa."

With a sharp turn of the wheel, Leni drove the vehicle off of the track and set out straight across the close-cropped grass toward one group of rocks.

"Where are we going?"

"I want to show you the most beautiful of the kopjes. You will be sorry not to have brought your camera," he said with a laugh. He zigged and zagged through the grass, passing stone giants to the right and the left. The motion pitched Erica and the loose packages in the back from side to side roughly. With one last turn, he pulled the car to a stop.

"We have arrived."

Erica stared at the mammoth outcrop silhouetted against the cerulean sky. Euphorbias growing in the soil wedged between the balanced boulders sported ripening dull red fruit. Erica wished she could pick one or two to bring home and donate to the Garden's collection. Leni was right; she was sorry not to have a camera.

As if he were reading her thoughts, he asked, "Would you like for me to take your picture on the kopje?"

"Isn't that against the rules?" Leni was rummaging through a satchel and finally came up with a small digital camera.

"There's no one to know." He stepped out of the car and came around to open her door.

This was better than a balloon ride any day. Erica stepped out of the vehicle. In all directions and saw nothing but blowing grasses and the towering rocks, which were farther from them than she had realized. She began to make her way through the sharp and crispy undergrowth—this was the longest walk she'd taken in almost two weeks. Being able to move alone across the terrain, without the chattering company of others, felt like freedom. What she hadn't been prepared for was the sheer scope of the landscape. Halfway to the rocks she looked back, and the Land Rover appeared a mere toy. In this setting, Leni, a tall, imposing figure up close, seemed no larger than a gazelle, and as delicate. She felt as small and insignificant as a termite, crawling over the scorched earth. She walked a little further and reached the lowest of the rocks. Hand over hand, she pulled herself up. The higher she climbed, the more startling the view. Under the overturned bowl of the sky, it was as if she were the last creature left on the planet. It was as dizzying as those long-ago nights under the starry summer skies, when she felt tethered to the earth by only the thinnest cord. She tried to climb higher, but found no purchase and was about to look for another handhold when a movement caught her eye.

Turning back to the jeep, she spotted the small figure of Leni, but instead of the camera, he was holding the rifle that had rested in the back seat. The barrel was trained straight in her direction. The scene grew fuzzy and she stared harder, hoping the wavering bands of heat in the air between them had created a mirage.

"Don't move!" he shouted.

Her mouth filled with a taste like copper pennies. The heat continued to roll like waves on the sea, but the howling wind had gone silent. The figure of Leni and his rifle grew larger and smaller, a funhouse image. Drop to the ground, she thought. Run. But she was able to do neither. Her legs were as useless as twin pillars of stone. Tears sprang to her eyes. She was no hero. She couldn't even save herself. So this was what it was like to face death. She'd been a fool to come here, and now she would pay the price of her foolishness.

A flash, and then, what seemed like an impossibly long moment later, a shattering explosion. Erica looked down. Blood spattered her bare legs. She waited to fall and braced for the pain. With her last breath, she tried to scream Cal's name, but she could only summon a feeble hiss. A putrid smell stung her nostrils. Was it coming from her? Bile filled her mouth and washed back down her throat. Everything was growing indistinct, and she fought to remain conscious. In the narrowing tunnel of her vision, Leni was running toward her, the gun still raised. She waited for the final shot. Now she knew who had been sending her those messages, but she would never know why.

Why was a question without an answer. Why would anyone turn a passenger plane into a weapon? Why aim it into a building full of people doing nothing more than trying to make a living? There was no why. Why was for another lifetime.

Leni was climbing—he was a few yards from where she stood. Erica knew it was only another moment before he reached her and ended her life. She slid backward against the burning rock and felt herself sway and begin to tumble. As she lost consciousness, she was once again searching a night sky full of stars, bouncing on the bungee cord between gravity and eternity.

"Are you all right?"

Such a strange question from a murderer. Was she alive? Dead? She was surprised to find herself resting in Leni's arms, his face bent close toward hers. Beads of sweat ringed his forehead; his eyes darted wildly from her to the boulders behind her.

Erica nodded abruptly. She bit her tongue, and it hurt. Alive then. He laid her on the rocks and turned in a slow circle.

"We have to get out of here. Can you walk?"

None of this made sense to Erica. She closed her eyes against the pulsing light. There was no pain, but neither could she summon the will to get up.

"We must go. It is not safe. I'm sorry." He lifted her to her feet. She found, oddly, that she could stand, and that's when she saw the blasted body of a hyena, blood and fur splattered against the earth, inches from where she had been standing. Already the vultures were beginning to gather overhead, alerted by the smell rising on the thermals. Other scavengers would be close behind.

"You have to walk. I need to have the gun ready in case there are more. There will be more." Leni propped her up as she staggered slightly. "Erica, do you understand?"

Slowly, she did. There had indeed been a kill, but it had not been her. She nodded mutely and rallied what strength she had for the trek back to the car, leaning heavily on Leni as they crept down the kopje and stumbling slowly across the dry grassland. Leni followed, walking backward, the rifle raised. It seemed like miles. The whole way, he muttered a garbled apology.

Erica couldn't believe she'd had such a horrible thought about Leni.

Once in the car, Leni cleaned the blood and guts of the hyena from her legs gently with the bottled water, apologizing the whole time. His words came through in disconnected rushes: *Sorry. Warning. Danger. Sorry.*

Erica could still not speak. Halfway back to camp, however, her voice returned in the form of wracking sobs. By the time they pulled into the parking area, she had regained some sense of composure. Leni, however, insisted that he had committed a terrible error of judgment and would resign from the tour. He pulled into the parking area and nervously began unloading the car, looking everywhere but at Erica. "I made an unforgiveable mistake," he said, finally. "I will tell Makinde and leave."

"But you saved my life!"

Leni pursed his lips and looked increasingly hang-dog.

"If it weren't for you, I'd be a hyena's lunch by now. I owe you my life. If you want to make this up to me, I insist that you stay. You're an excellent guide. If anything, I should by asking what I can do to repay you."

Leni looked startled and began to say something, then changed his mind and remained silent.

"I am shamed," he muttered, turning away. "But if you insist upon it, I will stay."

"Everyone makes mistakes," Erica said. But Leni was already striding from the area, carrying her pack. By the time she arrived at her tent, her things had been placed on her bed and there was no sign of Leni.

Erica pulled the tent curtains closed and stripped out of her clothes, which were sour with sweat. She would wash them in the shower and let them dry in the late afternoon sun. As she reached down for her shorts, she noticed a small folded piece of paper, yellow and crumbling around the edges, half hidden under the camp cot. She crouched and picked it up, but when she tried to open it, a corner broke off in her fingers. It was a piece of newsprint, nothing of hers. Perhaps it had been left behind by the previous guest or one of the camp workers. Erica sat on the cot and gently placed the paper on the blanket next to her.

The side of the page that faced up was covered in words in a language that she assumed was Swahili. As carefully as possible, Erica pressed her fingers into the mattress below the paper and with a little flick, flipped the paper over. On this side there was a faded photograph. She moved in closer for a better look, not daring to lift the fragile document.

A group of people clustered next to the opening of what looked like a cave. Erica squinted and bent low to the bed. She counted five men and a woman standing with their arms around each other, all but two of the group tall, lean, dark. Erica looked more closely at these two. To her astonishment, one was definitely Drew. She recognized him instantly by the ridiculous cowboy hat—possibly the same one he was wearing when she met him ten days ago. The other man, smaller than the rest, could that be Cal? Her skin prickled. How would such a thing have arrived in her tent? By now, Erica's nose was practically touching the paper. She felt a sneeze welling up and jumped back in time to keep it from blowing the photo to dust. Her heart tripped drunkenly around her ribs. Her hands were clammy. Holding her breath, she moved back in for another look. The man was slight with dark hair. His face was partly hidden in shadow, though. Erica strained to see. She rocked closer and farther away, trying to gain better focus, but nothing became any clearer. She turned her attention to the other four men and the woman. They were young. Barely out of their teens. The girl was holding something the size of her fist up to the camera and grinning broadly. Her white teeth contrasted strongly with her skin. Again, Erica looked at the fifth man. His head and shoulders inclined toward the woman and he was smiling broadly. It was a happy scene, then. A victory of some sort. There was no caption below the photo, or if there had been one, it had been cut away, as the clipping was trimmed close against the edges of the photo.

Who had dropped this? Accident, or message? It seemed like something Drew might send, but she hadn't received any letters since Billy's, and in any case, the clipping hadn't been in an envelope. They said a picture was worth a thousand words, Erica thought, but this one was an absolute cipher.

She switched on the tiny LED lights, but they offered little illumination. Erica put on her headlamp and clicked until she hit the highest setting. She aimed the beam at the photo. Even this did nothing to pierce the shadow that hid the identity of the second white man. But in the harsh electric light, his posture was clearly curved toward the woman in a way that was familiar. It seemed to indicate an intimacy, a protective affection for the woman whose forearm rested on his shoulder.

Quickly, Erica stood and walked to the little stand where her duffel rested. From one of the side pockets she fished out the gift that Karen had given her at the airport – the photo of Cal with the two of them at the zoo. It was the only memento she had of a wonderful day. Closing her eyes, she summoned the feeling of Cal's fingers stroking the fine hairs of her arm as they stood by the stone railing and the sharp amber smell of his skin as he leaned in toward her for the photo.

Her eyes fluttered open and she looked again. There was no denying it—Cal's unmistakable posture of affectionate familiarity in that photo was identical to that of the man in the clipping. The woman—was she his *love* that he mentioned in the letter to Billy? But he clearly wrote *loves*. Who, then, were the others? A hot bolt of jealousy skewered Erica's gut.

Rose

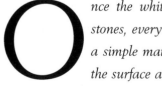 nce the white men had placed their value on our stones, everything began to change. No longer was it a simple matter of combing the ground or digging up the surface and carrying the prize to the city for pay-

*ment. Strangers flocked to the area like the clouds of flamingoes that
cover Lake Manyara in the wet season. My baba was forced to erect
a thorny* boma, *like the one we used to protect the cattle, around our
claim, and even so, we often found that thieves had broken in during
the night and dug our pits deeper for their own gain. Some of the* iloran
*began taking turns sleeping at the mines to protect our village claims.
Instead of keeping a sharp watch for the pad prints of leopards come
to steal the calves by night, they followed the sharp heel and sole prints
of the leather boots to find the thieves who stole the* jiwes *that should
rightfully have been our own.*

*Over time, of course, the mines have become not wide open craters
or deep pits, but narrow and treacherous tunnels dug deep into the
flesh of the earth, some one hundred meters deep. Today they are pro-
tected with razor wire and guns. The men who work the mines come up
after many hours shimmering in sweat, graphite and Tanzanite dust.
Those coming up from the belly of the earth collapse on the ground,
gasping, often too weak even to drink the water that is held to their lips.
Sometimes, of course, they don't come up at all.*

*In the future, men will claw their way even further into the earth to
get at these stones, as the rarity of the stones has made their price rise
higher and higher. Nowhere but in our beautiful country of Tanzania
can these gems be found. And nowhere in Tanzania other than in the
shadow of Kilimanjaro.*

*Once the government nationalized the mines, the area was divided
into plots, the best of which were sold to a company with experience
mining diamonds in South Africa. The rest were made available to our
own miners. My baba made his claim to several sites in Merelani. He
could do this because at nine years old I was able to read and write the
contracts that were required. When he died, only nine years later, he
left the deeds to me. My brother cared nothing for the mines, but only*

for his cattle, which by then were plentiful, and his new wife, Isima, who was with child. My possession of the claim made me the legal owner. Even so, as a woman I was forbidden by law to descend into the mines. I had to pay others to claw the jiwes from the earth, to oversee these men and to sell the stones to companies in Arusha. And what was left wasn't much of an income at all. Still, I remained, at least on paper, a miner. In the future this will change. In the future women will train to work the seams of jewels in their own mines. But that day will not come for many more years. And speaking of it only makes me regret that I will not be here, so I will speak of it no more.

By the time my baba died, I was living in Arusha and going to school there. I could see the world changing around me. Once a week I would take a bus back to visit my family and our mines, which were being looked after by my uncle. Week after week more of us Maasai came to Arusha to work and to live, and each weekend the buses back into the bush were full to bursting with people perched on the roof and hanging out the windows. Sometimes the bus would break down and we would all get out and sit in the red dust until another came along. Then that one would be twice as crowded. But eventually we would be home, where change came more slowly. Some of my friends from the village were parents now, and their young ones were herding the cows, learning at the school. Their lives were busy and hard and they rarely asked after mine, for which I was grateful. The words in Kiswahili that could explain half of what I knew hadn't yet been invented.

When I graduated, many people from my village came on the bus to see their Lucky Rose, the first person to have gone so far in school. They touched the shiny fabric of my graduation gown—as deep purple as the most prized stones—and they laughed at my pointed hat, with its tassel like a giraffe's tail hanging down one side. They brought the foods of my childhood and made a big party in the courtyard outside my apartment. They slept out there as if on the Serenget. It was the last time I saw many of them for a long time. Soon I would be living the secret life that not one of them would understand. And only my mother would remember to say my name.

I stayed in the city and began to teach in a tiny school for the children of factory workers. Among them were the children of those who worked in the glass houses where roses began to be grown by the millions. Our Tanzanian roses were flown all around the world. I liked to think of them as birds on the wing, roosting in the farthest places on this Earth. Often, these rose children would come to school with bandaged fingers from helping their parents remove the thorns from the long, stiff stems. The scent of the flowers wafted from their hair and their skin when I bent close to help them with their letters. It recalled for me the unfulfilled promise of the first rose I ever saw—the rose I buried under the baking grassland.

And how was it that I could still be a miner, my children would ask when I told them this story. That, I would say, is another story for another day, and now go to sleep.

Some stories, I did not tell my children. These I whispered to myself in the dark hours.

It was almost a year after my graduation from school that Calvin finally returned. One evening he appeared at my door as if he had left just that morning.

How did I feel when I opened the door to go out and found him standing there? I can no longer remember. The more time it has been since my feet touched earthly soil, the hazier these memories become. Especially this is true of the memory of feelings. Was I angry? Relieved? He hadn't even knocked. How long he had been standing there, wait-

ing, I don't know. I had gone to the door to let in the evening breeze. I dared not leave the windows open when I was away at work because of the large numbers of break-ins that had been taking place in the neighborhood. Each night when I came home, the rooms were unbearably hot and airless. At first, I had no idea who could be standing there and I leapt back, ready to slam the door or to fight. "Rose," he said. "My Rose." Seeing him for who he was, my head grew light and the hot colors of the street behind him spun and merged like the painted designs on children's spinning tops.

He did not ask if I had waited for him or had pledged myself to another. I did not even bid him karibu. *He simply walked through the open door and shrugged off the heavy backpack he carried. He drank the cool glass of juice I brought him, and then he lifted me up and carried me to our room. The eyes that I had once thought severe softened into deep, sweet pools and his mouth, as it found mine, was as tender as the rain. The first time, he cradled me and rocked me as if I were his own child and when he entered me it was as if we had melted together to become an entirely new creature. The next, he was like a leopard driven mad with thirst. When finally we slept, it was without regard to whose limbs were whose. Days passed like this in a haze from which we awoke to find the ants devouring the food we had left uneaten on our plates. The following week, we found a priest willing to marry us, but by then the twins had already taken root in my womb.*

We were an oddity even in my neighborhood, where people of many tribes and many nations lived crowded together. I cannot say there was hostility, but there were certainly plenty of stares and the occasional shopkeeper who pretended not to see us waiting. But with his graceful Swahili and his generous nature, Calvin gathered acquaintances, and maybe even a little respect. Later, even my mother accepted our love, if only for the joy and good fortune of her grandchildren. People in the street looked at him with a measure of unease, although I did not know why that should be. In any case, we kept mainly to ourselves and we were happy that way.

Each morning, I left the house early for the long walk to school. The children of the roses, as I had come to think of them, were growing in number until my whole classroom was awash with their fragrance. At the end of each week, many of them brought flowers to school for me, which meant that I returned home on Friday with a large bunch that perfumed our small house.

As I grew heavier with child, it became more difficult for me to visit my mines. By the end of each day in the classroom, my feet swelled painfully and I began taking the crowded bus back home to spare them further torment. We began to laugh at the picture I presented—my belly so distended I could balance my dinner plate on it. We were alarmed at how large and how quickly it grew. I sorely missed my mother and the women of the village who might share their knowledge with me in this area. At the same time, I feared their judgment.

After I became so breathless that I could no longer walk to school in the morning, Calvin made me go to the women's clinic. They smeared my belly with cold ointment and pressed circles in it with a wand as they watched gray images on a small television screen. That was how we found out about the second baby. Calvin strutted around proudly as any male ostrich. And he went out and bought a used Ford, saying that he would drive me to school. He offered to take over checking in at the mines, allowing me a day to stay home at the end of each week, with my feet up and my back resting as the clinic doctor advised. With the car, he pointed out, he could easily get there and back in one day. He said that it was a job for a man, in any case, and I was too tired to argue. I was grateful for all he did. I made the introductions to my uncle the next time he came to town and assured him that Calvin spoke on my behalf.

Calvin knew people in Arusha from his first trip to our country and he visited them often, looking for work, I assumed. For a while, he labored as a translator for one of the British companies that built office buildings in the center of the city. Sometimes, he was engaged by one of the safari companies beginning to take rich tourists into the bush. He was as good as a Maasai at bargaining, and they used him to acquire their provisions and hire the guides. He said maybe he would open his own company someday. He said that a good family business would give the babies security when they were grown.

But mostly, he grew to love the mines. He got the men to take him down into the pits, to show him how to recognize the veins where the gems would be found. He would return home coated in graphite dust, his exposed skin as black as my own. He described for me the scene that I, as a woman, would never see—the narrow ladder down into the dusty, hot hole, and the relief of reaching the main cave, its walls glinting with what he called "fool's gold." Sometimes he brought me a piece of boudin and we spent the evening chipping out its treasure. I would bind the uncut jiwe in wire and hang it from the lamp next to our bed or wear it around my neck bound in hemp.

These jiwes from deep in the earth were not the bright sunset shades of the first stones we found. Those had already been touched by the heat of the lightning. These new stones were a reddish brown and had to be specially heat treated before their hidden colors would emerge. I wouldn't have recognized them for what they were had I not known them as a child.

Calvin began to visit the mines several times a week, sometimes coming home after dark, sometimes covered in bruises and scratches—a fall from the ladder, he said, a stumble over some misplaced tools. I begged him to be careful, to leave the mining to those who knew the ways of the pit. The mines that gave us life also took their share. I did not want to become a mining widow with a baby—no, two babies—on the way.

This was our one fight: I asked him to stay out of the mines and he told me it was not my place to tell him what he could and could not do. These are my mines, I shouted at him, clutching the pouch of rolled up deeds and shaking it at him, and without my permission, you may not enter! His face turned as blood red as the stone dangling from our lamp and his arms, pressed tight to his sides, trembled with the urge to strike. I stood my ground, prepared for his assault. Without another word he stormed out of our house. I did not fear that he would fail to return. I knew the strength of our love. But I also felt the first sharp edges of something carving its way between us.

I grew larger and finally I had to stop teaching. It was one of the saddest days of my life, and also one of the happiest, for I knew my little ostriches would soon be born. And with Calvin watching the business, our income grew. My uncle had been helping himself to more than I thought, Calvin told me. With this leak patched, we were able to live quite well for a time, even without my school salary.

12

The safari was nearing its end; in only four more days they would be heading back to Arusha and from there, home. Erica would return empty-handed. In a way, though, this failure was liberating. So far, everything she had learned and intuited was baffling and painful. Drew's cryptic, scornful words echoed menacingly, and a bitter taste welled up in her throat when she thought about the photograph of Cal bent fondly toward that girl. She was jumpy and irritable, looking behind herself at the slightest snap or rustle. She felt a humiliating kinship with the rabbits that sometimes gathered at dusk at the Botanic Garden, their long ears swiveling and twitching with anxiety. Her appetite had dwindled noticeably. Just now, at dinner, she'd caught Bea watching her with concern as she pushed the food around on her plate. Erica ate a few mouthfuls to stave off any discussion.

And now, this. As soon as she entered the tent, she saw it—the latest note, white against the dark burgundy blanket stretched tight across the freshly made bed. She snatched it up and read. It was the harshest of the bunch. *Give up what is not rightfully yours or meet a thief's fate.* A thief's fate—what the hell was that in this country? Death? Dismemberment? The rose that accompanied this one had been shredded, its bruised petals scattered around it. Her fingers, grasping the scrap of paper grew white and cold—they were the fingers of a crone, aged and wrinkled—while the rest of her broke out in a sweat. As Erica stared at that unfamiliar hand, the usual social hum of the camp in evening faded to white noise and finally to silence. Fear crept like ice through her veins. And then she heard it—the familiar tune, "Hakuna Matata" from *The Lion King*, whistled slightly off key, accompanied by a rhythmic crunch of feet along the gravel path. Erica looked up to see Robert amble by her window. He must have seen her, too, through the screen.

"Hey, Erica—everything okay in there? No worries, right?" Without waiting for a response, he laughed and moved off, whistling.

An electric hum traveled from her soles to the roots of her hair. Was he taunting her? She dropped the note as if it had spontaneously ignited. Robert disappeared around the bend of the camp toward his tent without looking back. Erica gathered the petals and dumped them in the wastepaper basket by the bed. She snatched up the scrap of paper and crammed it into her back pocket. She would put an end to this. No matter how improbable she found it, there was only one person who had even the most tenuous connection to the address book and the threats. She stormed from her tent and set out to face her accuser.

Robert was inside his tent, still humming. He hadn't heard Erica's approach; she could turn back. Instead, she stamped impatiently on the wooden platform and was met with the buzz of the zipper. Robert emerged with his hair wet and a dab of shaving cream on one cheek.

"Erica! I wasn't expecting company, but, hey, come on in! Can I offer you a granola bar?"

"This is not exactly a friendly visit," Erica said, brushing past him. Inside, the tent was surprisingly neat and tidy. She had taken him for more of the toss-it-and-go type. Pushing this thought aside, she turned to him.

"Why are you harassing me?' she demanded, her chin thrust in his direction.

"Harassing you?" Robert seemed to find this amusing, which made her angrier.

"Who put you up to this?" She stepped forward until she was inches from him.

"This? This what?" He didn't look amused any longer.

"Whose idea was it to try and scare me with the notes and the roses?" Erica shook the latest piece of paper in his face. "Did you email them and tell them I was here? What could they possibly offer to make you behave in such a perverse and contemptible way?"

"Roses?" The word rolled slowly from Robert's slack mouth. His eyes narrowed, and a deep rift divided them. Erica had been expecting accusations, or maybe excuses, but this bewildered evasiveness was far worse.

"Is it the damn address book? Because if it is, you're too late. The blue monkeys got it long ago." She crammed the note into her pants pocket and glared at him. "Unless you're the monkey." She had assumed that whoever had left the rose had also left the zipper open, but here was a new possibility.

"Erica, I have no idea what the hell you're talking about."

"Just admit it!"

His mouth clamped shut.

Heat crept up Erica's neck. Sweat prickled her chest. Still, Robert said nothing. The silence lasted for an eternity. Finally, Erica spun around to leave and crashed into the zippered mesh. Moving quickly, Robert bent and unzipped it, and Erica fled like an animal released into the dark.

The next morning Erica woke groggy and disoriented and skipped breakfast, downing instead the pitcher of coffee that had been left for her outside the tent. Although Bea had saved a seat in Makinde's car, where Jane, Marcie and Robert were already ensconced, Erica slunk into the last available seat in Nini's. She felt Robert's glare follow her.

More and more, since that day at the kopjes, Erica had been riding shotgun with Nini.

"I think you would be most comfortable riding with me," she had said that morning. Erica wondered if Nini was offering protection.

For his part, Leni stayed as far from Erica as he could without calling attention to his behavior. As agreed, nothing more was said about the incident, but Erica couldn't shake the sight of that gun pointed straight at her. The flash of the bullet heading her way. Although Makinde remained oblivious to the narrowly averted tragedy, Erica felt that Nini knew what had happened.

Wrapped in misery, she saw nothing of the landscape as it rushed by. Now she saw her attack on Robert as a mortifying blunder. Fool, she reproached herself, you've let your own guilty conscience over that stupid address book make you believe that you are being targeted for some crime you've committed, just like you blamed yourself for your parents' divorce. When would she stop repeating the same senseless story? Maybe that's what she should have asked Elizabeth in one of those excruciating therapy sessions. Now she would have to avoid Robert for the rest of the trip. One minute she felt completely justified, and then the next she felt like she was losing her mind. In either case, her protective herd would be smaller by one. She would just have to limp through these last few days and get home. Back to a solid roof over her head, a lock on the door, and Karen only blocks away.

As Leni had predicted, they caught up with the migration that morning, just south of the border with Kenya. Erica was stunned at the sight of a valley so thick with wildlife that there was hardly any ground to be seen.

Nini pulled off the track and onto a spot overlooking the Mara River, Tanzanian soil under their tires, Kenya across the muddy water. The travelers watched as wave after wave of wildebeests flailed down a sharp bank and struggled up the far side. The group held its collective breath as crocodiles silently slipped into the water and floated toward the herd. With a sharp splash, one of the smaller animals was suddenly dragged below the surface and came up thrashing its skinny legs through a pink froth. Erica couldn't control a cry of dismay. She thought she'd been prepared for such a moment, but she had been mistaken.

The animals around the little calf burst into a frenzy of alarm. The whites of their wildly rolling eyes were visible as they churned the water to foam, trying to escape. Again and again, the ones at the head of the pack slid back down the slick banks as the ones behind mounted them and lashed at their hides with flailing hooves. The crocs slapped themselves against the water with excitement and dove at the slowpokes. The calf was dead in moments. The rest of the panicked herd continued to skid wildly up the muddy bank. Those waiting their turn to cross chewed their cuds in utter ignorance of the danger to come. Soon, they would follow their predecessors into the river and the scene would be repeated over and over again. The imperative to follow the long-established path could not be denied. Erica sighed with dismay, but Nini seemed not to notice.

At dinner the previous day, the travelers had been told a surprise was planned, and all morning the guides kept in radio contact with each other, although they gave nothing away in their brief, telegraphic messages. Now, as the sun reached its zenith, the four vehicles met up on the road to turn down a narrow track and came to a halt, in a circle, like Conestoga wagons crossing the Great Plains. In the center of the area were a cluster of tables already set with white linen, china and silver.

"Here we are, folks," Makinde called as he cut the engine of his jeep. "Our surprise gift to you—a real safari picnic!" The other passengers reacted with the delight of children on a snow day. They poured out of the cars.

"At last, we've arrived in Africa!" Marcie crowed, her arms outstretched to take in the entire landscape. Half a dozen voices chimed in with agreement. Only Erica hung back. Once burned, twice shy, she told herself about the opportunity to walk unimpeded out on the plains. She noticed that several of the young warriors who guarded the camps were already patrolling the perimeter of their circle.

"Come have a leg stretch," Bea called, setting off, camera in hand, toward a sculptural termite mound.

"Hooray, a little freedom at last!" Marcie shouted, jogging to catch up with her.

Erica waved, but did not join them. Instead, she leaned on the warm hood of one of the vehicles and watched a number of black dots in the far reaches of the sky, vultures and storks circling above what was likely a kill. She could see no animals in the bare land around her, but she knew they were out there, crouched and waiting in the grasses or curled into rocky outcroppings.

Hassam and Leni busied themselves unpacking baskets and setting a long serving table with silver and linens, while Nini and Makinde set up a washing table. After a few minutes, the travelers were summoned back for lunch. Erica sat at a table under a broad tamarind tree, and Bea, Marcie, and Jane filled in the spaces around her. They waved to Robert to join them, but he turned as if he hadn't seen them and made for the farthest table, where Mike and Priscilla were already reviewing the pictures they had taken that morning.

"Looks like someone woke up on the wrong side of the cot," Marcie whispered to Jane.

Erica busied herself applying additional sunscreen. Nini came and took the last seat at their table.

Lunch finally included some of the Tanzanian foods that Erica had been curious about: coconut bean soup, duckling cooked in coconut milk, banana and meat stew, *ugali*—a cornmeal mush—and also a vegetable dish that looked like sautéed cabbage. For the less adventuresome there were barbecued chicken and roasted potatoes.

"We Africans normally scoop the stew or meat into the cornmeal with the first three fingers of our right hand," Makinde laughingly demonstrated to the hungry group, "but today we will be giving you forks and knives. Enjoy!"

Bottles of beer were nestled in crates of ice at the very end of the table. The first swallow of stew burned Erica's throat—it had been a long time since she'd eaten anything spicy—but the next felt better and soon she was experiencing a pleasant capsicum high. In the seat to her left, Bea gnawed a chicken bone bare.

"I can't believe you can eat that stuff. It'll burn a hole right through your gut. I know a good gastroenterologist, though, if it does," she said.

On Erica's right, Nini ate in the traditional manner, delicately rolling stew into the scoop of *ugali* she had picked up with her slender fingers.

"Show me?" Erica asked. Nini's eyes flashed with annoyance.

"You should use your fork. A tourist who eats with her hands is still a tourist." Nini finished her food and excused herself from the table. Later, when Erica returned to Nini's jeep, she found a carton of dishes on the front seat where she had been sitting. Feeling chastised, she quietly fit herself into the middle seat of the car between Honey and Priscilla.

The food, the drink and the rocking of the cars along the track had lulled the travelers into a narcoleptic haze by the time they reached camp. Erica shook herself awake and nervously approached her tent. Last night's clash with Robert had been a disaster. She didn't know what she expected, but she had begun to feel that she couldn't leave this place a minute too soon; she was not safe here. And she had no way of rectifying a situation she couldn't begin to understand.

At the last moment, she veered away from her own tent and, clutching the fourth and latest note crumpled in her fist, Erica made her way across the camp to Jane and Marcie's. Her face was flushed hot with apprehension, and she was relieved not to cross paths with any of the other travelers. Down near the dining tent, one of the warrior guards was laying firewood in the pit. He glanced up briefly but took no notice of her. She hurried on in search of the comfort of her herd. Since that night at the campfire, Bea, Robert, Marcie, and Jane had surrounded Erica in what felt like a protective circle, for which she was grateful. Nothing survived long in this country without one.

A tiny dik-dik, the smallest of the antelopes, its head reaching no higher than her knees, was grazing on some green shoots quite close to her friends' tent. Startled, Erica halted abruptly. The little animal was as perfect as a porcelain statue, its oversized brown eyes and ears and the tuft at the top of its head giving it a Kewpie-doll appeal. Its slender tan legs ended in hooves as petite as sake cups. It ate in stillness, the only movements its jaws working and its cropped tail shivering. Erica crept closer and then stood, as motionless as the diminutive creature, panting through her mouth to still her ragged breath. The only sound was the splash of her friends' camp shower.

From the corner of her eye, Erica spied Marcie passing just inside the screened tent window. She would have liked to alert her to the dik-dik's presence. But Erica kept silent and savored the tableau alone, afraid to break the spell. As Erica watched the little female (no horns, she noticed) she felt touched by a sense of calm, like a cool hand across her forehead. The creature's willingness to feed in her presence restored a small sense of safety and peace. From inside the tent, she heard a zipper open and then the half-whispering voices of her friends. The dik-dik munched on, undisturbed.

"I like her, too," Jane said, apparently continuing a conversation that had been on pause while she showered. "But I'm starting to have serious concerns."

The dik-dik stopped chewing and looked around nervously.

"After what Robert said this afternoon, I'm kind of thinking she's unstable."

"I know what you mean, but shouldn't we give her the benefit of the doubt? She's been through so much, losing her lover, being shut out by his family. If your family did that to me, I'd be pretty disturbed, too."

Erica's hands flew to her throat with dismay, startling the dik-dik, which bolted wildly back into the tall grass. Marcie and Jane were talking about her.

"Robert was pretty freaked out. He said he had no idea what could have possessed her to turn on him like that."

"You'd be completely hysterical, I'm sure. Homicidal, possibly. As would I. And maybe one of us would go so far as to travel halfway around the globe on some crazy quest, but this business about the notes and the flowers—it makes absolutely no sense. No one would come all this way and spend all that money to send cut flowers and weird messages to a stranger."

They're right, Erica thought. Maybe I am crazy. Colors swirled before her eyes. She crouched and pressed her hands against a hot stone. The concentrated warmth steadied her.

"Poor Robert. I think he had a bit of a crush on her. It really hurt his feelings when she accused him of, well, whatever it was she accused him of. I couldn't quite figure it out, actually. Something about an address book."

Erica longed to bolt into the bush right behind the dik-dik. But she was rooted to the spot, a captive audience to their musings.

"I just find it hard to believe anyone would go to the trouble of stalking herself. I mean, what's the payoff?"

"There are lots of people who do crazy things to get noticed. Mothers who make their children chronically ill for the sympathy, people who fake their own kidnappings for the media coverage. A girl I knew in college even punched herself in the eye and blamed her boyfriend, just for the attention."

Erica shuddered as if a tsetse fly had flown into her ear. *Stalk herself?* Did they really think that? How could they possibly believe that she would do such a bizarre thing? But then Erica saw their point. She had accused Robert on the shakiest of grounds; maybe only a seriously unhinged person could have believed that he was an agent of Cal's family and had been engaged to get back Cal's swiped address book. Maybe she was truly losing her mind here, thousands of miles from home.

The cot creaked as one of the women sat down.

"I know you're right—about crazy people and all—but I just can't picture Erica doing something that absurd. She seems normal to me. Sad, but not mad," Marcie said.

"Still, I don't think I want to be involved any further. If this is really happening—if someone is threatening her—then it's time for her to alert Makinde or even the safari company. And if it's all some kind of weird hoax she's perpetrating, I don't want any part of that, either."

Erica couldn't bear to hear another word. As quietly as the dik-dik, she crept toward the back of the encampment and then fled to the privacy of her own tent. The remains of the mutilated flower in the wastebasket had filled the tent with a fetid aroma. Her stomach pitched. She shook the contents of the basket into the chemical toilet and flushed. The fragrance stubbornly persisted.

Erica didn't know what she should do. Three of the four people she thought of as allies and friends on this trip had turned against her. Maybe they'd already told Bea, too. Erica was being stalked by some danger she was at a loss to understand. As for the accusations, how could she prove her innocence when she didn't even know what she was had done? And nothing of any consequence had been done to her. It wasn't as though badgering someone with notes and flowers sounded like a serious threat. She couldn't imagine what Makinde would say if she were to bring this up to him. A rock and a hard place didn't come close to describing her position.

Later, in the dining tent, the only available space was at an empty table next to the door. She ate quickly and returned to her own tent without speaking to anyone. She was truly alone.

The following morning, Erica entered the dining tent with unease, bracing for a flashback to the middle school cafeteria. On the walk over she resolved to fill her plate and head straight for the nearest empty table. She'd even brought a book to read. This worked in eighth grade, why not now? In the end, she needn't have bothered. The tent was abuzz with the news that Bea had injured her ankle—Makinde thought it might well be broken—and was going to be driven to a lodge, where a tour bus was scheduled to leave for Arusha later this afternoon. In the meantime, Hassam had splinted and taped the ankle and given Bea some pain meds. No one looked Erica's way.

"She must have been walking in her sleep," Helena said.

"Don't be ridiculous; she tripped over the porch table on her way back from dinner last night and stumbled off the platform," Don said. The couple exchanged sneers and turned away from each other.

Erica looked for Jane and Marcie; they were nowhere to be seen. She assumed they were with Bea, helping her pack, keeping up her spirits, demonstrating the bonds of friendship. Her breath caught in her throat. Robert was absent from breakfast, as well. The herd had gathered around its injured member. She helped herself to some cereal and coffee and sat down. Erica wanted to offer Bea her assistance, but she wasn't sure it would be welcome. So she was particularly surprised and pleased a few minutes later when Nini came over and asked if Erica would accompany her on the drive to the lodge with Bea. Erica immediately agreed. Anything to get away.

"It is generous of you to give up your touring day for this," Nini told her. "I understand that you and she had become friends. The rest of the group will be visiting a Maasai school where my mother had been a student. We can stop there on our way back if it's not too late. It's a long drive to the lodge."

The school visit had been highlighted in the tour's literature. Many of the travelers had come prepared with school supplies and simple sports equipment to thank the school for allowing them to come. Erica brought the crayons and drawing pad she had hurriedly bought in Arusha to Makinde for inclusion.

While the others divided themselves among the three remaining vehicles, Erica visited a tearful Bea, taking some final pictures of her inside her tent and being helped into the Land Rover.

"This was not how I imagined leaving Africa," the woman said, leaning heavily on Nini's shoulder as they limped toward the car.

"I know exactly what you mean."

"I might be a little old to say this, but I'd like to come back some day."

Erica could not bring herself to say the same, so she concentrated on snapping pictures with Bea's camera.

It took almost three hours to get to Lobo Lodge, by which time the sun had bleached the sky and left the air scorching. As soon as Nini and Erica had settled Bea in on the Arusha-bound bus, they got back on the road. It was the hottest day so far, and the worst surface they had traversed—more ruts than road. Now, it felt as if they were twisting and turning in endless circles.

The vehicle jounced some more and Erica realized that all the water she consumed had finally made its way to her bladder.

"Nini, is there any chance we're near a bathroom?"

"Sorry, we're still over an hour from camp." The

car bumped over several more ruts.

"Well, I don't think I can make it. Is there someplace we could stop?"

Nini was quiet for a moment. There was a rural landing strip not too far away, she finally admitted. But it didn't have any approved shops or facilities.

"It won't be much," she warned, "and it won't be clean. But if it's really an emergency, I suppose we could stop briefly." She took a sharp turn and hit a rut that threw Erica into the door handle.

"Sorry," Nini laughed, not sounding sorry at all, as the car pitched about and finally found a level surface.

Finally, they pulled over on the edge of what looked to Erica like a runway for alien invaders. A cracked ribbon of macadam began at the side of the road and disappeared into the distant grasses. Further down the road were a couple of gas pumps and a corrugated tin shack that shimmered in the midday heat. At this hour, even the animals had taken cover. A few yards from where Nini stopped the car was a small cinderblock structure. An outhouse.

Nini looked at the gas gauge on the Land Rover and grimaced. "We've used more petrol than I anticipated. I will wait for you if you like, or get some at that station up the road." Erica was about to balk, remembering her recent experience at the kopjes, but this was different and she really, *really* had to pee. Nothing was likely to attack her in an outhouse.

"I'll just be a moment." She slipped out the vehicle's door and headed quickly toward the structure.

Erica opened the door to the tiny chamber. A blast of heat and stench flew at her, but that was all. The single window had screens on it to keep most of the bugs out. Okay then, she thought, deep breath, quick pee and I'm out of here. No real danger. The only object in the room was a porcelain toilet bowl propped on a pair of cinder blocks over a hole in the ground. I can do this, Erica told herself: Stand on tiptoe, hold my pants up to keep them from touching anything and go. She stepped in. The door banged shut against her back, and she jumped forward and turned around to face it. She peed as fast as she could, holding her breath the entire time, but just as she was done, the room went completely black. Where there had been a square screened patch of light above her head, there was nothing. Erica struggled with her pants and at the same time made a grab for the door handle, scraping her knuckles on rough wood. The handle clattered to the concrete floor, and Erica was left in blackness.

For a moment her heart stopped beating entirely. Then it resumed, quick and sharp, a rat-a-tat against her ribs. Her lungs felt starved for oxygen, but the air was thick sludge and made her gag. Panic dropped over her like a heavy blanket. Fighting for some semblance of calm, she squeezed her eyes shut. *I went on a picnic and here's what I brought...*

Despite the smell, she sucked in a great breath and screamed Nini's name until the air ran out. Again and again, she called for help, without result. Sweat and sunscreen burned Erica's eyes. This was no accident. Someone—Nini?—had purposely trapped her here. To frighten her? To kill her? Once more, she looked down the barrel of Leni's rifle that day on kopjes. That was no case of bad judgment. Either he lost the nerve to kill her, or he wanted to prove to her how easily it could be done. Those notes, the flowers, there was no denying that they were connected to this; she was the target of an intricate plan and this was its intended finale. But the notes still made no sense to her. They might as well have been written in Swahili.

Tafadhali—kuweka jiwe yangu salama.

The letter to Cal. *Tafadhali*—Please. That letter was a plea, a request for something. In a dizzying rush of blood to her brain, Erica understood that, with Cal gone, whatever had been demanded of him was now being demanded of her. She thought she had known Cal as well as she knew her own face. It was what she told anyone who would listen. Whoever was sending those notes must believe that, and must be convinced Erica would have access to whatever it was he had possessed. But now she acknowledged her ignorance. There was a dark side to Cal and Drew knew it. Maybe Frank did, as well. Had she ignored the clues? *Maybe I didn't become a medic to save people so much as to save myself.* She should have pushed him to say more. She should have accepted his decision to leave and moved on with her life. She should have found some other way to process her grief. Coming to Africa was a mistake—a deadly one. She was going to die. In a toilet.

Her ears buzzed as if her head were filling with flies. Her stomach heaved, and hot bile filled her throat. The last thing she recalled was the vision of two pairs of identical green eyes staring angrily in her direction.

ROSE

*L*ike all babies, mine were always clamoring for the story of their birth. And why not? One minute we are not in the world, the next we are fighting to stay in it with every fiber of our beings. What marks that moment? Who but our *mothers can be relied upon to note it in its every detail, to recognize it for the magnificent event that it is? I have read that in many Western countries women are put into a deep, deadening sleep for the birth of their children. At first, I refused to believe it.*

They would ask and ask for this story and when they were small I would answer like this:

Once there was a mother ostrich who on a bright morning laid a single giant egg in the wide, dry nest scraped up by her mate. Now, most of the other ostriches laid their eggs in the village nest, but this one ostrich and her mate had felt that something special was about to happen and they went off on their own. She sat and she sat alone all day and through the night and when she stood in the morning, there was that one large egg, glowing pink in the light of the newly risen sun. One egg? That was so unusual. Most ostriches, as you know, lay ten or even more.

At first, the ostrich was sad to think that she would return to her village with only one baby, when all the others would be surrounded by many chicks. But she looked at this smooth, glowing egg and was filled with love. She turned in a wide circle, making sure there were no lions, hyenas or jackals nearby, nothing to threaten the life to come, and then she sat down carefully to wait. Each long day she sat on the nest, and each night her mate took over the sitting while she foraged for food. For more than thirty days and nights this went on and she began to get impatient.

"When, oh when, will my baby bird appear?" she asked the empty sky, but there was no answer.

Then, one afternoon, she felt a strange craaack! *beneath her. At first she thought that she had broken her only egg and she cried out in fear. Her mate came running back from the grasses where he grazed. Again, she felt and heard the sound and this time she knew it for just what it was. Finally, finally, her chick would be born.*

"Was it me? Was it me?" each of the children would shout as I got to this part.

I would hush them and make them let me get on with the tale. By this time they would be too excited to stay still and they would be wriggling with excitement.

The mother ostrich sat patiently and let her chick work at cracking through the tough shell. There would be no point in helping. A chick too weak to break out of its shell would be doomed anyway. And then she felt it—the tiny body of her new baby bird pushing against her—and she stood to greet it.

Again, this was met by shouts demanding to know which of them it was, and as their voices rose to squeals I would at last relent.

There, in the half open shell, was Nitaana, her long neck stretched tall and her beady eyes wide. At my side, the child Nitaana would stretch her neck up as far as it would go, in imitation of her newborn self, and blink widely at us, proud as ever to have been first.

"But what about me? Where was I?" my son would cry out.

You, my little chick, my little Lembui, you were right there close behind her, the wonderful miracle that made me the mother of two chicks with only one egg. Lucky Rose.

Never mind that their actual birth took place in the steaming, blood-tinged heat of a tin-roofed shack, a women's health infirmary in the pulsing core of Arusha. The cries of the marketplace, the sirens of police, and the moaning of the sick and dying were loud enough to drown out their first precious cries. The initial pains struck me as I was returning from the early morning market. In no time, they bucked through me like a water buffalo defending herself from a hungry crocodile. Despite my protests, my husband drove me to the clinic, where they took all my clothes, wrapped me in a paper robe and wheeled me into a sterile room. Even the midwives were astonished when I delivered two large, healthy babies only an hour later. Heedless of their advice that we stay at least one night, I wrapped up my children in the bright clean cloths I had brought with me, and their father drove the four of us home later that same afternoon.

After Calvin left—for good this time—I went back to teaching. The day of his departure was not long in coming after we began to have our one fight, over and over. It was never love that failed. When he touched my face each morning to waken me, when we curled around each other in our sleep, that love was reaffirmed. But the sustenance we found in one another began to fall away and starvation was setting in. Its imprint was pressed on the gaunt cheeks I saw in the mirror each morning. Although he said nothing, the way he looked at our babies and then at me spoke of desperation. We became like a pair of secretary birds frantically pecking in the dirt to find a meal.

One night I woke up just before sunrise and he was gone. I rushed into the babies' room to make sure they were still here. They were lying in their cots, snoring with the self-importance of any three-year-olds. I checked in the front yard to see if he had gone outside for a smoke, but in my soul, I knew better. He had gone back to America, taking only the worn gray backpack with which he had arrived. A flock of white-throated bee-eaters flashed by overheard on their way to their southern breeding grounds.

I believe for his escape he took advantage of the migration of a flock of wild birds, *I whispered. And like my namesake in* The Little Prince, *I hid my tears,* for she was such a proud flower.

As when he arrived, I found myself forgetting to eat and drink. I believe I might have wandered off into the grassland had it not been for the needs of my babies. Children are greedy and do not allow a mother to die of a broken heart.

One day, I asked Lembui and Nitaana if they remembered their father, if they could describe him. I thought they would recall the many times he carried them high on his shoulders through the market, or sang them to sleep with songs in silky languages I didn't know. But no, they remembered none of this. Like a candle, Nitaana said: tall and pale. No, said Lembui, like a mountain: all hard muscles and rough-skinned. I suppose all brothers and sisters have different parents in the end.

As I said, I returned to teaching, but the smell of roses was gone from my classroom. In its place was the smell of diesel and of sweat. Things were changing everywhere. One day the director of the school called us all together and told us the school was closing in two weeks. We had been losing students for a long time, so it came as a shock, but not a surprise.

One Saturday shortly after Calvin left, I boarded the bus for Merelani and the mines. It was time for me to take up my responsibilities as a miner again. I hoped that my neglect hadn't caused the mines to be destroyed or stripped bare. The bus rocked and leapt from rut to rut in the long road as I clung to an overhead rack. A man motioned to me and stood up from his seat. Grateful, I nodded to him and eased onto the hard bench.

"Rose? You are Rose, yes?" he asked. I did not recognize him. "I am Maitera, your cousin. Nampozo's son."

Of course I didn't recognize him. He wasn't even an iloran *when I saw him last, and here he was, with strands of silver in his hair. It was his father I was seeking in Merelani, to ask him humbly if he would once again manage my mines for me. I expected that this would require some pleading. His pride had no doubt been wounded when Calvin took his place at the mines. I brought gifts of supplication—fine woolen fabrics in purple and red, sandals made by machine to take the place*

of the hand-stitched tire treads most of the men of the village wore. I
had wrapped sweets for the children and a packet of rare copper beads
for my aunt.

I was pleased to see Maitera. It seemed a good omen to find family
so easily after such a long time. He told me that my brother continued
to prosper; that he was certain everyone would be glad to hear I was
well. He expressed his sympathy that my mother had passed on. Mai-
tera was meeting his father at the mines. I was welcome to join them.
The heavy weight that I had been carrying in my chest since Calvin left
felt a little bit lighter for the space of those hours on the road.

The bus screeched to a stop on the track outside Merelani, and
my cousin helped me down the steps. At the side of the road stood my
uncle, older than I remembered, of course, but as straight and tall as
ever. Like all our men, he carried a spear-tipped herding stick. He was
wrapped in a blue and red checked fabric that was darkened by graph-
ite dust that spoke of his life in the mines. As his eyes swept from his son
to me, something disquieting crossed his face. It was gone in an instant.

"Jambo, jambo," he greeted us both warmly. "Karibu, e-inoti."
Welcome, daughter. But his eyes said something else entirely.

We walked to his jeep, talking of family and village gossip. The old
names on my lips were like honey. I lingered on each one, sucking the
sweetness from the memory of them. When we got to the mines, though,
I was a little shocked. Razor wire marked each claim; men with shot-
guns stared stone-faced toward the bush.

"It is not as you remember," he said, although it was unnecessary
to tell me this.

Then we entered his encampment and the tin shack that was his
office. I should have known something was wrong as he put his hand
up to warn my cousin to wait outside.

It wasn't his idea, he said, immediately. Calvin told him that it was my idea, in fact. That I wanted the money from the sale of the mines to use for my children and I could not wait for the slow drip of profits. I sat dumb, listening. Terrified, I scrambled to touch the pouch around my waist that held my deeds. I couldn't have been more distressed if my own children were hanging over the precipice. The pouch was there, as I knew it would be, and I felt the security of the rolled up papers inside. The only time I had ever let it out of my sight was the day I birthed my babies. Trying to maintain my composure, I placed the small bag on the table and untied the leather wrappings. Rolled up for so long, the papers were in danger of tearing and I smoothed them carefully as I spread them on the table between us.

But where I remembered the clean black letters of the legal form on the cream paper, and the large signatures of my father (an X) and myself, there was a blood-red stamp.

Sold.

My uncle said nothing. Then he unlocked a safe on the floor behind him. A new set of papers, signed by him and by my husband, transferred legal ownership to him and my cousin.

And then he made me an offer. "Do you remember the great stone you carried home all by yourself when you were just a girl? The stone with the many jiwe in its belly?"

Did I remember? It was the stone that was my babies' first plaything, the object that welcomed the evening breeze into our house, holding our door open to the sunset, the symbol of our family's love and the last reminder of my lucky girlhood. It was the stone that decided my fate. I could more easily forget my own name than that stone.

He continued. "Well, if you still have that particular jiwe, I would trade the deeds to all three of your mines for it." He looked at me expectantly, but I had no words. Perhaps he thought I was trying to drive a hard bargain. Or that I was trying to tot up the value of the stone versus the mines. No. That stone disappeared with Calvin the night he crept from our lives forever and returned to the city of the tall nyumbas.

I believe the seeds of my final illness were planted at the very moment I realized this, to take root like the baobab all these years later. The world became gray and then black, as if smothered in coals.

When I opened my eyes, I was in a dark place. The sting of smoke and the hard, slick surface under my back told me immediately that I was in a nyumba, *lying once more on a dried cowhide bed. For a long moment I wondered if everything had been a dream—if I would rise in another minute to the sound of my little brother shouting at the cows and my mother brewing chai for breakfast. Of course it was not so. Sold. That was all I could take in. Sold. I was no longer a miner. And if not, what was I?*

I was not a wife, not a teacher, no longer a daughter and, for a long time, unable to be much of a mother.

Nitaana and Lembui and I went back to the village to live with my brother's family. I was sorry it was too late for my mother to have known them better. Of all the mistakes we make in our lives, it's never the ones we recognize that will cause us the greatest regret.

I lived for several years as a shadow in my village until Enkai sent death to greet me. My babies grew—Lembui herded the cows with his cousins and sometimes worked at the mines, and Nitaana walked the long miles to school. They have made their own contract with the new world and have learned to move freely between the village and the city.

Death, in the end, slips over us as cool and simple as a breeze flowing down from the highest mountain. But taking another's life is a labor that lasts until the end of time, ceaseless and without respite. That is what I would like to warn my babies. Both of them are angry and seeking revenge—stricken with a sickness of mourning and unable to find the road back from the house of death. If I could tell them one last story, it would be this one, but my time for stories has ended. They will have to tell their own stories now.

13

As consciousness began to return in swollen waves, the first thing Erica noticed was the smell. Rubbing alcohol and the odor of a body, not her own. And then a faint buzzing that felt as if it was coming from her teeth. She opened her eyes to find a rail-thin figure—so wiry it was unclear whether it was male or female—bent close to her face. Erica reached out to touch the stranger, not entirely convinced of its reality. The person flinched slightly and straightened up, smoothing a crisp white apron against graceful hips. Erica struggled to assemble impressions into sense. Pale blue cap on closely cropped hair; white uniform stark against ebony skin—a nurse. Erica tried to sit up, but her head spun and she dropped back against the thin pillow. Around her, the room was in shadows, the only light a humming fluorescent tube on the wall over her head.

"Where am I?" she rasped. Her mouth was painfully dry. Her lips cracked as she formed the words.

"You're in hospital," the woman answered in a voice as round and mellow as a bell.

Africa came flooding back.

The nurse lifted a cloth from a porcelain basin and applied it gently to Erica's forehead. Again, alcohol fumes prickled her nose. A drop of liquid trickled down the side of her temple, and she reached to wipe it away, then was surprised at how exhausting it was to make this simple gesture.

"Why am I in the hospital?" A note of panic slurred her words.

"You will have to ask the doctor," the woman replied, firmly but not unkindly. "She will be to see you in the morning. Would you like some juice?"

"Please," Erica said. The nurse turned and walked a few steps away, returning with a glass of pale orange liquid and a straw.

"Please that you don't drink this too quickly," she warned Erica. "Slowly sip."

Erica did as she was told, but the sweet, cold liquid felt so miraculous as it slid across her tongue that she sucked harder and harder. And, indeed, she did get dizzy, but it was a fair price to pay for the relief of cold sweetness slipping down her parched throat. She closed her eyes with pleasure for a moment, and when she opened them, the woman was gone. The glass was no longer in her hands, the room completely dark. She let herself slip back into a thick, syrupy sleep, helpless as a fly sliding down the neck of a carnivorous pitcher plant.

When she opened her eyes again, sunlight was flooding through a window to her left. The light reached her through a cloud: a veil of mosquito netting hung from a ring suspended from the ceiling over her head, softening her focus on the room around her. Even without making the effort to sit up, Erica saw that she was alone, although there were two other beds and a pair of cribs. She wondered weakly if there was a crib next to her bed, as well. The walls were painted a sickly yellow ochre and the narrow beds were bare, unpainted metal and low to the ground. The faucet on the cracked sink against the wall across from her was dripping, and a green stain followed the water's established trail down the porcelain. A slow fan circulated hot air, but it drifted down from the ceiling with such lethargy that no breeze disturbed the netting. Outside, flies buzzed and batted themselves against the window screen, trying to get in.

What was she doing here? Erica drew a blank for several moments as she conducted a mental scan of her body for areas of pain. There were none, only a bone-deep weariness that held her heavily against the thin mattress, the springs pressing into her back. Then she remembered the dark and the heat. Inside of that was the stink of her own fear, sour and acrid, existing in tandem with, but separate from, the general eye-stinging reek of urine and feces, as she cowered for what seemed like hours. After that, nothing. Just thinking about it brought on a profound and unnerving vertigo that made her squeeze her eyes shut. She gritted her teeth and held tight to a slippery awareness.

"Excuse me, I was told you had awakened in the night and wanted to see me," a voice above her said. A different accent— English, or maybe Australian. Once more, she blinked her eyes open. The netting had been swept back. Standing before her was a short blond woman with a stethoscope looped around her neck— the universal symbol for doctor. The woman's suntanned face was strewn with freckles, like constellations in a clear winter sky. Erica squinted to read the badge on this woman's chest: A.M. Adamson, MD. Dr. Adamson had already lifted Erica's hand and was taking her pulse with cool, dry fingers. A whiff of flowers replaced the alcohol odor for a moment, then was gone.

"You arrived here unconscious, with severe heat prostration," she said, before Erica could ask. "You also have a couple of stitches on your jaw, just in front of your ear, although you probably can't feel them yet. You will. The wound was deep, but it will heal."

Erica reached up and fingered the stiff surgical bandage sur-rounding the wound. She tapped it. It was completely numb.

"Can you tell me how you came to be in such a state?"

Erica wasn't sure where to begin, but she told the doctor what she remembered of the landing strip and the outhouse.

Dr. Adamson replaced her hand under the sheet. Whatever she made of Erica's story, her face gave away nothing.

"You must have been trapped in there for several hours," Dr. Adamson said. You're lucky to have gotten off so lightly. People die of dehydration and heat exhaustion all the time. Or suffer ir-reparable brain, or heart, or kidney damage, which you did not, as far as we can tell from your blood tests. Your electrolytes are still off, but your cardiac numbers looked okay after we got some IV fluids into you. Thank your lucky stars you were close enough to our facility. Your veins were already so shrunken we could hardly get a needle into one. Another twenty minutes and I don't think we'd be having this conversation."

Erica wondered about those lucky stars. They hadn't felt lucky when she was trapped in the outhouse. The smell of it was still in her nostrils and clung to her hair. How many showers would it take to erase it? Before she succumbed to that dark, steaming pris-on she had grasped, with razor-sharp clarity, that it was Cal who had trapped her there. Nini's words echoed in her head. *He has no friends in Africa.* Drew's coarse laughter. Sammy's comments on the mutability of human nature. And as much as she found the notion incomprehensible, she felt with horrible certainty that it was Cal's punishment she was suffering. There were lies and half-truths hidden in his tales. And something more sinful that she didn't want to know, but feared she could no longer avoid.

"Erica?"

Dr. Adamson was still standing by her bed.

"You are in this country on safari, are you not? Please don't tell me you're with the CIA or something like that."

Erica smiled weakly and shook her head.

"Then someone must have driven you to that landing strip. There's only bus service there twice a week and you're not likely to have gone unnoticed on the bus."

"Yes. It must have been a mistake. I was out with one of our guides. I don't really understand it myself." Nini. Nini left her there. She was so tired. Just the act of thinking made her long for the refuge of sleep.

Dr. Adamson put a cool hand on Erica's temple and nodded.

"I'll let you rest now, but I'll be back to see you later this afternoon." The doctor smiled mischievously. "I'm sure someone will come looking for you shortly. Safari companies hate to lose paying guests. Bad for business. Have the nurse page me if you think of anything that might help explain this."

"Wait!" Erica called just as the woman was about to turn into the corridor.

"Yes?"

"You said I arrived here. Where, exactly, is 'here'?"

"You're at the Mara district hospital. A Roman Catholic archdiocese hospital. Well, actually, the hospital's dispensary outpost. We're a small local outpatient department and HIV clinic. But we have sixteen beds for labor and delivery, and male and female admissions. You're in the room we usually reserve for our new mothers. They rest here about ten hours after giving birth before going back to their *boma*, but you seem to have arrived on a slow day for babies."

That explained the tiny cribs. She wished for a moment that at least one of them was occupied. It would be nice to consider new life.

"But someone must have brought me," she continued, as Dr. Adamson again turned to leave. "Who?"

"I don't know. Apparently you were left at the emergency room doorway, barely conscious. And you gave off a terrible stink. Nurse gave you a sponge bath, which also brought your temperature down. Fortunately, you didn't convulse. Whoever got you here didn't wait around for a diagnosis." She left the room, another whiff of flowers following in her wake.

"Wakey, wakey! Can't sleep all day," came a cheery voice the next morning, startling Erica from her fitful sleep. Dr. Adamson adjusted the blinds as she entered and the light burst through the open slats as if it had been pounding since dawn to be allowed in. Dust motes danced in the rays, and Erica blinked in the sudden glare. Even that small movement made her wince. Overnight, sensation had returned to her jaw and that sensation was pure pain. Sometime before dawn, she'd thought about calling for the nurse and asking for medication, but then decided against it. This was a physical pain with nowhere near the potency of the emotional ache that originated in her chest and spread until it filled her entire core. Concentrating on the bodily hurt was the only thing that managed to push the rest back. Eventually, she managed to fall asleep.

"I brought you some breakfast." The doctor put the tray on a bedside table. A wooden bowl of maize porridge and sweet plantains with small cubes of meat, along with a glass of juice and a mug of tea. The aroma, redolent of cinnamon and spices, was tantalizing, but Erica ignored it.

"You should eat. You need to get back your strength," the doctor said. "And anyway, I cooked it myself. Relatives usually bring the food here." She laughed. "I'll be back in a little while and expect to see an empty bowl."

Erica began picking at the food, but became more enthusiastic as she realized how delicious it really was. She had just started to dig in when loud voices, all talking at once, approached quickly from down the hallway.

"You scared us almost to death!" Makinde boomed as the door flew open, and he pushed into the room, several steps ahead of Leni and Nini.

Startled, Erica dropped her spoon and then quickly moved the tray to the bedside table, wiping her mouth and pulling up the thin cover.

"What were you thinking, doing such a dangerous thing?" he demanded. "Did you not realize what could happen to you?"

Behind Makinde, still half in the hallway, Leni and Nini were arguing in Maasai.

"But Nini..." Erica began, glancing sideways at the pair.

Nini and Leni broke off their argument, and Nini came rushing up to Erica's bedside, wringing her hands and wailing loudly.

"I thought you had been dragged away. I looked and looked, but you had disappeared. I told you I'd be right back. It was unsafe to step away from the jeep. Where did you go?" Nini looked wild-eyed with dismay. She moaned with distress and tugged at the pendant around her neck, stepping back into the group.

Erica stared at her, stunned. She had screamed Nini's name until she could no longer force sound from her throat. Now, Nini was acting as if Erica had wandered off like a disobedient child and was to blame for her own troubles. From across the room, Leni and Nini watched her intently, their faces as still and unreadable as masks—suddenly Erica saw them as a pair of lions sizing up their prey.

Give up what is not rightfully yours or suffer a thief's fate.

"You could have died out there," Makinde scolded her.

"Yes, but I was told—"

"All your friends on safari are worried about you. We told them you were well and safe, but they will not believe us until they see you themselves. If you and the doctor think you are sufficiently recovered, we hope you will rejoin us for our final days together. If not, we can arrange for your trip directly back to Arusha."

Her friends? She had no friends here. They had cut her from the herd. She doubted if any of them were as concerned as Makinde made it sound. Jane and Marcie probably thought she had rigged the entire event herself. Robert no doubt thought she was a delusional harpy. Tears stung her eyes even as she continued to watch Nini, who had shrugged away from Leni and was now standing alone, staring down at her feet, fiddling with the sheath on her belt.

"I'm feeling better, thank you, and I'm sure that Leni and Nini have many more interesting things to teach me about this country." She gave each of them a long stare, and they shrank from it noticeably. "I'm not sure about coming back. I'm very tired now, but I'd like to take to you later, Makinde." Nini looked up, startled and wary, reminding Erica of nothing so much as the dik-dik in the moment before she bolted. Clearly, her suspicions were well founded, if completely inexplicable. She was struck once more by the wide, gray-green eyes shared by these two. At that moment, Dr. Adamson returned.

"Ah, I see you found her," she said.

"Yes, doctor, thank you," said Makinde, reaching out to shake her hand. "It was good of you to take such excellent care of our friend. We're happy to report that she says she is feeling much better. We hope she will soon be ready to continue on her journey through our beautiful country."

"I hope you're not planning to misplace any more of your safari friends," Dr. Adamson answered. "It's not like you, Makinde, to lose track of them this way." The two of them laughed, but Erica noted that the man looked chastened. "I think you all need to let Erica rest. I'm planning to send some medical supplies out to Serena Lodge tomorrow and the driver can give her a ride back to your camp, if she feels up to returning. Otherwise, I assume you'll arrange transportation back to Arusha for her. Right now, Makinde, I need you to come with me and sign some papers."

Leni stepped out of the room ahead of Makinde and Dr. Adamson. Only Nini was left behind. She moved to follow her friends.

"Stop," Erica said. Nini froze. "Nini, turn around."

Nini remained in the doorway with her back to Erica, but she did not leave the room.

"You did it. You locked me in that stinking box to die. I dare you to tell me I'm wrong."

After a long moment, Nini turned in Erica's direction. Slowly, she said, "It seems to me that you keep getting yourself in trouble and we keep saving you," The skin on her face was stretched tight and her eyes twitched, focusing on a spot on the wall behind Erica's shoulder. With one foot she pushed the door closed behind her.

Was Nini mocking her?

"You and Leni. You're the ones who have been tormenting me with those notes and those flowers. What are you after? Money? You think I'm a rich American who will pay well for my life? You're mistaken." Nini's face betrayed nothing. No sign of guilt or even hostility. Outside, a bird screeched and children shrieked as they kicked a ball around the dusty courtyard. The only sound in the room was the plink of water from the leaky faucet. Nini began to turn away once more.

"Nini, answer me or I swear I'll scream until I bring every person in the hospital into this room." Nini paused and stared at Erica. If Erica had had the strength, she would have risen from the bed and slapped that impassive face.

"You know what is owed to us." The girl's taut lips barely moved.

"Owed to you?"

Nini's dry whisper was almost inaudible. "When Sammy—our cousin—told us you had come to our country, that you wanted to go on safari, I became hopeful that you had come to return what was stolen from us. But as he spoke of your false ignorance of such things, I became certain of one thing. You would return what is owed or you would die."

"Return what?" Erica demanded.

"You should have been killed by the hyenas on that kopje. A fitting death. My brother was a fool and a coward not to let them feast on you. And leave your bones for the jackals."

Sammy? The hyenas? Suddenly Leni's remorse took on new meaning. Erica recalled the fight she witnessed between Leni and Nini. Nini had called him a coward then, too.

Nini continued. "Yes, I told him to let the hyenas have you." She blinked once, but not a muscle in her face moved. Instead, Erica watched her hands twist together in mounting agitation.

Erica's body went icy cold while her face flushed with heat.

"He could have claimed you insisted on going up there. Tourists are so demanding; they risk their lives for their stupid photos." A note of frustration had crept into Nini's voice.

Erica could hardly believe what she was hearing. When Leni raised that gun in her direction it was not to kill her, as she'd feared, but it was a failure to let her die. Back at camp, he must have suffered Nini's scorn at his weakness. She thought about these last days of riding with Nini, her presumed protector, her would-be murderer. For a moment, Erica was speechless with shock.

"I'm telling you, I have no idea what I could possibly owe you." Erica's voice cracked, and she hated how weak she sounded, but that very weakness seemed to trigger something in Nini.

All efforts at evasiveness gone, Nini stepped forward boldly, staring stony-eyed, directly into Erica's eyes for the first time since entering the room. The rage Erica saw there horrified her. Almost before she could register the movement Nini was beside her, one hand pinning Erica hard to the bed, the other pressing the long knife flat against her throat. Erica felt the razor sharp edge and what she hoped was only a drop of sweat slide down her neck. Nini hissed, "What is owed by your precious Calvin then."

The name fell hard, foreign and mysterious coming from the girl's lips. Cal-veen. In that moment it was Cal's name uttered from Nini's lips that shocked her even more than the attack itself. Her thoughts tumbled drunkenly. She could neither move nor cry out. If she screamed or struggled, the sharp blade would easily pierce her skin. It would be over in moments, her throat slashed as easily as Nini cut the throat of the hyena that had threatened her family's calves.

"He has stolen," came the furious voice at her ear. "And you must return what he has stolen. Or die."

"Nini, what the hell do you mean? Calvin? Cal's dead." Erica rasped with difficulty. "He owes nothing to anyone."

Despite her terror, her mind raced. How could Nini even know Cal? Was she old enough to have been alive when he was in Tanzania?

Heavy footsteps were approaching down the hallway. Erica prayed it would be Makinde coming to say goodbye. The steps approached the room and then, finding the door shut, lumbered on without pausing. There would be no rescue this time, Erica realized, with surprising clarity and acceptance. I will die here, she thought. As Cal died. As everyone dies in the end. As the vultures had predicted. But not, she vowed, before knowing why. She held onto her last shred of indignation, clutched it like a shield, because she was unsure if it disappeared what would take its place.

"What could a stranger possibly owe you?" Angry tears soaked Erica's cheeks. She blinked her eyes and tried to compose herself, to let this hideous charade end once and for all.

Suddenly, the door swung open and Erica felt, but could not see, another person enter the room. Nini froze, but did not back off. It would all be over in a moment.

"Take one more step, and this knife does its work," Nini warned.

The other person in the room took a slow, deep breath.

"Nini."

One word, but Erica felt Nini tense. It was Leni. To rescue her again, or help Nini finish the job, she did not know.

"Get out. I will take care of this myself. She will swear to return our *jiwe* or die."

"Nini. This will stop. Now," he said. "*Tafadhali*. You will step away from the bed and leave with me, or I swear in the name of Enkai, I will kill you and then myself. And in our deaths our mother's memory will end for all eternity."

"You are a traitor to our mother then." The look on her face shifted from fury to pain, as if a knife twisted somewhere inside her, too, but her grip on Erica did not diminish.

"No, you will be the traitor. Without our memories she will be completely gone from this world. And it will be you who forced my hand. The choice is yours."

Nini let out what Erica interpreted as a string of curses. Leni did not move from his spot in front of the door.

The blade that rested against Erica's throat backed off just a bit, but it was enough for her to ask once again.

"What could a stranger possibly owe you?"

Outside the window a troop of baboons shrieked their way through a nearby grove of trees. A car engine sputtered and caught and a child squealed with delight. The smoky scent of Africa trickled in with the breeze, making Erica's nose itch. Inside the room, the silence was absolute. Even the faucet had stopped dripping. Erica knew there would be no backing down for Nini. Pay attention, she told herself. This is where it ends. Instead of fear, she felt total alertness. She thought once more of Cal, and of the others trapped in the certainty of death. Always, she had imagined the utter terror of their final moments, fear and horror inescapable, stretching into infinity. Now she understood that there might instead have been an oasis of calm finality for each of them, not unlike this one. She found a certain comfort in it as it enfolded her, silent, still and absolute. She allowed herself to drift within its grasp.

A small movement from Nini brought her back. Nini had withdrawn the knife, released the pressure across Erica's chest. Erica took a huge gulp of air and looked up into a face ravaged with torment.

"Not a stranger. He was our father," Nini spat out in disgust. A moment later she and Leni had disappeared through the door, and Erica was alone in an empty room.

14

E rica dumped the wrinkled contents of the duffel onto her couch and the smell of Africa rose to greet her. Although it was a warm day for October, the heat was blasting in the apartment, and the windows were shut. Erica felt the prickly onset of fear. How long would it take for her body to stop tripping into panic mode at the presence of dark or heat? She certainly wasn't looking forward to her first rush-hour subway ride. Her native city felt like an alien landscape. *If you see something, say something*, warned a series of posters along the walls of the airport corridors last night. The same message graced the back of the cab. Erica was sure those hadn't been there when she left New York. So much change in such a brief amount of time.

She moved through the rooms, opening all the windows to let fresh air dissipate the memory-laden tang and began checking on her plants. The cacti in the living room window were as turgid as when she'd left, but several of her other plants had wilted badly in the time she'd been away. These she ferried to the kitchen sink, where she submerged them in a restorative bath of tepid water. Both now and in the shower this morning, the simplicity of turning on the taps and getting an endless supply of crystal clear water struck her as slightly miraculous. The familiar routine of caring for her plants felt uplifting. It was good to be home.

Erica reached up to rub gently at the swollen scab on her jaw where she had fallen, which itched unbearably. In another couple of weeks the scab would heal and fall off, but the scar would remain, a permanent memento of her journey. In the bathroom this morning, she'd studied her reflection in the mirror. Her face was still a little bruised from the fall and would look different still when the scar emerged. So much change in only a matter of weeks.

Her final two days in Africa had mainly been spent arranging a flight to New York. With the help of the tour company, the hospital booked her a place on a small transport plane that would ferry her to the main airport in Arusha. The ten-seater prop plane left from the same run-down landing strip that bordered the outhouse in which she'd been trapped. Erica kept her gaze averted until she was in the air.

She had never returned to the safari camp, but asked Makinde to pack her things and send them to the hospital. She wondered how much he'd known about what had taken place and whether he had discussed it with any of the other travelers. She wished she could see Jane and Marcie's faces when they found out that her fears had been real and not pathological. Maybe one day she'd hear from them.

Bending over the couch Erica gathered up an armful of the worn clothing and headed for the hamper, then changed her mind and stuffed them into the garbage under the sink. They stank of sweat and disappointment.

In order to survive, Erica had to acknowledge that nestled amid her deepest beliefs was one big lie. Too late, of course, she recognized the half-truths and the wishful thinking that had pushed her to the brink of death. Not only had she been successful in believing the fantasy she and Cal were two halves of the same coin, but apparently she had projected that certainty so strongly that others, most notably Leni and Nini, were equally deceived. In this, Erica might have been complicit in her own fate.

If either Leni or Nini had shown up again at the hospital, Erica was prepared to make this confession. Actually, the more she thought about it, the less she feared another attack from Nini. The look of triumph on the girl's face just before she fled the hospital room made it clear that the revelation of Cal's identity was her killing blow, and she knew it had struck its mark. In that moment, the entire fabric of Erica's belief had been shredded like a narcissus in an early spring blizzard. And it wasn't Cal's deception that had been her undoing, but her own.

On the flight from Arusha, crammed between the fog-smeared window and a man in a military uniform who spoke not a word but played solitaire on his seatback table for hours on end, Erica had expected neither sleep nor emotional relief—and she was not disappointed. She was besieged by despair. She had gone to Africa to compile the biography of a hero and was returning empty handed, a failure in so many ways. The image of Cal she carried in her mind was as cracked and faded as an aging snapshot.

Even after she finally climbed into her own bed in New York, sometime in the wee hours of the morning, she endured a replay of the events that had sent her fleeing Tanzania. Bitterly, she'd chewed on Nini's words. They cut like a lash. Cal was Nini's father. Leni's father. That woman in the news clipping swam before Erica's eyes. The final scrap of the Cal Erica thought she knew sifted into dust. *I can't give you what you want,* Cal had told her. *Marriage, kids.* Because he had already given those things—and then turned his back on them. "We can adopt," she had said to him. Now she burned with humiliation at her naiveté. Eventually, Erica fell into a fragile tissue of sleep, laced with cruel and inchoate nightmares. A harsh, choking stench, a sickening drop through the dark.

The message light on her answering machine was flashing. Probably Karen, she thought, pushing Play.

"Hello, Erica. This is Margy. Cal's sister." Erica clutched the edge of the desk as the air turned thin around her. She felt the blood in her head plunge toward her feet. Taking a deep breath, she fought an urge to hit Delete and managed to let the message continue. "I don't know if you're back yet—I heard from Frank that you were going to Africa—but when you get this, please call me. I think we have something important to discuss. Thanks."

Erica sat heavily. This could not be happening. After all she'd been through, was she going to have to withstand accusations of theft from Cal's family? The idea was unbearable. She wanted to tear the tape from the answering machine and slice it into a thousand pieces. But what good would it do? Margy would call again. And again. Like Nini, she would hound Erica to the bitter end. For a sickening moment she thought that maybe a quick death at Nini's hands would have been preferable. Maybe death was the only way these things ever ended. She felt the shadow of depression descending over her like a sack. This wasn't something her therapist could fix with talk and tape recording. It was an endless loop. No. It would stop now. She dialed Margy's number.

Erica counted slowly to five before she opened the door to Margy's knock. She prepared herself to get this over with quickly and cleanly. The woman standing in the doorway looked years older than the last time they met. Her hair, previously black like Cal's and his mother's, had turned a steely gray and she seemed thinner and more fragile in stature than Erica recalled.

"Thanks for agreeing to see me," Margy said as she crossed the threshold. She glanced at the duffel bag and travel items strewn around the room. "It looks like you just got home. You really could have waited until you were settled back in. But it was good of you to call so quickly."

Erica cleared a space for the woman on the couch and took a seat in the chair across from her. "Look, I know why you're here. If you want me to admit I took the book, I'll do that right off the bat and save us both some time. But I can't return it because it's gone. Lost somewhere in Tanzania, and there not a damned thing either of us can do about it." She started to push the chair back and stand. "So if that's all you came for..."

"I'm not sure what you mean. That's not what I'm here about. Wait—you took something? When? What?"

Erica felt heat creep from her chest all the way to her scalp. She must be as red as a baboon's butt.

"I thought you knew. I thought...when I left his apartment that day...It didn't seem like anything that would matter to anyone but me."

"Please. Stop. I don't care about Cal's *things*." The woman held both hands open in front of her as if she were trying to stop a boulder rolling downhill.

"But then what?"

"There are things you need to know." Margy clasped her hands together under her chin and Erica worried that she was about to launch into prayer.

"I already know them."

"You do?"

"I know that Cal walked out on his family in Tanzania and came back to the states to live what I imagine was an easier life. I admit I'm completely humiliated to have gone around telling people what a wonderful human being he was and that we were closer than any two people on the face of this earth. I couldn't have been more deluded." Erica's voice was reedy and constricted. She cleared her throat.

"Wait, no—or rather, yes. Look, I'm not here to make you admit anything. I'm here to tell you what I think you need to know. My family has spent years not dealing with any of this. We were pretty sure Cal never told you, and we figured that was his call to make. Even after...what happened. When I heard from Frank that you were interviewing people and that you'd gone off to Africa, I realized we were wrong. We should have told you."

"You didn't think I deserved that courtesy before?" Erica asked, stunned. "Cal and I were together for three years, and that didn't give me the right to be privy to the family secrets? Or to be acknowledged at his memorial?"

"You guys broke up."

"We were about to get back together."

This time it was Margy who looked taken aback. She reached into her purse and brought out a bottle of water, pausing to take a long drink. "I didn't know. I'm sorry. Cal and I were always really close. Maybe because we were less than two years apart and our other sister and brother were several years older. Or maybe we were just most alike. Anyway, growing up, we trusted each other with secrets. He knew where I hid my diary and I knew where he hid his *Playboys*. Good secrets make good siblings, you might say." She started to laugh and then winced, as if death had made the quip less funny. "In any case, I'm probably the only person who really knows what happened in Africa. But he hadn't told me about the two of you getting back together. I would have been happy for you. Whatever you learned in Tanzania, I'm pretty sure you still don't know the whole story."

"I know enough. I was stalked and hounded as a thief and almost murdered for his desertion and my ignorance, and I will be sporting this scar as a lifetime memento." Erica grimaced as she reached up to touch her chin. "All that, and what I still don't know is what his children want from me. Obviously, I can't return their father." She paused and glared at Margy. "I was told that the Maasai are too proud to ask for anything directly. But Nini said I must return their *jiwe*. I think they want a piece of tanzanite, but Cal never gave me any jewelry. So what then? Do you know?"

Margy looked thoughtful but made no reply. Although it didn't change a thing, the fact that Margy had to admit ignorance of Cal's plans gave Erica a tiny bit of satisfaction.

"Okay, so you already know that Cal had gone back to Tanzania, not to the Peace Corps—that made a good cover, later—but because he'd fallen for a Maasai girl, Rose, who he met there on his semester abroad. My parents figured it was just a thing, that it would end and he'd come home, but of course I knew better. Cal wrote me that he was waiting for the 'right time' to tell Mom and Dad they'd gotten married. After he was gone about a year or so, I went over there to see him. I think my parents expected me to bring him back home. But by then the twins had already been born."

Twins? Erica caught her breath. Leni and Nini were not just siblings but twins? The closest bond a pair of beings could possess. Nine months floating in a shared womb, years united in shared resentment. And the growing desire for revenge. Erica reflexively reached up to touch her scar again, but she said nothing. Margy continued.

"I almost didn't recognize my brother when I got there."

"What do you mean?"

"He was, like, transformed. When he left, he was kind of a jerk, I guess, but not in a bad way. You know—putting cold spaghetti under my pillow when we were kids and threatening to beat up the guys I dated if they were bad to me. Stuff like that. Kind of frat boy."

Erica recognized that Cal. She could hear him shouting *"girlie girls"* in that stupid accent as he pedaled past the other bike riders.

"But when I got to Tanzania, there he was, changing diapers and blowing raspberries into fat baby bellies. One whimper out of either of those kids and he'd scoop them up and dance around the room singing old Chuck Berry songs until they giggled. He couldn't stand for them to cry."

Erica's chest tightened. She tried not to visualize what Margy was saying, but the picture of Cal as a dad was making it hard for her to breathe. Erica thought about the little boy on the bike tour, the one whose father had almost choked to death on the jawbreaker. The natural ease with which Cal approached the boy and reassured him. At the time, it had moved her. But now it just made her angry.

"Yeah, he loved them so much, he abandoned them, along with their mother," Erica spat out bitterly.

"That's the part only I know."

"Sorry, it's still just so hard to believe."

"I don't blame you for being defensive. This isn't easy for me, either," Margy said gently. "We should have spoken sooner."

Erica lowered her eyes. "Yes, we should have." She twisted the hem of her skirt tight around her fingers, cutting off the blood as if that would cut off the memories.

"Rose was a beauty, there's no denying that. Tall and regal; she walked down the rocky road barefoot and looked like she owned the earth. Cal clearly adored her, but I couldn't entirely understand how they expected to make a life together, either there or back in the States."

Erica looked up in surprise.

"Yes, Cal asked her to come with him to America, but she wouldn't leave her people. Or her tanzanite mine. And yes, she owned a mine, so he figured it couldn't hurt to stay there and make a living. I was a little sad, truth be known. I thought I might never see him again. And I wondered how I was going to explain all it to my folks."

The phone rang, but Erica didn't move to answer it. Whoever called hung up when the answering machine picked up.

"Anyway, he tried a lot of things to make money. He wrote me long letters veering between optimism and disappointment. A tour business, some kind of go-between for American companies interested in laying down a footprint in Africa, he even worked as a broker for the flower trade. Roses. Now they're a huge industry in Tanzania, but not then. Nothing really panned out for him. So he went to the mines. Rose's uncle was running her mine while they lived in Arusha and Cal believed the man wasn't quite on the level. Cal even went down in the pits himself for a while. But it was pretty ugly down there. Not just the heat and the bad air, that you might expect. The men weren't accepting of the white guy who married their cousin. They beat him up a couple of times. Once, he had to be hospitalized for a concussion. Anyway, toward the end, Cal and Rose were so broke they were about to get kicked out of their house. That's when Cal sold the mine to her uncle, who had been hanging around like a fly at an outhouse."

Erica winced at the reference, but again, didn't interrupt.

"This guy was dying to get his hands on the mine. Offered more than it was worth, Cal thought. And no—before you ask—Cal didn't tell Rose, which was wrong. The guy had offered him a deal where he could buy the mine back—at a profit, of course. Cal was convinced he could use the cash from the sale as seed money for a new business that was a sure thing and he'd get the deed back before Rose knew it was gone. Well, you know how sure things can be —you get desperate and it's like everything you touch turns to mud. The money was gone, the mine was gone, and now he was borrowing from loan sharks to keep the four of them afloat."

Erica clasped her hands together, anchoring herself, and stared hard into the fabric of her skirt. She refused to allow herself to cry in front of this woman, but one fat tear leaked down her cheek. She ignored it.

"To make a long story short, Cal owed the shark a bundle and when he couldn't pay up, the guy began making threats against Rose and the babies. Cal was distraught. He told me in no uncertain terms that there are no idle threats in that country.

No idle threats—Erica could see the words on the wrinkled onionskin stationery of Cal's note to Billy.

"Calling the man's bluff was out of the question. Finally, he got the guy to agree to let him go to America, telling him that he could get the money from his family. Cal had two months to get him the money he owed, or else. It must have killed him to leave them behind. But also, our father was dying. Mom had been writing to Cal almost every day trying to get him to come home. She was so relieved to see him, she put the money in his account immediately, no questions asked. Well, not until later. In any case, Cal sent back a check right away, and nothing happened to Rose and the babies."

Margy looked at Erica like she expected an expression of gratitude for the belated revelation.

"But why the hell didn't he go back to her? To them."

"He'd betrayed her and sold her mine. There was no way he could get it back. He left her and their kids with no word of explanation. He couldn't face her after that. If there's one thing I know about Cal, it's that he totally adored Rose and their babies. His exile was his self-inflicted punishment, and it must have been agonizing. He tried sending her money, you know. Through his friend Drew. Did you meet Drew?" She sniffed with dismissal. "The cowboy."

Here at last was a point on which Erica could agree with her.

"She refused the money every time. And she told Drew to tell Cal never to write to her or set foot in her country again."

Erica stared, unblinking, at Margy, who was fiddling with her wedding band. If Cal loved anyone in his life—and at this point Erica wondered whether he had been capable—it must have been Rose. The thought burned like acid. For a long moment the women were silent, and Erica wondered if Margy was waiting for thanks for sharing the story.

But it was Margy who broke the silence.

"It took me a long time to see this, but in the end, he was something of a hero after all, no?"

"Hero?" Erica sputtered. "He broke her heart. He left nothing but hate in his kids' hearts. That's some hero."

"I understand what you're feeling. I felt that way, too, for a long time. But after praying about it a lot, I came to see it differently."

"How else is there to see it?" If Margy went all spiritual on her,

Erica thought, she might scream.

"We Americans want everything tied up in a neat package. All good or all bad. You ever wonder about the men who plowed those planes into the Trade Center?"

"Ever wonder? I think about them all the time."

"As do I, but some time you might try thinking about the fact that they had mothers and lovers and probably kids, too. And that every now and then, they probably did something sweet and kind and good. They made love to their wives and they rocked their babies to sleep at night. But that didn't stop them from being terrorists. People are good. And people stink. The very same people. That's about the long and the short of it."

"Pleochroic," Erica whispered, remembering Sammy telling her about the three colors visible in each crystal of tanzanite.

"What?"

"Nothing." Erica glanced at Margy and then at her watch. Taking the hint, Margy began to gather herself to leave, but then stopped.

"When I got here you said you took something of Cal's. What was it?"

"His old address book. It was so silly. And I lost it in Africa anyway."

"Still, you felt bad about it, but you couldn't bring yourself to tell me." Margy reached back into her purse and brought out a large file folder. "We've all made mistakes. I have something I want to give you. I don't know when it was sent, or by whom exactly, but it arrived after we closed up Cal's apartment. I had his mail forwarded to me. Keep it. You can read it after I leave."

The two women stood and Margy gave Erica an awkward hug before letting herself out the door.

An open envelope, inside the folder, was yellowed and the ink on its front was fading. It was printed with an official looking seal from the Meru District in Tanzania.

White, Rose S. it said, in shaky letters. *Date of death: October 7, 2001. Cause of death: pneumonia.* Inside the folder were two thin, folded pages.

Rose

*T*he oldest story is also the briefest.

Long ago, in a dusty schoolyard, the paths of two foolish strangers collided. Like many foolish strange before them, and many since, they fell in love and   tried to build a life together. And failed. And grew into strangers once more.

The end.

In our case, however, these strangers brought additional life into this world, and it is in the name of that life that I write to you today.

I will not dwell upon my feelings in the weeks and months after you left us. Suffice it to say that your eyes staring at me from our children's faces were all that tethered me to this earth. But now, almost twenty years later and despite the best efforts of the doctors here, I am about to depart this world.

I have asked our children to tell me their memories of their father. They say they no longer have any. I don't believe them, but neither do I press them for more than they want to share. They have been good children. They have worked hard and respected their mothers—myself and their land. After we left Arusha and returned to my village, they grew up as proud Maasai. Nini has graduated from high school and Leni has risen in his uncle's mines and has a good head for business, if not for cows. Both have the eyes of falcons and love and respect all creatures.

Once I wrote to you and asked you to keep my jiwe safe. Here is what I wish to ask you after all these years, and I ask it on their behalf.

If you still possess my jiwe, always for me the symbol of our home and our family, I would ask you to return it to the place and the people to whom it belongs. I ask this not because of any monetary value, but because that stone remains the missing piece that deprives our children of their wholeness of spirit. It is around that treasure that their anger gathers. Its absence feeds a rage inside them that burns me more than these pains of the flesh I endure. Perhaps its return will bring them some peace. When I am gone, at least allow them to have something as solid as that rock on which to fasten their love.

Tafadhali. It seems not so much to ask, and also too much to ask. But ask it I do. And having asked, I will return to the earth believing that no matter where you are or what you have become, you will grant this last appeal. If not for love, then for justice.

15

Erica carefully refolded the paper and, with trembling fingers, replaced it in the envelope. She ought to be crying. She ought to be furious. She ought to hear the shards of her heart tinkle against her ribs like shattered glass. But all she felt was numb, even as the stitches in her jaw pulled tight. Numb and very, very tired.

There was no longer any way to deny it. Everything between her and Cal had been a horrible sham. She'd lived in a fog of self-deception. She was worse than a fool. She was a fool who believed her own foolish stories. And his. Never would she trust her instincts again. She thought of the memorial service. The way his family had overlooked her place in the hierarchy of his love. They had known. They must have found her pathetic.

White, Rose S.—it was all abundantly clear. The flowers, Rose and her twins—Leni and Nini—Cal's own children whom he deserted. Those were Cal's eyes staring out of their faces—once revealed, the likeness was impossible to ignore. As was the fact that Cal's heart had never belonged to Erica. It was Rose who owned his love, who was his true soul-mate. Now she had a name for the woman in the photo, his torso bending toward hers, toward the life they had created together. Jealousy and grief boiled in her gut like acid. She understood why Leni and Nini hated him. And hated her, too. She had been a thief, albeit an unwitting one.

At least allow them to have something as solid as that rock.

A rock? They want a rock, she kept repeating to herself. It couldn't be that dusty doorstop that Cal left behind in her apartment, the one on which she'd mashed her toes so many times. Could it? She remembered the care with which Cal had unwrapped the bulky thing the day he brought it to her apartment. The tenderness with which he looked at it. At the time, his affection for an ugly stone made her laugh. A *jiwe*. A jewel. Cal couldn't leave Tanzania with nothing to remember them by, so he took a big chunk of raw tanzanite boudin that they had in their house. Rose's *jiwe*. To her, it symbolized their love, their family, their future.

What was taken must be returned. Erica walked slowly through the apartment and stood looking down at the stone where it stood, patiently waiting to be restored to its rightful owners. In the morning she would carry it to post office and send it to Leni and Nini in care of the safari tour company.

Erica picked up a framed photo of Cal in his EMT uniform that sat alone on an end table. It was taken at his graduation from paramedic training. In the photo, Cal's brow was slightly furrowed, and he appeared to be contemplating something just beyond the photographer's shoulder. Erica stared deeply into the picture, wondering what Cal was feeling at that moment. She would never know.

In the end, he was something of a hero after all. Erica was dismayed to find her weary brain replaying Margy's bewildering pronouncement. But was it so far from the truth?

Although Cal had managed to save his family from the threats of a loan shark, he had returned to America a man consumed by shame. He trusted no one, not even Erica, to forgive him. Instead, he nurtured his disgrace in isolation. It was shame that put him through paramedic training and shame that urged him out night after night to save others. It drove him from his home with Erica. It sent him racing into that doomed building. No matter how many people he rescued, absolution would always hover just beyond Cal's reach. Like the little prince, Cal had banished himself from his beloved home with its baobabs and its one precious Rose. And like the prince's, his path to forgiveness was through death. It made Erica want to weep.

One night, as Cal readied himself for his shift in the FDNY ambulance, Erica asked him what it was like to do a job where someone's life hung on the quality of his work. Where his own life might, as well.

"I disappear," he said, shrugging into his dark uniform jacket and slinging a stethoscope around his neck. "I step out of my own way and do the job. The world becomes as simple as this: his body, my hands, the small space in which we're both breathing. Everything else, past and future, dissolves. It's a great relief. It's almost painful to come back to myself, when it's all over."

Now she knew what he meant. In those brief moments, full of trauma, he was finally able to escape his own pain by helping someone else.

Maybe I didn't become a medic to save people so much as to save myself.

Cal had done some appalling things and made some very bad decisions, but he was never the despicable monster he must have believed himself to be.

And he had, indeed, died a hero.

The thought stung Erica like a trek through a field of nettles, making her flesh prickle from ankles to scalp. Cal had left Rose in a sad attempt to protect her and their babies. What, then, had sent him fleeing from the home he shared with Erica?

I can't give you what you want.

Cal could not marry Erica, nor could he bear to explain why. His only recourse, he must have felt, was to bolt. Maybe he did love her, as he swore, maybe he didn't; she would never know. She pulled the copy of *The Little Prince* from the bookshelf and read the final lines that he had underscored:

"But the eyes are blind. One must look with the heart."

And next to them, in blue ink: *What if one can't bear to look at all?*

The real tragedy, she suddenly realized, was not that he had come so close to working through what made it impossible for him to accept their happiness together, but that he had come so close to confronting, and maybe finding relief from, his own guilt and self-loathing.

"Oh, Cal!" Erica cried out to the empty room. In rapid succession she tumbled through the states of desertion, grief, confusion, anger, and even greater abandonment that had driven her tens of thousands of miles since Cal had walked out on their shared life and then been torn from this world. Even now she wished she could tell Cal of her journey. Not about the wild and planetary landscape of Tanzania, but about her voyage to understanding—both him and herself. Here at the end of the ride she recognized how her own loneliness and need made her blind to the many hints of his unhappy deception. I looked at you and saw my perfect self, she wanted to say to him. And if I had known, if you had told me about Rose and your babies and that wonderful and terrible chapter in your life, what would I have done? Here she came up mute.

Erica tucked the letter from Rose inside the book and replaced it on the shelf.

Next time, she told herself, next time I love (this was the first she'd admitted to the possibility of there being a next time) I will love clear-eyed and whole. Even as the thought surfaced, she knew she was fooling herself; that such a thing was not possible. Because falling in love is about hope—it paves the discernible path ahead with only the smoothest stones and softest moss. Who has ever been in love and thought, Oh good, here is another flawed human being with whom I can endure a lifetime of friction and disappointment with only the most remote prospect of joy and contentment? And yet, we aim our inner compass toward finding that joy.

She slid to the sofa and wrapped her arms around her knees. She wasn't sure if the epiphany made her feel better or worse. It would take time, she knew, for her insight to sink in deeply enough to turn grief and disorder into some measure of acceptance. Might the arrival of the stone in Tanzania trigger a similar understanding within Rose's children?

Erica shuddered at her memory of the frustration and loathing that radiated from Nini that day in the hospital. The woman had nurtured the rage of her father's abandonment for a long time. It had etched itself as deeply into her as an obscenity slashed into the bark of a tree—had twisted her to the brink of murder. Erica hoped that the wound had not, however, penetrated the heartwood. Despite all that happened, she wished Nini and her brother peace and healing. And yes, as much as she wished to assuage their pain, she wanted to quell their hatred of her. In their state of loss, the three of them had more in common than they knew. She hoped the return of the stone would serve as an olive branch.

Somewhere in the grassy plains, Erica thought, Leni and

Nini are going on with their lives. They, too, must believe they had failed in their mission to regain their mother's treasure. Erica imagined how Nini would weave these past weeks into her family chronicle. And how, when the *jiwe* arrived, the tale would transform, like a tight, dense bud breaking into fragrant flower.

THE END

Acknowledgments & Thanks

Asante sana to Barney Easterday, Dean Emeritus of the University of Wisconsin, Arnold Makinda, and all the wonderful people of Tanzania who shared their beautiful country and its many stories and languages with me. Dik diks and baby warthogs still wander through my dreams. Thanks as well to Deb Brody, who shared a tent (and posed the ever-popular question: Who gnu?!) and to Kathryn O'Donnell, who taught me so much about the world's flora.

As always, this book could never have approached my aspirations for it without the nurturing of the remarkable and generous writers who share their devotion to craft and to our writing group: Natalie Danford, Moira Trachtenberg-Thielking, Allison Lynn, and Ellen Kahaner (long lost friend!). My love and admiration for you women knows no bounds! Special thanks to the talented Alex Martin for cover art and design.

And to Mark Dallara – husband, honey, fellow nerd, and builder of perfect writing studios – expanding universes of love and hugs for sharing your air miles and for listening to me conjecture, whine, procrastinate, work out plot points, freak out, and all the rest, on the road to the farm and to the words THE END.

A graduate of the MFA writing program at New York University and the graduate program of journalism at Syracuse University's Newhouse School of Public Communications, Ellen Greenfield is a poet and novelist living in Brooklyn and Jefferson, NY. Her debut novel, Come From Nowhere, *was a finalist in the Pirate's Alley Faulkner Society's competition for Novel-in-Progress.*

The author is available for reading and book club appearances, in person and online.

ellengreenfield.com

Also by Ellen Greenfield:

Come From Nowhere

In the early hours of July 13, 1977 in New York City, seven female characters — ranging from a nine-year-old girl and her Greek immigrant mother, to a young chef losing her vision, to a brown rat — share the same subway platform. They are unaware that the next 24 hours will see them struggling to find their way home, both literally and metaphorically, when a historic blackout hits the city. For the women of Come From Nowhere, this blackout is personal: it brings revelation, self-awareness and, for at least one of them, tragedy.

Enjoy Chapter 1 here.

Chapter One

July 13, 1977

"M ami, tell me the story!"

"Which story?"

"You know which story!"

Althea sighed and brushed her thick black hair off her forehead with one hand. With the other, she ushered her nine-year-old daughter through the subway turnstile, down the platform and onto an empty bench.

"Ay, Celia, *kukla*, not again," she smiled to herself. "You already know that one. You could tell it to me." She unfastened a button at the neck of her blouse and pulled the lapels sharply away from her skin to lure the damp breeze that drifted from the dark subway tunnel. Even for July it was too early for it to be so hot. Not even 7:30. And too early for her to feel so bone weary, as well. Although she'd been up since six, she now had barely enough time to get her daughter uptown to her mother's apartment, and get herself to work back in midtown. She could hardly afford to be late – again. She'd been warned twice. Althea listened hopefully in the direction of the uptown train. Silence. She could not afford to lose this bookkeeping job – their only income and barely enough to cover their rent and living expenses.

There were only three other people on the platform this morning, all women, and none of them looking in her direction. She unfastened one more button. From her purse Althea took a small round box of dusting powder and plumped its fleecy puff against the skin between her breasts. The lemony smell of Jean Naté clouded around her head, momentarily replacing the subway stench.

Her daughter jumped up onto the scarred bench and stood resolutely on top of it, arms and legs splayed wide, one hand clutching a bagel with guava jelly that Althea had made for breakfast and served to her on a plate, but which Celia insisted on saving to eat on the train.

"I am the starfish, Mami! I live in the sea and you are walking past my house with your little speckled goat."

Althea tried to look stern. "Celia, stop playing around and sit down. You're too old to be acting like this. If you're not careful, one day you're going to get hurt."

"Then tell me. Tell me the story. Tell me, tell *me*!" The girl jumped down and began to spin in a slow circle, waving her fingers like fat tentacles. The wide legs of her flimsy, blue-and-white-striped shorts flapped around her bony knees. The pants were too large. But they were Celia's favorites, a gift from her Aunt Eleni back in Greece.

Althea knew her headstrong daughter wouldn't give up. Althea's own mother had cursed her with this – that she should have one just like herself. And here she was. A wild thing – always racing away down the sidewalks of Manhattan, as Althea herself had galloped the cobbled paths of Skiathos. But the streets of New York held many more dangers than the urchin-strewn cliffs of that rocky Mediterranean island. In the end, Althea knew she would have to give in if she wanted Celia to be still. The puny breeze from the tunnel had died away. The hope for a train was a false hope. Althea patted the space beside her on the wooden bench and Celia sat down and turned her face up expectantly. Althea planted a kiss on top of the girl's head. The sweet smell of her daughter's scalp melted the last of her resistance.

"Once, on the pine green island of Skiathos, a little girl laid down the first of the morning footprints in the sand where the sea had slept, tossing and turning through the night," she began. The words, sinuous and familiar even in her adopted English, wove their spell, stilling Celia and binding mother and child just as endless retelling of ancient myths had bound the Greek people.

"Following behind her, a small goat – as black as the little girl's eyes and with speckles as tan as her skin – laid down the second set of tracks. Each morning they walked, the girl heading across the pink sands to school, and the naughty goat, who had slipped out the gate, sneaking along behind. The girl knew the goat was there, and the goat knew the girl would have to take him home if she turned and saw him. But she didn't turn, and he didn't hurry, and in that way they walked the crescent of beach until she disappeared into the school-house with its red tiled roof, and he settled into the shade of an old olive tree to nibble the sparse, dry grass."

Celia was humming under her breath as her mother spoke. Humming and kicking her legs as she sat on the edge of the bench. A bit of jelly stained the corner of her mouth. Althea looked down the tracks for a sign of their train, but there was none, so she continued on with the story before her unruly daughter leapt up once again. It was a fulltime job, keeping Celia safe from her own untamed impulses.

"The sun, rising higher and higher in the tile blue sky, made the day hot. Inside the schoolhouse, the children's eyes grew heavy, hooded; outside, the little goat beat the bare ground with his hooves, making the dust rise before he bent his spindly legs and lay down to sleep, his head in the last sweet patch of grass. Eventually, the special rhythm of the little girl's feet on the sand woke him and he tottered up to follow her back home. Each time, she turned to greet him, pretending surprise.

"'Why, Tragos, how did you find me here?' she crooned to him, slipping her arms around his bony head in a hug. Then they walked side by side, their six feet lapped by the waves."

As she spoke, Althea ran her fingers through her daughter's hair, marshalling the frothy curls into a pair of high, dark pigtails held with a pair of elastic bands she had pulled from her purse. Her daughter wriggled under the attention, but remained seated.

"One day, the goat stopped and lowered his horned head to the water. When he raised it, his nimble lips held a small pink starfish. Quickly, before the animal could swallow the creature, the little girl grabbed at it, and it came away in her hands – minus one pink leg, which the naughty goat dropped back into the sea to be carried away on the next slip of a wave. The starfish's single red eye, in the almost-center of its body, winked with what the little girl saw was a tear. She stamped her feet at the goat. 'Bad Tragos!' she shouted – and in her fury she threw shells and sharp stones until the goat ran from her. From the satchel on her shoulder, she pulled a cup, which she filled with seawater. Gently, she slid the starfish into the cup, and then she hurried the rest of the way home, careful not to spill. She placed the starfish in a large bowl – the one her mother used for pickling – and filled it with more water drawn from the sea."

"But where was Goat, Mami?" Ceci suddenly asked. "What happened to Tragos?" The question troubled Althea. Celia had never asked it before – she had always been more interested in the survival of the starfish – and Althea did not answer. Where *had* the goat gone after she chased it away in a rage? Her brothers told her that it was surely dead, food for the vultures and gulls that wheeled over the rocky spine of their small island. Her mother said it would probably find its way home eventually. And indeed, the following week, a mottled goat – skinny and ragged – came wandering in from the parched hills behind their house, but it never followed Althea to school again, and she knew that it was not her Tragos. Her father slaughtered it the following Easter.

Sitting on the platform, Althea just sighed. The goat had been her responsibility. In one moment of misplaced fury she had failed it. Her gaze wandered now, unfocused from time or place.

"This is what can happen to you in the world," she said, sadly. Her hands floated up, palms open and helpless.

Celia was off the bench again, sweeping away down the dirty platform, her arms and legs once more splayed like those of a starfish. Althea jumped up after her, her heart racing, and quickly looped one arm around her daughter's shoulders as she tottered at the edge.

"What do you think you're doing?" she asked. Her daughter froze, staring.

"Mami, look! What's that?"

Althea followed Celia's hand, still clutching the last bite of bagel, pointing to the tracks. At first she saw nothing beyond the usual accumulation of damp and crumpled newspapers, fast-food bags and gum wrappers. Then a slight movement caught her eye. From under the third rail, a gray and hairy shadow broke, weaving from side to side between the rails, twitching, stopping and moving on at a jerky, broken pace. It was about the size of her two fists held together.

"It's a rat, Celia," she whispered. "An ugly old subway rat. Look at something else."

"But Mami, it's missing a leg."

Althea looked again. Sure enough, the rat's jerky pattern was caused by the fact that it ran on only three legs, giving the creature a little lurch at the end of each step. Celia was as observant as she was energetic.

"Will it grow back, Mami, like the starfish?"

"No Kukla, it won't."

The other three women waiting nearby – all except the one with her nose in a book – were now shooting uneasy looks at the animal and then around the platform. Their eyes flickered in a brief unity of disgust.

But Celia had already lost interest. Now she turned to stare at a homeless woman, mountainous in layers of soiled clothes, who sat slumped on a bench, a paper cup for begging set on the floor at her feet.

"Mami!" Celia began.

Althea took her daughter by the hand. Would there never be a moment of peace?

"Shh, Celia. Come away," she said, tugging. "Nobody likes to be stared at."

༄

Judith took three small steps backward on the platform and then three forward, toward the tracks.

A-do-nai s' fa-tai tif-tach, u-fi ya-gid t' hi-la-te-cha, she chanted in a bare whisper. Open my mouth, oh Lord, and my lips will proclaim Your praise.

The gusts blew from left to right down the platform. With each one Judith adjusted the scarf she had draped over her hair and steadied the onionskin pages of the battered leather-bound book in her hands. This time, the sour wind from the tunnel stole the page from her moist fingertips just as she was about to turn it herself. From left to right, which would have been a hindrance had it been any other book, but with her prayer book it was a *mechayah*, a blessing.

Boruch (she bent her knees) *atah Adonai* (she straightened again)... "Praised are you, Lord our God..." A few stray hairs blew from the edges of the flowered scarf tied around her head and tickled her nose. Ignoring that, she fastened her concentration more deeply on the blessed words before her.

...*E-lo-hei-nu, Vei-lo-hei a-vo-tei-nu,*
E-lo-hei Av-ra-ham, E-lo-hei Yitz-chak, Vei-lo-hei Ya-a-kov,
Ha-eil Ha-Ga-dol Ha-Gi-bor v'Ha-No-rah Eil Eil-yon...

Her lips and tongue raced each other through the holy invocation. It was not enough just to read these blessed words each morning; one must say them out loud, or as she was, in a fervent whisper. Praised are You, LordourGodandGodofour-ancestors, GodofAbrahamof IsaacandofJacob, great, mighty, awesome, exalted God who bestows lovingkindness, Creator of all. You remember the pious deeds of our ancestors and will send a redeemer to their children's childrenbecauseofYourlov-ingnature. Amen.

"This is what can happen to you in the world," she heard a voice say dreamily. A young woman, not much older than herself, with an indefinable accent – Spanish? Italian? – was talking to a young girl beside her; the woman's bare arms raised, palms open, toward the ceiling. Judith followed the direction of her hands. The paint above their heads was peeling in thick, ragged strips. A greasy stain underneath oozed and sweated like skin. But the woman's half-closed eyes looked neither at the ceiling nor at her little girl.

Judith turned her back against the subway wind, and faced down the length of the concrete platform. Under a partially shredded poster still hawking the March opening of *Star Wars*, a beggar woman struggled to her feet gripping the sides of a shopping cart half-filled with rags and sacks. Judith wished she could have plinked more than one quarter into the dirty paper cup at the rag-wearer's feet. It was a *mitzvah* to give to the poor, but it was one Judith could ill afford now that she had to pay for rent, food, books and tuition out of the small salary she earned at her aunt and uncle's jewelry store. Hashem had showered her with so many blessings – chief among them the love of her family. Judith gave thanks daily for them and for the work that allowed her to pursue her aspirations. She watched as the woman rose laboriously and worked her way onto a bench by the wall. Judith looked away, not wanting to be caught staring. Someday, God willing, I will be a doctor, she thought. Will I be able to touch the bodies of women such as this, unwashed and doughy?

Judith adjusted the scarf, which had slipped down around her neck, so that it covered her hair again. As an unmarried woman, she didn't have to wear the headcovering, but modesty was expected in the shop, and the many *frum* customers would assume that at her age, almost 23, she was married. She wanted no speculations raised. She wanted no *shidachs* made, either – no sweaty, nervous young men paraded by in hopes of making a match. Under the scarf, her hair was damp from the shower and from the beads of sweat that were beginning to make her scalp itch. Judith turned her attention back to morning prayers and anchored her heart more firmly to the words before her.

❧

Ratus Norwegicus. Back when she was an intern, Johanna had seen more than one case of rat bite and the infection that often followed. The suppurating skin and willful fever that left its young victims fretful and moaning. Pediatrics. Her last rotation. Unless you counted Psych. A quick yawp of laughter broke from her throat. Quite an education, being on the sharp end of all that Thorazine, now wasn't it? How long ago was that? She scratched deeply through the layers of clothes that encased her thick torso, from the shapeless pink sweater on down, and took a furtive glance around the platform. Up and down. Up and down. And then again. Of the four people standing before her, waiting for the train, only one seemed unaware of the loathsome creature prowling the tracks at their feet. And that person was talking to herself, her nose in a book.

Johanna watched through hooded eyes as the women darted nervous looks at the rodent and then blinked away, as if they could tolerate the sight for only seconds at a time. But over and over their eyes were drawn back, keeping track, making sure that it didn't get too close – God forbid it should race up onto the platform and touch one of them. She could practically feel these women's toes curl against their fancy shoes. Again and again, the rat darted in and out from under the tracks, looking for food that the filthy pigs who traveled these subways were only too happy to provide, with their greasy McDonald's bags and sugar-smeared doughnut wrappers. European Brown Rat. Most reviled mammal in the world by these same exalted humans who pissed in the corners of the station late at night when they thought no one would see.

Johanna hunkered down on the bench and pulled on a heavy gray wool coat that she yanked from a shopping cart full of her possessions. Even that didn't stop the trembling. She knew – she was a doctor, goddamit – that she needed Amoxicillin, 500 milligrams, *qid*. Her tongue was thick in her throat. She dug through her pockets and found the mirror half of an old folding comb. Sure enough – her tongue was coated. Probably strep. When she wasn't sweating in this hellhole, she was shivering. Fever and chills, fever and chills. Baked Alaska. Another of her hoarse laughs echoed through the station.

That kid – the first to notice the rat – was now staring at her. The child was skinny in that little girl way. Stick figure arms and legs; her torso, not yet touched by puberty, was lost in her tee shirt, which hung from neck to waist like a sack. She was the little girl with the ratbite fever. She was the little girl with the strap marks on her back. Daddy's little girl. Burns on her thighs. She was six and ten and seven and nine. Makes thirty-two. My age? I was born in the year of the Rat. Exactly. Or maybe not. Johanna's mind rolled and tumbled, then halted like a stubbed toe.

The girl on the platform was staring at Johanna and scratching one ankle with the toe of the bright pink sandal on her other foot. Soon her mother would turn to see what her daughter was looking at. She'd pull the girl closer and whisper. *Don't stare. She's nobody.* Or, *that could be you if you don't listen to your mother. Wash your hands when you get to school. Don't touch the strange dog. Nobody likes to be stared at.*

Nobody – that's me, all right. I'm nobody. Who the fuck are *you*? If I were nobody, I'd like to be stared at, too. I used to be somebody. I used to be somebody. I used to be…who?

She had stopped shivering and begun to sweat. The heat made her feel thick and dozy. Johanna lifted one swollen leg onto the empty bench, and leaned heavily against the straw basket she had propped against the arm for padding. She reached out to lift a pen off the desk and wrote herself a prescription. Take two of these three times a day with water, she mumbled. Don't drink and drive. Call me in the morning. Let Hertz put you in the driver's seat.

She dozed then, with one leg still on the ground until the train rushed shrieking into the station with its hot electric breath. The sound split her eardrums. It rushed into the station and screeched to a halt, then stood there panting with fury before rushing away, taking everyone. Taking the little girl away. She'd never see her again. Gone. Johanna opened her eyes and spat at the receding lights – a big soapy gob of spit. Then she pulled her other leg up to the bench and dropped off into the black and airless pit that passed as sleep.

ॐ

Phnf....phnff....phnf.... Rat's soft gray body twisted out from
the silver rail following her nose.

Food, where? Here? Not here? No. Here?

There up there under soot black sky.

Toss it here toss it down dammit here. Nasty baby claws.
Pink

and flutter. Fuck it all drop it here. Nasty baby fingers
nasty gnawing baby teeth.

Climbandbite. Grabthefood? Bite hernastylittlehand.

Phnf...phnf... Mine. Food-is-mine. Foodismine belly-
fullbitch.

Whereismine?

Food? Greasy paper crumple. Greasy-meaty-sharp-and-
meaty.

Bait? Poisoned? *Phnf...phnf...* Good then. Food then.
Fucking good. Fuckinggreasygood.

Metal roar. Steelroar wind. *Phnf...phnf...*

Steelbeastwindrush. Windrush?

Over and under overandunder overandunder.

Where to hide? Metalstink. Wheretodragfood?
Phnff…phnff…

༄◉༄

TAKI 183. Swollen letters, green and black and red.
Could that really be *TAKI 183*? Pia's arms prickled with electricity, her breath caught in her throat. And again, *TAKI 183*,
TAKI 183, TAKI 183 – the individual subway cars flashed by. It
was all Pia could do to keep herself from running the length of
the platform in an effort not to lose them. Her eyes filled – but
maybe that was just in response to the stinging subterranean
wind. When the train finally slowed to a halt, it was not TAKI
183 but another tag that marked the car in front of her. She
felt let down.

The train that swept into the station brought Pia more
than mere relief from the stagnant heat on the platform – it
delivered the surging energy of rogue art that made each day's
journey uptown a carnival – dizzying and aggressive. PIS-
TOL, TRACY 168, BLADE ONE, CAINE 1, STAY HIGH
149. Graffiti tags raged across car after car. Some turned an
entire car-length into a vivid mural. Others just screamed
FUCK YOU in violent fuchsia. In the brief pause before the
train doors opened, Pia's right hand shot up and traced the
broad, angry strokes of a tag that slashed across the car's sid-
ing. TEENY 128. A broad swath of green rimed with orange,
purple, black. Her fingers curled around a phantom spray can,
forefinger crooked over the nozzle. She dreamed of being part
of the crews that blazed their marks by flashlight, moonlight
and sometimes even torchlight.

This city, she discovered upon arriving only five weeks
ago, was literally awash with graffiti, from the strident and
malicious to the subtle and the just plain mundane. Advertis-

ing posters sported handlebar mustaches, sure, but also, more often than not, poetry. Along the seedy blocks of Brooklyn's Crown Heights neighborhood, where Pia was living with her father's aunt, there were virtually no blank walls. Steel shuttered storefronts wore Mardi Gras colors and abandoned buildings bore vivid memorials to those who'd died in the neighborhood's angry streets. Out her window onto Prospect Place, she gazed upon a 10-foot portrait of a dark, doe-eyed young man. Eighteen-inch letters proclaimed *Shawan James - Never Forgotten 1960-1977.* Smaller testimonials ringed the memorial. *Yo, Man you the best - Mel*; *Solidarity, Peace. T, Wherever you gone, I'm coming - Linda.* Every block had its fallen warriors. No one dared paint over their markers.

Aunt Ida clicked her tongue dismissively when Pia told her how the portrait of Shawan moved her.

"Shoot, those boys ain't nothing but criminals," she sniffed. "They just tearing down the neighborhood with they nasty selves." She slammed down the ashtray she was dusting. "Shawan James broke his mama's heart long before that bullet stopped his," she said, sweeping out of the room. Pia never mentioned it again. The whole city was up in arms against graffiti, she knew. It went hand in hand with crime, filthy streets, drugs, and a palpable mounting rage. Still, she savored new tag sightings like an ornithologist tracking rare birds. She had to admit it: her first glimpse of the infamous TAKI 183 made her cry.

In her most secret feral heart, Pia roamed the city's dark byways armed with spray gun and paint. All the while, the rest of her traversed its streets outfitted demurely in the two-piece, polyester-blend armor of the mild-mannered job seeker she was. With her, she toted the large black portfolio full of the drawings she hoped convince some art director to give her a break. She had three more interviews lined up today. Any of them could be The

One. Better be. The clock – and her money – was ticking down.

In the beam of headlights that had preceded the train into the station, Pia watched a rodent dive for cover under the electrified third rail. Rats. The city was crawling with them, her aunt had said, but this was the first one Pia had seen. If it came toward her, she could fend it off with her portfolio. Maybe she could find a seat on the train and sketch it before she lost the details. Pale, matted fur flecked the color of pewter, the texture of a moth-eaten pony jacket she'd once found in the attic of her father's cottage on the lake. Whiplike tail. Delicate pink ears, onyx eyes. Harder, though, to capture its gait – more hop than scurry, really, as it swung itself out of danger at the last possible second.

But when the doors slid open, it became apparent that there would be no way for Pia to dig through her bag for her notebook and pencils and draw. This was one of the few air-conditioned cars on the train. Despite the early hour, it was elbow-to-elbow and hip-to-hip with bodies. Blue suits, white shirts, arms hairy and smooth – Pia worked her way through the fleshy obstacles until she could grasp a few inches of space on the pole in the middle of the car, and there she staked her claim.

༄༅༈

Danielle's closed eyelids twitched impatiently. From the moment she'd changed to the express, at 72nd Street, she had held them shut. She steadied herself with her breath. Air in, air out, air in, eyes closed. This is what it will feel like to move through the world blind, she told herself, gripping the slick silver pole with both hands, swaying in the dark as the train lurched around bends, bouncing lightly on the balls of her feet as the subway bumped and screeched along the downtown track.

Even with her eyes closed, Danielle knew what surrounded her on the train. Crushed and tangled pages of yesterday's *Post* and *Daily News* whispered at her feet, and the burnt smell of coffee – a rusty umber scent in her personal mental conflation of tastes/smells/colors – rose from abandoned paper cups printed with whimsical depictions of the Parthenon. The walls and windows of every car were etched with knives or spray painted with the names of faceless thugs who shared an overwhelming need for recognition. Her nose told her that at least one person had relieved himself in this car.

The announcements from stop to stop were, as usual, an auditory jumble, practically indecipherable, but Danielle counted off the successive stations in her head: 42nd Street - Times Square, 34th - Penn Station, 14th Street, Chambers Street, Park Place and now, finally, they were approaching Fulton Street, her stop. There had been a long delay between 14th and Chambers with no explanation. Now she would have to hurry to get to the fish market. The fans went off, then on again, the lights flickered, and finally the train lurched back into motion. It took real guts to keep her eyes closed during the wait. Like a feral creature, she sent mental feelers out into the space around her to sense whether anyone was coming close. No one was. The people on the train this early in the day were drawn into themselves.

The car in which Danielle rode was sweltering. She could scarcely bear to think what it would be like in another hour or so when the hordes of rush hour travelers and gaping tourists began to heave themselves into already-packed coaches. The train shrieked around the last bend and slowed to a stop. The doors receded along their metal runners and the recognizable smell of the Fulton Street station – yeasty and yellow-green like fermenting fruit – rushed in. She had reached her destination. Danielle took two steps away from the pole before she allowed herself to open her eyes. She stepped gingerly across the palm-wide gap between train and platform – she'd have to remember that when she was forced to navigate in the dark – and onto the concrete.

Made in the USA
Columbia, SC
16 June 2017